HER BEST FRIEND'S KEEPER

CALLE J. BROOKES

Lost River Lit Publishing, L.L.C.
Springs Valley, Indiana
Est. 2011

OTHER TITLES BY CALLE J. BROOKES

PARANORMAL

DARDANOS, Co.

The Blood King
Awakening the Demon's Queen
The Healer's Heart
Once Wolf Bitten
Live or Die
The Seer's Strength
The Warrior's Woman
The Wolf's Redemption
A Warrior's Quest
The Wolf God & His Mate
Out of the Darkness
Warrior Blind
The Witch
Balance of the Worlds
God of Nightmares

DARDANOS, CO: THE ADRASTOS

The Outcast
The Forlorn
The Beloved

ROMANTIC SUSPENSE

PAVAD: FBI ROMANTIC SUSPENSE

Beginning
Waiting
Watching
Wanting

Second Chances
Hunting
Running
Redeeming
Revealing
Stalking
Burning
Gathering

FINLEY CREEK

Her Best Friend's Keeper

SUSPENSE/THRILLER

PAVAD: FBI CASE FILES

PAVAD: FBI Case Files #0001
"Knocked Out"
PAVAD: FBI Case Files #0002
"Knocked Down"
PAVAD: FBI Case Files #0003
"Knocked Around"

COMING SOON

The Healer's Soul (Dardanos, Co.)
Shelter from the Storm (Finley Creek)
The Price of Silence (Finley Creek)
Falling (PAVAD: FBI Romantic Suspense)
The Betrayed (Dardanos, Co: The Adrastos)

ISBN: 978-1-940937-11-3

CALLE J. BROOKES is first and foremost a fiction writer. She enjoys crafting paranormal romance and romantic suspense. She reads almost every genre except horror. She spends most of her time juggling family life and writing, while reminding herself that she can't spend all of her time in the worlds found within books. Calle J. loves to be contacted by her readers via email and at www.CalleJBrookes.com.

For my grandfather, the best man
I have ever known.
You will be missed.
Oct. 2015

For my grandmother, who gave me the
courage to try. Without you and your love
of romance, I never would have made it
this far.
Feb. 2016

HER BEST FRIEND'S KEEPER

FINLEY CREEK
BOOK 1

I would rather walk with a
friend in the dark,
than alone in the light.

-HELEN KELLER

CHAPTER ONE.

* * *

THE desk had been his father's. The position, as well. Elliot Marshall Jr. never thought he'd do more than share a name with the greatest man he'd ever known.

His father's murder had made sure of that.

The decor had changed in the ten years since his father had occupied this particular office with the Finley Creek post of the Texas State Police. But the desk...the desk was still the same one.

Elliot didn't know how he thought about that. About how he'd handle the memories of what had been lost.

His father had been damned good at what he did, the best police chief the Texas State Police had ever had. It was what had gotten his father killed, along with Elliot's mother, younger brother, and sister.

Or so the rumors went.

They'd never found the bastards responsible. Speculation was rampant that Elliot Sr. had run into a nasty and powerful man. The rumors spoke of bribes and kickbacks. Corruption. The very word had a particular stench all its own.

Good or bad. No one really knew the truth about his father. Had his father been fighting the corruption or had he been a part of it? Questions were still whispered when the infamous Marshall Murders were mentioned.

Truth, no one seemed all that interested in finding it. There was no way his father had been a dirty cop. It went against everything the elder Elliot had stood for. Everything his father had taught him.

Sitting in his father's chair hurt more than Elliot had ever thought it would.

He had his father's old office now, a personal assistant of his own, and a whole hell of a lot of responsibility. The Texas State Police was the smallest law enforcement body in the state. The Texas Rangers outnumbered the TSP ten to one. This post where he sat was the second largest post of the ninety-two spread out across the state. Only headquarters in Wichita Falls, fifty miles to the northeast, was larger.

He was going to run it as best as he possibly could.

Nothing would stop him. Hopefully, along the way, he'd find the answers he'd spent ten years searching for. Maybe *then* he would find peace.

"Will you be needing anything else, Chief Marshall, sir?" Officer Magda Journey asked. His assistant was an attractive young woman with an impeccable record at the TSP and a cool manner he respected. Professionalism was what he prized in his people. Everything else was just secondary. She'd been temporarily assigned to him before he'd arrived in Finley Creek but she'd impressed him with her efficiency fifteen minutes after he'd met her. It would be a permanent position if she wanted it. Elliot was rarely wrong in his assessment of people, and he'd peeked at her personnel file, as well. Very impressive for someone of her age. He hadn't accomplished half as much when he'd been in his middle twenties.

"I think I'll be good for tonight, Magda, thank you."

He needed time to process the changes life had brought him.

His appointment to the position had come from the governor of Texas directly. His cousin Marcus, the governor, had told him it was a last minute replacement, and he'd snapped up the appointment without thinking it through. Now he was starting to question himself and the *why* of the position.

He'd certainly never made any friends in Marcus' office. He and the governor weren't exactly the closest of cousins, let alone *friends*. The biggest question he had was *why* Marcus had put him there.

Why any of it, at all.

And what in the hell was he supposed to do here in Finley Creek now?

CHAPTER TWO.

* * *

GABBY Kendall didn't know what to do.

No real surprise there; that was kind of what Gabby was used to, was known for, even. It was just the way things always ended up for her.

But this…this was a bit scarier than she had expected. She was fighting off a full-blown panic attack and failing. Miserably.

It had been ten years, three months, and sixteen days since her world had tilted on its axis and made her afraid of every shadow in the room. She'd thought she'd gotten herself past all of it. Thought she'd convinced herself the world was actually a pretty safe place after all.

The call from her stepfather had erased ten years of hard work in five minutes.

Gabby closed her eyes and forced herself to breathe again. To think.

It was just coincidence. If someone was gunning for her, they wouldn't have far to look. Gabby had lived in Finley Creek almost her entire life. She was safe. They were *not* coming for her.

Of course...it could be because they hadn't found her yet.

They hadn't found her yet. If they were smart, they weren't even looking. They'd probably faded into the evil-people sunset or been arrested on other crimes long ago. Maybe they had even been eaten by rabid coyotes or something.

Unable to make good on the promise to find her and kill her they'd made ten years ago.

Yeah, that was what she hoped. She'd just have to convince herself of that, somehow.

Her partner pushed her own chair back and said Gabby's name. Gabby looked at the redhead across the table from her. Brynna was staring at her. Again. Brynna stared at Gabby a lot. "What?"

"Something's wrong. What?"

"Just some bad news from my stepfather. Nothing to worry about. Nothing that I can't handle." *Breathe deep. Breathe deep.* She didn't have to have a total freak-out in the middle of the computer forensics lab.

Not exactly professional. And not exactly like it hadn't happened before...even this week. She tended to freak out—a lot. Her teammates, at least, were used to it. And they had *quirks* of their own, anyway.

"What is it? Tell me."

Gabby thought about it and thought about not telling Brynna, but…Brynna was more than relentless when she was worried. It was the way her best friend was. "The Marshall killers may have struck again."

Sara Marshall had been her best friend in the world all through junior high until they were sixteen. Until Sara and three members of her family had been brutally murdered.

One night when things had gotten particularly tough for Gabby, she'd broken down and poured out the entire story to Brynna and Brynna's older sister Melody. Their father had been friends with the murdered family. Mel and Brynna had been on *their* way to Sara's house that night, too. It had been luck that had their father stopping at a gas station. If he hadn't...well, that was something Gabby refused to think about.

Gabby had needed that connection at first. That shared understanding of what was lost.

Their friendship had grown since then.

Her stepfather Art had always kept Gabby safe, and today's phone call was just another way for him to do that. "In Oregon, there's been a case that's similar."

"Similar, but not a guarantee. We see lots of similar cases in this business." Brutally frank, that was Brynna's way. "It doesn't mean anything yet."

Brynna always spoke the truth, didn't she?

No, there was never any guarantees, but she knew the truth—until they had the killers in custody and could compare forensics, they had no way of knowing if it was the same or not. She'd just be left wondering, and wondering. Probably forever, wouldn't she? "Still, it was enough to have Art calling me. Warning me."

"I see. What are you going to do?"

Exactly what she had done every time a similar case hit Art's radar. *Absolutely* nothing. "I'm not sure there is anything I can do. The case has been cold for ten years." Gabby had never understood that. With such a high profile case, she'd have thought it would have been at the front of the TSP's case load every day since.

It wasn't. And in the five years she'd worked at the Finley Creek TSP it had *never* been. Even though a good portion of the people at this branch had been there when the Marshall murders had occurred, it was rarely talked about. That was one thing she and Brynna had never fully understood. They talked about it a lot—but not usually within the walls of the TSP.

"The new chief starts today."

Gabby looked at Brynna again. Her friend had a habit of wild conversational jumps at times. Brynna was on the autism spectrum and sometimes Gabby had a little difficulty keeping up with how Brynna's mind worked. When that happened, they talked about it so Brynna would have a chance to recommunicate her thoughts. And so Gabby didn't miss anything. "So? I heard we were getting a new guy after Chief Blankenbaker's retirement."

The former head of Finley Creek TSP had taken early medical retirement to help his wife battle breast cancer and spend time with their teenage children.

Gabby had always liked working for him and hadn't bothered to ask who the emergency appointment to the position was going to be. It wasn't like her position came into contact with the chief that often. Most of her direct work was under Bennett Russell, chief of the entire Computer Forensics division of the TSP, not just Finley Creek. Most anything extraordinary that they dealt with had Benny's name on it.

She and Brynna *liked* it that way. Gabby lived for anonymity, but Brynna just didn't like people all that much.

In the four years since she'd been promoted from the IT department to the computer forensics department of the TSP, the chief had entered her office exactly three times. Gabby liked it like that.

People in authority made her nervous. *People* made her nervous. When she got nervous, she rambled. When she rambled, she said something royally stupid. When she said something stupid, she got embarrassed. When she got embarrassed, her skin turned beet red and her blue eyes watered. When she turned red, and her eyes watered, she looked ridiculous. Not exactly how she wanted her career to go. Gabby would rather just hide in the computer lab most days. Her supervisor could handle anything with people in authority that came her way, right? It had worked this long.

"I *said*, the new chief starts today." Brynna was still looking at her with her pale brown eyes so serious. No surprise there, Brynna was serious most of the time. Brynna serious, Gabby freaked. Both of them a little bit more than weird.

"So? You're going to have to elaborate, Bryn."

"You know *who* it is, right?"

"No. I missed the memo...and the meeting." Gabby tried not to feel too guilty. She wasn't good when shoved in a small room with bunches of people. She was better when they left her alone with her computer. Brynna was the same way. One of the reasons why the two of them got along so well. "I covered Benny's calls. You were with Major Crimes that day."

If people just left them alone to do their jobs, there pretty much wasn't anything they couldn't accomplish together—with the computers, that was.

The former chief and the rest of the officers and detectives they worked with understood that.

Hopefully, the new chief would be the same way.

"You know *who* it is, right? Gabby!"

"No. Who?"

"It's Sara's oldest brother, Elliot Marshall. *Junior*."

Gabby just stared.

"Maybe he can help you."

That was definitely something she would never have expected. Elliot Marshall was back in Finley Creek. Back. Wow. "Unh-uh. No way. Elliot Marshall wouldn't have *anything* to do with the Texas State Police. Especially here in Finley Creek. I heard he quit almost five years ago to go to the FBI. And he definitely wouldn't believe me. He always thought I was nuts. That I didn't see anything that night. And he wasn't all that nice to me before that." Sara's two oldest brothers, Chance and Elliot, had already been adults with their own careers at the time Sara and the rest of her family had been murdered. They'd both had sudden other plans the night their family was killed. It had saved their lives; Gabby didn't doubt that at all. Chance was around eight years older than her and Elliot was a few years older than him—she hadn't known them well. They'd scared the timid kid she was back then.

"Well, a lot has changed in ten years. You have, right? Maybe *he* has, too."

Somehow Gabby doubted it. "I don't know, Bryn. I guess I just need to think about what I want to do before I say anything to anyone else. Besides, Oregon, where this latest case was, is a really long way away. It was probably not related. I hope."

"I understand. Just...keep your doors locked, ok? Statistically, these probably aren't the same killers. But why play the odds? Why don't you come home with me tonight?"

"No. I'm ok. If I start hiding with friends instead of facing things head on, I'll never be able to live my life without the fear, right?" A hard lesson she'd had to learn over the past ten years.

"Sometimes I just don't understand your reasoning. You'd be safer with us. Dad and Mel both have guns."

"I know. But thank you for offering. It means a lot."

If someone was coming for her, there was no way she'd want Brynna and Mel—or their younger sisters and father—in the line of fire. No way. She'd stick it out in her own apartment, with Bug the Cat and her panic attacks for company.

If someone was coming for *her,* she would never want her best friends standing between them. Ever.

CHAPTER THREE.

* * *

ELLIOT chose to dive right in the next morning. The former chief had left everything ruthlessly organized, and Elliot appreciated it. No one knew if Elliot's appointment would be permanent or temporary, and he wanted things to go as seamlessly as possible for everyone. He wasn't even certain he wanted the position long-term.

He'd had the choice of early retirement after he'd taken a bullet during a case over a year ago. That hadn't been an option at the time, and he'd kept going with the TSP.

Who retired at thirty-six? Elliot didn't know what he'd do with himself if he didn't have law enforcement, didn't have the Texas State Police. It had been everything he'd worked for since he was a kid. Ten years ago that want had shifted to being his best tool for finding the answers he needed.

The call for this appointment couldn't have come at a better time. The first thing he had done was gather all the personnel files for everyone under his command. He had one hundred thirty-two officers, eighty-six detectives, fifty-six support staff, and twenty-four forensics technicians. It was the second largest post of the TSP in the state, a far cry from his former position with one of the smaller posts in Garrity.

But he would run it as he had run his previous assignment. He prized integrity and efficiency amongst his staff. Held himself to the same high standard. Elliot would start by knowing the people he led. He needed to get *out* of his office and actually see the Finley Creek TSP in action.

Elliot wasn't one of those leaders who stayed hidden away; he'd always believed in hands-on like his father had taught him a leader should be. This place would be no different, though he had a strong suspicion he'd be facing more politics and less police work than he ever had before.

Elliot wasn't made for politics, and he would be the first to admit it.

He waved Officer Journey away and headed for the main elevators. He needed to poke around downstairs, see how his people operated when they weren't expecting him.

Every operation had a unique feel to it; it was far past time he found out what this post's was.

* * *

IT seemed well ran. Finley Creek had some of the best people in the organization—at least by reputation. Elliot put more faith in history than reputation. From the moment he'd accepted the appointment he'd quietly started pulling cases, going back forty years. The TSP had been in existence off and on since 1870 and had a tumultuous history—and not always a great reputation.

Today it dealt with a variety of crimes and worked in conjunction with the Texas Highway Patrol, Rangers, and Attorney General's office, just among others.

Elliot wanted to know all of the cases that had crossed the doors of the Finley Creek Post, the second largest in the state.

It was going to take a while, but he was determined to at least touch on as many cases as he could. His wasn't a political position, he was there to run the Finley Creek TSP to the best of his ability. Not win favor for later positions in the future. That wasn't his way.

Elliot hated politics.

This was the first real opportunity he had to get his hands on the Finley Creek TSP files from ten years ago. Which would most likely be in the computer forensic department's archives, as most of what they had on his family's murders was digital. A decade-old digital, at that.

Everything they had hinged on the video taken of the murders that day.

Or so he had always been told.

Elliot would speak with the head of the TSP's computer forensic division as soon as he possibly could. Bennett Russell was a pioneer in the Computer Forensics field and had spent his entire career in his hometown of Finley Creek.

He was one of the ones with the reputation of greatness that the TSP was known for.

Elliot's father had spoken highly of Benny's computer skills when they'd worked together. He'd tried to get Elliot interested in computer technology when Elliot had been ten. But that wasn't Elliot's plan at all.

For him, it had been Texas State Police from the beginning. He'd lived and breathed *cop* from the time he was old enough to understand what his father did for a living. Had childish fantasies of catching all the bad guys and making his father proud.

Now was as good a time as any. Elliot headed toward the Computer Forensics department on the first floor.

At one time, when Computer Forensics first became relevant and Benny was pushing hard to grow his division, the department had boasted three times as many people. Of course, technology had changed so much in the last several decades. Fewer people were needed to do the same jobs.

Today, the Finley Creek TSP Computer Forensics department was still one of the best in the nation—but it had only sixteen people.

Most likely Benny kept his best on day shift, which meant they'd be there now. If Elliot was inclined, he could pull one of them to find what he was looking for.

It would be taking them away from whatever pressing cases there were, and there were always pressing cases. A ten-year-old cold case wouldn't be one of them, no matter how much he wished he could focus the whole post on finding the bastards responsible for his family. He could wait. That didn't mean he couldn't take a look at the Computer Forensics department now, though.

A glass entrance separated the lab from the reception area of the two-story annex. Elliot wasn't so sure he liked how isolated the CF department was. He may need to move them out of the annex and into the main building, to be nearer the rest of the officers and detectives. The space downstairs was being wasted—there were too many empty offices and conference rooms in the computer forensics lab. Offices that could be used to house detectives.

He'd picked up an entourage—exactly what he'd hoped to avoid—about half a dozen supervisors and support staff trailed after him, asking questions.

He understood it; he was new and their boss. The unknown. And the TSP was their livelihoods. They wanted to make a good impression.

Bennett Russell was in the small conference-slash-breakroom with two of his staff. They had half a dozen laptops, a tablet, iPhone, and three-ringed notebooks spread out among them. And a dozen glazed donuts and soda on the table.

It looked like a study session, rather than a criminal forensics department. Informal.

Interesting. Nothing at all like the sleek professionalism of the TSP departments in the five-story main building he'd just left.

Elliot nodded at Russell then took a closer look at the two techs seated next to him.

Pretty. Very, very pretty. That was the first thing he noticed. Elliot was a healthy man, after all. These two would get noticed anywhere. But they were a hell of a lot younger than he was expecting.

They stopped their conversation and they stared at him, then stood. Their shoulders touched, and they looked at each other. Then at him. Back at each other.

He fought a smile. Something about the two of them side-by-side amused him. He didn't know what, but it did. Maybe the wide-eyed nerves? Was it because he was the Division Chief?

"*Elliot*!" the blonde on the left said, drawing his attention immediately. Her cheeks flushed. "I...uh...mean ...Sir...it's good to see you again."

Elliot looked into big blue eyes behind purple-framed glasses. Eyes that looked familiar.

CHAPTER FOUR.

* * *

"ELLIOT. I mean...Chief Marshall...it's...well, it's good to see you again." The woman's cheeks went bright pink. Her pretty cheeks. Behind the thick glasses she was a very stunning woman, with long pale blonde hair and a soft mouth. He'd put her age at a good ten years younger than his own thirty-six.

She reminded him of someone, and it took him a moment to put it together.

"*Gabby*." He didn't hold out his hand toward her, a slight that he didn't mean. He realized what he'd done when she pulled her hand back and wrapped her arms around her middle. He could almost see the nerves running through her.

But hadn't she always been that way? She *had* always been a bundle of nerves, hadn't she?

She hadn't been quite as pretty ten years ago, though. Just an awkward and very geeky teenage girl—that was how he'd always remembered the girl who had been his sister's best friend.

Gabby Deckard or Duncan, or something like that, had been at his parents' house almost every weekend, side-by-side with his sister. They'd been almost inseparable. Until the night she'd watched his family die.

He had been busy down in the Gulf building his early career with the TSP and had only seen her about half a dozen times in the year before his parents' and siblings' deaths. She'd been a young girl, and he'd been a man in his mid-twenties. His return visits to Finley Creek had been consumed with catching up with his friends and making time with women his own age. They hadn't included the teenage sister he had had so little in common with, or the brother two years older than Sara who he hadn't known much about at all. It definitely hadn't included their friends.

Elliot would always regret not being close to Sara and Slade before their deaths. Always.

"You really look…well." She was backing away from him. Until she bumped into the table, sending a bottle of unopened soda rolling to the floor. Her redheaded friend nabbed it before it got too far. Elliot tried to put his finger on why she was so nervous of him.

Was she frightened of him? *Why*?

The words he'd said to the girl at his family's funerals came rushing back. He hadn't exactly been nice to an obviously grieving kid, had he? Gabby was definitely one of his *regrets,* too. Life was about regrets, wasn't it? Maybe she was a regret he could somehow mend? "Gabby, it is nice to see you. I didn't recognize you for a moment there."

He'd just found out that she'd witnessed the whole thing back then, and he'd been angry. He had lashed out in a moment of grief. At her and the federal agent who'd accompanied her to the funeral.

He'd blamed the agent for the case not moving forward, and he'd blamed her for not being able to give the FBI or the TSP the information they needed.

But he'd really been angry at himself. He'd hated himself—and his brother Chance—for them not being there that night.

He was *supposed* to be home the night his family had been murdered. A last minute date with a woman he'd been chasing had had him changing his plans. He'd never forgotten how disappointed his mother had sounded when he'd called to tell her. That was the last conversation he'd ever had with his mother. Sara's birthday. And his sister had wanted a dinner with the entire family and her best friend.

Sara had been web chatting in the living room with her friend—with *Gabby*—when four armed men had broken into their home, dragged Slade and Elliot's parents into the living room and killed all four of them.

While her best friend watched.

Gabby had dialed 9-1-1, but his parents had lived forty miles from the Finley Creek city limits. By the time help had arrived it was too late for his sister and parents, who had all died instantly. Slade had died two days later in the hospital. Elliot's eighteen-year-old brother hadn't wakened in those forty-eight hours. Elliot and Chance had had to make the difficult decision to have Slade taken off of life support when it became clear he probably would never recover.

She was still staring at him, as were the rest of the half-dozen people surrounding them now, from the larger forensics division, not just computer. They were waiting for him, weren't they? To acknowledge? To tell them what he wanted down there today. Elliot pulled his thoughts back together. Now wasn't the time for the past, was it? "It's nice to meet you all. I look forward to working with each of you. Gabby, would you like to escort me back to my office? We can catch up for a few minutes."

"Uh…now?" Her voice rose in a squeak that surprised him.

He didn't miss the crowd's surprise, either. The speculation in their eyes. What were they thinking? He smiled slightly and addressed the room at large. "I knew Gabby as a child. She was a close friend of the family's. Though it has been over ten years, hasn't it?"

"Yeah. At least. It's good to see you again. I already said that, didn't I?" She shot a confused look toward the redhead. The other woman nodded. Gabby sighed. "Sorry, I tend to repeat myself sometimes."

"Not a concern. Shall we?" He motioned to the elevator. Elliot didn't miss the look of pleading she shot at her friend. Who shrugged.

He almost smiled. These two were interesting, weren't they?

Did she think he was the big bad wolf going to gobble her up? He hadn't gobbled up an innocent young woman like her in at least…ten years.

That thought sobered him. It always came back to that night, didn't it?

That was the last time he'd focused on his own selfish needs rather than living up to his obligations first. If he'd been with his family, he would have been armed. He would have been able to save at least some of his family that night. Of that, he had no doubt.

Gabby darted into the elevator in front of him. Once the steel doors slid shut, cutting them off from everyone else, he looked at the woman who'd once been a grieving young girl. Who had once been more a part of his family than *he* had.

She still had the thicker glasses; this pair had dark purple plastic frames, and she still wore her hair in two loose braids. She was—and had always been—a mix of sheer geek and green hippie. But now her awkward teenage angles had smoothed out into some very feminine curves. Her eyes were just as blue as they had been back then. Beautiful. And staring at him with wariness and…fear. Why the fear?

Because of what he'd said ten years ago?

He'd been grieving. But he'd also been a total ass. To a kid who hadn't deserved it. A kid who'd lost people she loved, too. His family had loved *her,* too. That had sat on his conscience for a very long time. Now wouldn't be too soon to apologize, would it? In fact, it would probably be far past time, wouldn't it? "Gabby, how long have you worked here?"

"Almost five years. Here. In Computer Forensics. Before that, I was with IT." She still eyed him like he was a rabid dog. It was starting to irritate him. He wasn't going to bite her. Although, he bet she tasted as sweet as she looked. "So…how long are you going to be chief here?"

"I don't have a clue. How have you been?" He stepped closer, testing to see just how she would respond. She didn't disappoint—or surprise. Gabby backed up until she was flush against the rear of the elevator cart. She really was trying to get away from him. Why? "Seriously? Doing ok?"

"I…I'm fine. Of course, I am. Why wouldn't I be?"

Because she looked like a big-eyed squirrel caught in the talons of an owl at the moment? "I'm glad to hear it. I've wondered how you were over the last decade." He'd wondered, regretted. He'd thought of just calling her and apologizing for his words back then. He just never had—what was the point in dredging up old wounds? For the both of them?

"Fine. Just fine. And here for the last four. How have you been? Chance? I saw him about two years ago. And he calls occasionally. We had dinner once. About three years ago, I think."

That surprised him. His brother wasn't often in Texas, especially this side of the state. They both had their demons; Chance's involved their late brother, and Elliot doubted Chance would ever stop running from them. "Chance is doing…fine. We both are."

"Fine." She tilted her head back and looked up at him. He studied her; her skin was flawless, except for three small freckles beneath her left eye. He bet she was as soft as she looked, too. Her lips were full, and she was chewing on the bottom one as she eyed him.

He made her nervous, didn't he? Elliot was man enough to admit he liked that.

In a different world, maybe he would have acted on that.

"Fine."

CHAPTER FIVE.

* * *

FINE. Yeah. That was the word she'd used. Him, too. Over and over again. And he was definitely *fine.* He looked like his brothers—all the Marshall boys had favored their father—but Elliot was definitely the hottest of the brothers. Now.

Of course, she'd only known Slade when he was a teenaged boy. She'd never get the opportunity to see him as an adult.

She'd missed him almost as much as she'd missed Sara those first few years after the murders. Slade had been her first real kiss.

Two weeks before he'd been killed he'd asked her to his senior prom. She still had the dress she'd picked out shoved in the back of her closet. Slade Marshall had been a boy—Elliot Marshall was a full grown man.

His hair was sable brown with a touch of silver at the temples. His eyes were dark green. His face was all hard angles and planes; rough but manly.

Just like his father's had been.

She missed the senior Elliot Marshall to this day. She hadn't had a father figure until him. She'd met Sara when she was eleven years old. And without her own father in the picture—he'd joined the military and left Gabby and her mother high and dry three years earlier—she had developed a relationship with Sara's father. He'd taken her to her first father-daughter lunch at the community church. He had been there for that first junior high dance. He'd been the closest thing to a father she'd had as a girl.

It had taken her stepfather a long time to earn that same spot.

Her mother had married Arthur Kendall, the senior FBI agent who'd been assigned the Marshall family's case. He had made a promise to Gabby the day after Sara's funeral. Art had vowed to keep her and her mother safe from anyone who'd hurt them.

And he'd kept that word.

Eventually Gabby had come to love him, and his daughter Elizabeth, like the family Art and her mother had tried to make. *Had* made. She had three more siblings, thanks to them. Family.

She'd had a real family.

Eventually.

Of course, it had taken a whole lot longer than that for her to feel reasonably safe. To not wake up terrified that the killers were in her bedroom, waiting to kill her with little thought, or hindrance. Along with everyone she had left to love.

"So."

He looked at her. Something about the intensity of his eyes had her fighting the urge to squirm.

Gabby knew herself well, and she knew her quirks. Every last quirky one of them. She didn't do well when confronted by those in authority. She didn't do well with tall, broad-shouldered men who looked at her like *that*, either. She tended to turn into a complete babbling idiot. *Babbly Gabbly*—that was her.

Not a big surprise, really. She'd always had issues with being shy, and hating any attention her way. Was it any wonder she felt like a stupid raging river of babbling?

That was true even before Sara was killed. And whenever facing that subject, the babbling was worse than a river. "I…wow, you really look like them, don't you? I remember your dad looking just like you do now." But there had been laughter in the senior Elliot's eyes. Laughter and love that had never truly gone away.

"You knew them well, didn't you?"

"I was at their house almost every weekend from the time I was eleven. You were already out of college when Sara and I became friends. She worshiped you and Chance. Did you know that? I used to be so jealous. I didn't have a sibling. Not then. I have some now. But not then. And they're kids, but I try to be a big part of their lives."

His face tightened. "I used to feel the same way about Sara and Slade. There were ten years between Sara and me. I should have made a point of knowing her better. Slade, too."

She could see it, couldn't she? The real hurt in his eyes? Surely he knew that Sara had idolized him? Had he spent the past ten years thinking that? "Sara understood you were busy. And to be honest, you were old. We had other things to do…Well, sorry. That was incredibly rude, wasn't it? What I meant was that Sara understood you were older and had your own life. She *loved* you."

"And I loved her. You did, too. I'm sorry for what I said at her funeral. I shouldn't have, and I've regretted it."

"You were hurting. I figured that out eventually." Gabby hadn't expected that. She would have bet good money on Elliot Marshall never apologizing for anything. Arrogant guys like him rarely did. And he was arrogant, wasn't he? Well, he definitely had been back then. She remembered a cocky guy drawing all the girls his way. Chance had had the same flare. Even some of her and Sara's friends had thought Elliot and Chance Marshall were the greatest things on male legs.

She and Sara had giggled over that so many times.

He still looked pretty good, though. For a man closer to forty than twenty. He looked...kind of yummy, really. Gabby felt her cheeks heat again. Sara must be looking down on them from heaven laughing at Gabby for that stray thought. There was no way Gabby found Sara's big brother drool-worthy.

His face was too hard to get much of a reading on him now. She knew so little about him, and the ten years they'd not seen each other had just widened that gulf. What was she supposed to say now? When confused, her standard fall back was to…babble. "So…what are we supposed to say now? Hi, how are you? We don't really know each other. Personally or professionally. So what do you really want to talk about?"

* * *

HAD she always been so direct? He honestly didn't remember. "I wanted to apologize, and wanted to see how you were doing. My family cared about you ten years ago. And it was wrong of me to push you away. I'd like to make amends for that."

"No amends necessary. And your family was close to me, but *you* weren't. Chance wasn't. So no obligation there. It was good to see you again. I saw Chance by accident. He was looking good, too. Good genes apparently ran—run in your family."

Did she ever stop talking?

Thankfully the elevator reached their destination at the top. When the doors opened, he waved her through into the hallway just outside his office.

What was he even going to talk to her about, anyway?

He hadn't been thinking when he'd first realized who she was. He'd just recognized her and then acted.

She went to his office ahead of him, and he took a moment to study her from the back. She had definitely filled out from the teenager he'd once known. He waved Officer Journey back to her seat. "It's personal."

Gabby had to be in her mid-twenties now, didn't she? Like Sara would have been. Was she seeing someone? Did she have a family? A man waiting for her to get home in a few hours? Had things ended up good and normal for Sara's friend? He damned well hoped it had. She deserved it. He wanted to think of her as being *happy* over the past ten years. More than he or his brother had been, at least. Gabby settled in the chair across from his desk, then crossed and uncrossed her legs. Long legs.

She stared at him. "Wow. This is completely awkward."

"Maybe. And maybe I just need to see a familiar face for a few minutes." He grasped at thin threads, just to get some sort of conversation going. "So…you said you had siblings? How many?"

"Three. Plus my step-sister Elizabeth. Remember Arthur Kendall?"

"Yes. I kept in touch the first three years after the murders. But he never got anywhere with the case. And so I stopped calling." Tried to move on. Or at least not make it the entire focus of his life.

"He married my mother six months after the funerals. They have three kids now. And he had a daughter a year older than I am. Art's great. We spent some time in Seattle after Sara…and he sent me to his sister in Spain for a little while."

"I'm glad things worked out for your mother. I knew Kendall retired."

"Yeah. He took an early pension. To…well…to keep me safe."

He definitely hadn't expected that. Elliot leaned forward. "From what?"

"You don't know, do you?" She blinked at him; then a flush hit her cheeks again. He had a fleeting thought—did that flush cover her from head to toe? Or did it start right there, just beneath the collar of her purple shirt?

"Apparently not."

"After…well, about a year *after* that night, I started getting emails from someone. Art thought it might be one of the killers. They were threatening and knew too much, I guess. That's when I went to Spain. The emails stopped about five years ago. But Art…he still keeps an eye out for similar cases. He's hoping someone will stop them somehow. I told Chance this that night we had dinner together."

"Chance didn't tell me." He didn't like the idea of her and Chance having dinner together. Chance would hurt someone like this woman, simply by being Chance—and taking off in the middle of the night, disappearing for months. The idea that his brother *hadn't* told him something as significant as her getting threats from the killers pissed him off. And was something he'd be discussing with his brother the next time he saw him.

Not that Elliot knew when that would be. Last he'd heard, Chance was somewhere in Missouri working. Chance was a private investigator, licensed in several states surrounding Texas. They didn't talk much about what his brother did whenever Chance would blow into whatever town Elliot was working in. He saw his brother maybe three times a year. And that hadn't changed since the year after the murders. Just another of Elliot's regrets.

"Art said it might not be the killers, either. Just some stupid nuts wanting to scare me."

"Damn it, Gabby. I didn't know. If I had..." He'd have what? Protected her? Art Kendall had done a fine job of that. He just didn't like the idea of her dealing with the fear all alone.

"It's ok. I'm safe here. I know I am."

CHAPTER SIX.

* * *

GABBY was glad to be home, and she was glad to be with a friendly face. Her day had been tilted on its axis since she'd left Elliot's office.

Elliot Marshall, Junior, in the flesh. Wow, wow, wow. He'd grilled her about the emails until she'd been ready to pull her own fingernails out and scream at him. There was such an intensity in the man, and she'd been unsettled from the moment she'd laid eyes on him again. She'd finally claimed Benny probably needed her and she had to leave his office. Escaped.

She'd run and hid in the lab where she felt the safest, of course. Gabby had stayed there until her ride home arrived at the door to get her.

Detective Jarrod Foster was one of her favorite people at the TSP, grumpy though he always was. She knew he cared—about her, about Brynna, and about his former partner, Brynna's sister Melody. She sometimes thought he'd had a crush on Mel when they'd worked together. Still thought he might. "Thanks for the lift, again."

"Hey, it's on my way." He lived two floors up from her, and he routinely checked on her after hours. He knew of her...*issues*...with night time and going places and driving and just about everything else. And in a particularly low moment, she'd told him why.

There had also been a few hot kisses between them that had gone just about nowhere. They'd decided they weren't meant to be lovers in this lifetime, but friends.

Friends worked better for her anyway. Even though those had been some seriously *hot* kisses worth remembering.

Friends was a lot less scary than lovers. Gabby needed less scary, didn't she? There was always the next lifetime for her and Jarrod to hook up. Or so he had always teased.

"So what's between you and the new chief?"

"What do you mean?" Huh? There was nothing between her and Elliot, except the nastiness of the past.

"Apparently he couldn't look away from you. And seemed to watch you like crazy when in the room. At least that's what the rumors are speculating. Because there was something *interesting* in how he said your name." His voice showed no inflection, and his face was only mildly curious. But Gabby knew he definitely wanted to know. Jarrod wouldn't have asked if there wasn't some serious curiosity going on in his handsome head.

"He was Sara's older brother. One of them. He blamed me for a while, I think. After she was killed."

"It wasn't your fault. I've looked over the case files. You acted as fast as you could. And it wouldn't have mattered—they were dead before you finished dialing 9-1-1. Where they lived, no one could have gotten to them quickly enough to stop it. *No one.* Hell, their driveway was a mile long itself. Add in that they were fifteen miles from the nearest help. Nine and half minutes is the absolute best a well-trained team of responders could have made it. They did make it in twelve. By that point three of the four victims were dead."

"And Slade was dying. I know. In here..." She pointed to her head. "I know that. But in my heart...and at night...I still manage to do something different. To at least save Slade, if nothing else." Slade would probably have survived if he hadn't been deprived of oxygen for as long as he had. If she'd gotten him help just five minutes sooner. It had taken her a long while to come to grips with *that.*

"And you'll end up driving yourself crazy thinking that. The cards for the Marshall family fell the way they were supposed to. You got to just accept that." Grumpy, but very accepting of fate—that was her Jarrod, wasn't it?

"I know. You'd think ten years would have been long enough, right?"

"Time heals some wounds, but not all." There was a dark expression on his face that told her he had a few serious wounds in his own past.

She knew very little about him when it came down to it. Jarrod kept everything to himself. That didn't matter—she still loved him. "Guess not. Well...so what are the greatest speculations?"

"That you and he have a checkered past. Apparently, he was a bit of a player back then."

"Ten years ago, definitely. Anyone tell you how old I would have been the last time I saw him? Sorry, TSP grapevine, no illicit affair. I don't know if I could even spell *illicit* back then unless it was a tenth-grade spelling word. He missed Sara's birthday dinner because of a last minute date." And she remembered how hurt and angry Sara had sounded on the webcam that night. Sara had idolized her two oldest brothers, though she was much closer to Slade. That both Chance and Elliot had canceled on her, for her birthday, had really hurt her friend. "I was going to the movies with Slade the next night. My first *official* date, Jare. I was hoping he'd kiss me again afterward. Instead, I spent that night in the police station with Brynna's dad, praying the killers wouldn't come after *me*. Or my mother."

Sara had originally wanted just her family at a special family dinner. But after they canceled on her, she'd messaged Gabby to see if Gabby and her mom wanted to join the Marshalls. Gabby had been at her computer and answered via web chat.

That was the last conversation she'd ever had with her best friend—Sara complaining about her older brothers. She'd never forgotten that.

She cherished the three best friends she had now even more. Jarrod, Brynna, and Melody were the most important people in her world, next to her family.

Her family had moved away two years ago for her mother's job. She missed them like crazy. Mel, Brynna, and Jarrod had become her world here in Finley Creek.

She'd wondered before why she didn't move away from her hometown. It would have made the most sense, wouldn't it? But she just couldn't. Something kept her in Finley Creek, and that was where she was supposed to be.

Sometimes she really thought she was crazy. And then she'd think and plan to move away.

Then...she would freak out even more at the idea of leaving her friends behind. They just *got* her better than anyone else anywhere.

At least since Sara.

They were what mattered to her, and she'd never forget that. She knew she clung a little too tightly to Mel,

Brynna, and Jarrod, but they understood. "Hey, Jare…I love you; you know that?"

"Wow. Way to make a man uncomfortable. I don't have a ring if that's what you're angling for."

"Hardly. It's more like a brother thing anyway. Minus a few silly moments between us, that is."

She just wanted to cuddle up on his lap and be safe for a few minutes. She didn't dare, though. Jarrod would climb the curtains if she even tried. Well, *maybe*... Jarrod was a healthy guy, after all. Things could happen.

"Hey, those silly moments have sustained me in my celibacy for a long while now."

He seemed to know what she needed, though. He held open his arms and she hugged him tight. Just for a few minutes. No sense tempting fate, after all. Still, if there was ever a guy she trusted enough, it would be this one. If only… "Ha ha. So they really think there was something between me and Elliot Marshall? And I thought I was crazy."

"Is it? You're a beautiful blonde with one hell of a hot body. You have to know that. And that is *always* a guy like Marshall's type. And he called you *Gabby*." He grinned at her as he turned onto their block.

"Jare, *everyone* calls me Gabby. That's my name, after all." She would never get it, never understand the way men's minds worked. Maybe they were from Mars, after all. "And we knew each other when I was a child. Hardly anything romantic there."

"And I'll see that gets around the post. But people probably won't believe me. An old family friend is far less salacious than former lovers. And there's the fact that the rumor mill has you and me as lovers for the last three years, at least. Apparently, I am doomed because

Marshall is more important on the TSP food chain. People are assholes, babe."

"Really? You and *me*? I thought it was you and Mel who were doing the tango on your off time." She hadn't known there were rumors about her and Jarrod. Gabby didn't pay much attention to idle gossip. It wasn't her way. She preferred the more direct, honest approach. Or hiding. Hiding was her favorite way of life, after all. "Why do they say that?"

"Because I spend so much time in the computer forensics department, apparently. A man can't be friends with three extremely hot women without there being some speculation. And since Melody was my partner, and Brynna is…well, *Brynna*…that leaves you. Beautiful blonde, living in my building, who rides home with me every night. Theory is we spend our nights together, too."

Gabby thought about it for a moment. If she hadn't known the truth, would she believe she and Jarrod were lovers? Maybe. It made a sort of sense, after all. "Well, we do. Just not in any romantic way. Oh, well. I don't really mind if you don't."

"Hmmm. It does make it a bit difficult to put the moves on other women." He leered at her. "So I think you and I should just go with it. Give the people what they want."

"Been there, talked about that. Decision made, right? Yet you never do put the moves on anyone, anyway. Who would you even try with? I know you. You don't date within the TSP, duh."

"Sigh. All my dirty secrets." He parked his car and turned off the engine. "All joking aside, you need to be aware that there is speculation. Already. This guy has the younger people curious and the older who remember his father wondering *why* he's here. I don't know what you want to do about it, but you don't want your name linked to his right out of the gate. That will only make it hard for you if you want to progress. And for him to take over. He'll need to earn respect. Fooling around with a young blonde tech won't help *him* either."

"As long as my supervisor and my department know me, I really don't care what people think of me, Jare. I'm happy doing what I do. And I am happiest when people don't bother me. There are some days Brynna and I won't see another soul in there for three or four hours. I like that." The thought of more than that gave her hives. Seriously.

"My two favorite hermits."

"And you're our favorite misanthrope."

"Yeah, yeah. Now you're just getting sentimental."

* * *

SHE was glad to be alone, both at work and in her apartment. Yeah, sometimes she worked herself up into being convinced someone was watching her through the window, but she knew that was most likely her imagination. But when it came down to it, Gabby liked to be alone—as long as she knew she was safe.

Surrounded by her stuff, in her own personal space. She'd asked for an apartment with as few windows—entry points—as possible. On an upper floor, which had ended up being the sixth. Jarrod was two floors up and two doors over. She could reach him from the fire escape in less than a minute. They'd timed it. Rehearsed it.

It made her feel a little better when the sun went down.

Her friends knew about her fears, and they understood. She hadn't exactly broadcast the fact that she was an almost twenty-seven-year-old woman who was still afraid of the dark.

Only Mel had suggested Gabby seek therapy after a particularly bad panic attack late one night in a theater parking lot. A group of men had crossed the parking lot, hooting and catcalling, directly after she, Mel, and Brynna had exited the theater. Gabby had totally freaked. Mel had thought she might have PTSD. And thought that she needed more help than she was getting.

Gabby didn't disagree.

She just wasn't sure she wanted to go the therapy route again. Her mother and stepfather had insisted she go to weekly sessions those first two years after the tragedy. And it had gotten her through. But she was in a good place now. She knew that. Well, maybe a *better* place than she had been in.

She'd come a long way from the girl who'd refused to leave her mother's side for two years.

She was in a good place, wasn't she?

Gabby still checked out the window of her bedroom four times before finally closing the blinds.

Sometimes, *sometimes* she was convinced there were eyes out there. Watching her. That was pretty much one of the definitions of crazy, wasn't it?

It was so tempting to go up two floors and crash on Jarrod's couch.

Again.

CHAPTER SEVEN.

* * *

JARROD was called out on a case fifteen minutes before she was scheduled to go off the clock the next day. That meant Gabby was pretty well stranded unless she caught a ride with Benny. She'd done that a time or two before. Mel used to drive her and Brynna in each day, but that ended when Mel retired. Brynna was just as against driving as Gabby, for her own reasons.

Brynna was paged to the Commander of Major Crimes' office to work on a cold case that had suddenly opened up again. She was one of the man's favorite technicians, and he always asked for her. Brynna would be getting some serious overtime in the next few days which meant more comp-time. The TSP didn't pay overtime to its employees, but when they had to work past their regular shift, they earned paid time off. Brynna liked to save her comp-time and visit her sister in St. Louis whenever she could. That left a taxi for Gabby—not her preferred method of transportation, but one she'd used before. She'd survive.

She used her cell to call the service she always used, then waited by the window.

One day, she'd have to get her driver's license, wouldn't she? For self-sufficiency's sake, if nothing else. Independence.

It was an argument she'd had with herself on multiple occasions. She'd never really resolved the argument satisfactorily.

She wasn't entirely certain why she'd developed a weird fear of driving a car. *Probably* because she'd spent most of her sixteenth year in therapy addressing some very real fears, and hadn't wanted to get her license. She hadn't been able to deal with the pressure of having other people's lives in her hands.

Sara had received her driver's permit the week she had been killed. She'd been so excited, and had driven Gabby home from school twice.

Something else that had probably left a deep impression. Sometimes she felt she'd never unravel the ties Sara's death had wrapped around her.

"Waiting for the bus?" A male voice asked from directly behind her. Gabby spun around, bumbling half the personal notebooks in her hands. She narrowly managed to keep the half full fountain drink in her left hand from hitting the Chief of the Finley Creek TSP smack dab in the center of his broad chest.

Elliot Marshall had always had one of the best guy-chests she'd ever seen.

And—come to think of it—she'd seen that chest naked once. When she'd been fifteen, Sara's family had taken her on vacation with them to the Gulf. Elliot and Chance—and their girlfriends—had surprised their parents on their wedding anniversary by showing up at the small vacation bungalow. The next two days had been filled with festivities and swimming.

That was the first time she'd seen Slade without his shirt, too.

That had been the weekend she got her first real kiss. All of her attention had been focused on Elliot's youngest brother, but that hadn't stopped her from noticing how nice Elliot and Chance had looked in their swim trunks and nothing else. From noticing how strong and perfectly made the Marshall brothers all were. She'd never forget the look that had been in Slade's green eyes when he'd smiled at her.

Eyes that had been so much like the brother's now looking right at her. That's when she realized she hadn't answered him. "Yeah…well, a cab. I don't drive."

"Any reason why?"

"Never got my license. I'd delayed Drivers' Ed. And I never bothered getting it when I was sixteen. I had too much else going on."

His face tightened for a moment as they both remembered what it was that had happened. "Let me give you a ride. An officer is bringing my car around."

"I…"

"It'll be no trouble."

"You know what people will think?" She darted a quick look around the lobby. Yeah, people—people she worked with, knew and had for the last almost five years—were pretending not to watch them.

Yeah, real subtle there, TSP people.

"What? That I'm giving an old family friend a ride home? Unless you're afraid to be in a car with me. It's a simple ride, Gabby. Nothing more. A safe way for you to get home."

"That's what you think. Don't you know you were dropped right into the middle of Finley Creek TSP—Texas's real life soap opera? We leave here together, and rumor will have us together in the morning, too." *Babble, babble, babble, Gabby.* Sometimes she just needed to *stop* talking. "Probably engaged with six kids on the way."

Had she really just said that? To the chief?

"I don't care, if you don't. We'll work out the wedding details later. And half a dozen baby names. But I get to pick the honeymoon destination, though. How do you feel about silk sheets? Decision time; here's my car."

Taxi or *him*?

His hand wrapped around her elbow, warm and strong. And there were enough people close by for their conversation to have been overheard.

If she turned him down that fact would go through the rumor mill faster than water over the Hoover Dam. Yeah, that wouldn't be a good thing, for either of them, would it? "Let me cancel my taxi."

Sometimes she thought she really was crazy.

CHAPTER EIGHT.

* * *

THE ride lasted far too long, even though it was only sixteen blocks between her apartment and the TSP. He dropped her off after she'd thanked him and that had been the end of it. No mountain. Not even a molehill. Just a simple ride home.

There wasn't anything Gabby liked more than coming home. To her reinforced door with three extra deadbolts, thanks to Jarrod and his handiness.

Today was no different. She needed time to think, to figure just how she felt about having Sara's brother so close. Why did he disconcert her so darned much? Was it because of how much he resembled his father? Or because having him there had brought every fear and hurt she'd experienced at the loss of the Marshall family back up to the surface?

Or was it something else?

Whatever it was, she was just glad that she wasn't looking at him straight on, wondering what to say or what to do and feeling like a tongue-tied dork.

The cat greeted her when she unlocked the door, like always. She picked him up and snuggled him against her chest. He wasn't very big, and one of his ears was slightly smaller than the other; his tail has a kink in it. It had always hung slightly to the left. He was her baby, and she wasn't ashamed to admit that she was fast turning into the crazy cat lady of the sixth floor.

Most of her evenings included a short reheated dinner, a few television shows, some internet surfing, chatting online with friends, and reading.

She was one of the most boring people she'd ever met, and Gabby liked it that way. Boring was less likely to get murdered in her own home.

Sometimes when the boring got to be too much she'd head up to Jarrod's apartment, and he'd feed her something other than cheap frozen dinners or canned soup. She very rarely cooked for herself, though her mother—and Sara's—had spent many hours teaching her how. She cooked when she wanted to—she just didn't want to all that often.

Elliot's mother had been one of the best cooks Gabby had ever met. When she'd been killed Gabby had sort of lost the desire to cook much at all.

Maybe she should try again?

She would. There had been a chocolate oatmeal raisin cookie that she used to love. She probably still had the recipe somewhere in the old cookbook Anne Marshall had been making for her.

Sara's mother had been a cookbook author. She'd been designing one specifically targeted to young girls just about to go out on their own. She'd had Gabby and Sara try recipe after recipe and Gabby had loved being with her. Sara would act all embarrassed by it, but Gabby knew her friend had loved it, too. And they'd gotten paid for it.

But the time they'd spent together would be what Gabby always remembered. Always.

It took her a few moments of digging, but she finally found Anne's last project.

Gabby's stepfather had brought it to Gabby right after the funerals. She'd always appreciated it, although it had been four or five years since she'd really looked at the handwritten notes and photos.

There had been several photos of her and Sara, as well as quite a few of Sara and her mother. And all three of them together. Slade had hung out in the kitchen sometimes, and he'd always had a camera around his neck.

A small curl of heat went through her stomach when the idea that Elliot might like to have copies of the photos hit her. The least she could do was scan the pictures into her computer and give him a zip drive or something. What he did with the photos after that was up to him.

It wasn't as hard this time to look at the photos; not like it was the last time. Maybe time did dull some of the pain? She would always miss Sara's smile, how it turned in at one end just like her mother's had.

Like Elliot's still did.

The only thing he'd gotten from his mother was that smile.

He was in one of the photos, one taken when he'd stopped by for a few hours about four weeks before the murders. She had been more consumed with Slade than Elliot so she hadn't done much more than say hello.

Now she studied the photo a bit more closely.

He was already in his twenties when the photo was taken. His hair was longer now than it had been then. He'd worn it militarily short back then, and he had his dark green TSP uniform neatly tucked and pressed.

He wore the TSP uniform so well. She'd seen many an officer and detective whose shoulders didn't fill their uniforms quite as well as Elliot Marshall, Jr.'s had—even ten years ago. She bet he looked awesome in his dress uniform *now,* too.

She finished scanning all of the photos onto a spare memory card then turned to the more personal items in the file box. Art had grabbed her everything Anne had been working on back then. And she'd never been able to get through the entirety.

It had hurt too much. Even five years ago.

Elliot's presence was what had brought it all up, wasn't it? But instead of being quite as painful, she felt more nostalgic.

Perhaps ten years was long enough? Maybe it *was* time she went through it all.

She dug through the notecards with recipes and alterations and everything paper clipped together, then grabbed the purple binder that held all of Sara's mother's personal notes and observations. The small leather journal that Elliot's father had given her to keep as a record of her progress rested in the bottom of the box.

The first page had hand-drawn flower doodles and Gabby smiled. Elliot's mother had doodled on everything. She'd always had a pen in her hand. A pen or a wooden spoon. She'd been forty-eight when she died.

Gabby really missed her.

Her cell rang and she set the journal aside.

Only a handful of people ever called her, especially during the week. One quick look at the display told her it was Brynna.

Exactly who she needed to talk to. Sara had been her best friend, no doubt about it; her loss had almost destroyed Gabby. Her mother and Art had helped Gabby heal, but *Brynna* had been the first real friend Gabby'd had since Sara'd died. Brynna made her *be* a friend again.

Through Brynna had come Mel, and even Jarrod. Gabby hadn't wanted another friend, but when she and Brynna had been assigned to work together the other woman was relentless. They were going to be friends, no matter what. Because Brynna had *decided* so.

She'd cared about Gabby, and she'd somehow made Gabby care about her. She would always love Brynna for that. "What's up?"

"I'm checking on you. I don't want you sitting in your cave brooding." Brynna never sugar-coated anything, and Gabby had often wondered if that was because her friend was autistic, or simply because most of the Becks were straight-shooters on everything. Brynna's sisters and her dad were the same. *"What are you doing tonight?"*

"I'm fine, Brynna. I promise. I'm going through Anne's stuff right now. Her last cookbook project. I helped her with it. There're quite a few pictures."

"Is it making you sad?"

"A little."

"I'm coming over. You can show me and talk about her."

She thought about refusing, but she wanted the company. She just felt too alone right now. Bug the Cat just wasn't enough right then. The cat meowed at her as if he knew what she was thinking. She pulled the phone away from her ear. "Don't look at me like that, Bug. You know I love you."

"You're talking to the cat again even though he can't talk back. I'll be right over. I'll get Mel. She can get the pizzas. It's her turn."

"No. I have a recipe here. I'll make some. I still have some of your fake cheese and purple sauce here. I can make the pizza allergen free, too. Give me an hour."

Anne's recipe. It seemed almost right, didn't it? Sara's mother's recipe for pizza fed to her two best friends in the world. Who had both loved Anne, too. Fitting, wasn't it?

It would be the first recipe she'd made from that cookbook, and it was more than right that it would be shared with the best friends she had.

CHAPTER NINE.

* * *

BRYNNA'S older sister Mel had a look of fierce warrior bitch in her eyes when Gabby opened the door to her and Brynna half an hour later.

Gabby got out of her way. She'd seen that look before. "Hey, Mel. Here, let me take that."

She held out her hand for the purple backpack that went with Mel everywhere. Mel was down to one forearm crutch now but was still unsteady when carrying heavy objects. Or walking prolonged distances—like from the elevator to Gabby's door near the end of the hallway.

Mel waved her hand away. She was extremely stubborn and determined to get herself as mobile as she possibly could. And Gaby thought she was doing a damned fine job, considering the doctors had predicted she'd most likely never walk again. She'd proven them wrong on that. "I've got it. I'm getting pretty good at swinging around with this thing. I've only fallen twice this week. It's a record. Brynna tells me something's going on. What is it?"

Leave it to Mel to get right down to the heart of everything. She had no doubt her friend would march out and slay any dragons she had—if Mel had been able to march, anyway.

The bullet had come so close to her spinal cord that she'd almost died. It had been touch and go whether she'd be completely paralyzed, too. Mel had fought the odds and learned to walk again with assistance, but her entire future had changed. She was still adapting.

Gabby was just thankful her friend was *alive*. She'd had to wait until Jarrod got off his shift before she'd been able to get a ride to St. Louis the night Mel had been hurt. That car trip had been the longest nine hours of her life. Mel had still been in recovery when she'd arrived. She'd never forget the terror at almost losing another friend. Mel's dad had been beside himself—Mel had been on her way to visit her older sister Carrie, who was in labor. Just before Gabby had arrived Carrie had been taken back for an emergency cesarean. The sisters had been in surgery one right after the other. Their father and younger sisters had practically gone nuts waiting for news.

Mel would most likely always need the forearm crutch, but she was getting steadier and stronger thanks to physical therapy.

There had been many times when she'd witnessed Mel fall and pick herself right back up off the ground. Mel was the strongest woman—*person*—that Gabby had ever met. Sometimes she wanted to be Mel when she grew up. Her friend didn't seem to be afraid of anything and was smart and beautiful on top of strong and brave. Mel knew how to be in charge; that was for certain.

"I want to make pizza first." Mel had been Sara's friend, too, though Mel was bit older. Some of the photos she'd found had pictures of the Marshall family with the Becks. There was even one photo with her, a ten-year-old Brynna, a thirteen-year-old Mel, a just turned twelve-year-old Sara, and a nine-year-old Jillian. Mel had been holding her two-year-old sister Sydney. She vaguely remembered that cookout—it was the first time she'd spent the night at the Marshalls, and she'd felt so awkward. She'd stared at that photo for a very long time. Anne had meticulously labeled the back with everyone's name and age in her neat handwriting.

Connections. They mattered, didn't they?

She'd met Mel and Brynna a few times as a child, but they hadn't been in the same grades or lived in the same neighborhoods, or even attended the same schools. It had been so casual. It wasn't until Brynna had been hired by the TSP and Mel started coming down to the computer lab to see her sister that they'd put it all together. Figured out that they'd all known each other before. Figured out that they'd all been *there* the night Sara had died.

That connection was the main reason they'd become friends.

But now...

It had been so hard for Gabby to let them in, hadn't it? She'd been so scared to get close to anyone. She looked at the two as emotion filled her. "I love you both. You know that, right?"

Mel looked at her for a serious moment. "Of course we do. And we feel the same right back. What's going on, Gabs? What's got you so spooked? Talk to us. Let us help."

"Mel means more spooked than usual. I think." Brynna closed the door behind herself and locked all of the bolts carefully. Brynna rarely freaked over anything. Cool and logical, that was Brynna's way. Maybe that was what made them such good friends? Logic, Panic, and Strength—the Three Musketeers of Finley Creek.

"Something like that." Mel took the closest chair. Gabby kept the area around that particular armchair clear of any obstacles for when her friends visited.

Bug the Cat waited semi-patiently for Mel to get settled and then he hopped up in her lap. He was in love with Mel and would stick close to her side the entire time Mel was there. His infatuation was practically pitiful. Sometimes she suspected he *pined* for the other woman.

"I was just...thinking of Sara again."

"No surprise. I heard Elliot was back from Brynna. I worked with him a few times in Garrity. He's grown even better with age."

Gabby felt heat hit her cheeks. "Really? I didn't notice."

Mel laughed. Mel had always had a very pretty laugh. "Liar. I think you noticed right away."

"So? It was kind of hard not to. He was right there, after all. All big and muscly and...looming. I didn't know what to say." So babble, babble, babble—like always.

"So you said something typically Gabby-ish, didn't you?" Mel grinned. She'd always told Gabby to embrace who she was—goofiness and all. To *be* who she was without excuses. Yeah—Gabby was still working on that one. "So...what was it?"

"I don't remember. I was just babbling. Babbly Gabbly, that's me."

"Ouch."

"I don't think it was that bad. He has a nice smile. And he smiled at you a lot." Brynna always took the end of the couch near the window. She was a definite creature of habit.

Well, so was Gabby. One reason why the two of them clicked so well, probably.

They went to work; they went home. They did it all again the next day. Habit was the only way to go.

At least Brynna and Mel had each other and the rest of their family, didn't they? They went home to the house they shared with their father and two younger sisters. Heck, Mel was even a band parent for Syd. She was as close to being a soccer mom as she could get, without having an actual child of her own, anyway. They were a family and a close one, at that.

They had each other.

She had Bug the Cat, who was busy making moony eyes at Mel and ignoring Gabby completely. Silly cat traitor.

She was so boring that even her cat preferred someone else over her. Hard to swallow, wasn't it? "It was bad. But...it's not like we ever had any good conversations before. It was just awkward. What was I supposed to say? *Hi, how have you been since the funerals of most of your family?* That probably wouldn't have gone over all that well."

"Probably not," Mel said. She was quiet for a moment. "He's always been so sad. I worked a few cases with him, and that always stood out."

"He has another brother," Brynna said. "Whatever happened to him?"

Chance. She knew him better than Elliot; he'd come around asking questions about the murders a time or two over the last ten years. He was a few years younger than Elliot, she thought, and looked a lot like his brother. But darker, leaner. Like his father. He was different than Elliot, though. More intense. Much more frightening. He was someone she definitely wouldn't want to meet in a back alley—whether he was the good guy or the bad. Talk about some seriously scary mojo—

Chance Marshall had it in spades. "Some say he's gone off the deep end. I half believe it. He calls me sometimes, just to ask me a bunch of questions that I usually can't answer. Freaks me out again every single time."

"Do you think they'll ever find the people who did it?" Brynna pulled a blanket off the couch and wrapped it around her shoulders.

Gabby understood. She felt the sudden chill in the air, too. "I don't know. I'm afraid of what the cost of finding them might be. What if they're out there, just ready to hurt someone else? What if they're out there just waiting for me? I think of that all the time. All the time; I can't get it out of my head. I'm not so sure I ever will. I'm not so sure Elliot Marshall being back is all that great."

"The fear that it'll get dragged back up again? I can understand that. The way it is now is safer. You don't have to face it with it as buried as it has been." Mel shifted on the chair, stretching her legs out in front of herself with a grimace. She'd said once she'd been told she'd most likely always feel pain from the shooting; Mel so rarely complained. She held out a hand toward Gabby and Gabby took it, barely resisting the urge to cling to the most stable friend in her life. The strongest. Mel continued, "The sting is still there, but the grief—maybe the grief has finally found a quiet place to rest. Seeing a guy like Elliot Junior who looks just like his father, and just like the rest of the Marshall family, it makes it raw. Makes it real again. And it hurts. It hurts to remember. Hurts me, too. I got my first period while spending the night with Sara when I was thirteen. Her mom was great about helping me. To lose them all—it'll probably hurt forever."

"Yes, it definitely does."

"Then let's shove the nastiness of that last night away for a while. I smell pizza. *Good* pizza, not like that cardboard dairy-free tomato-free stuff Brynna likes to buy at the grocery store."

"Hey, that's the best pizza." Brynna had a list of strange and weird food allergies that she had to watch for. Gabby kept a list of Brynna-safe foods stuck to her own fridge for when she did actually cook for her friends. And special dishes to reduce cross-contamination issues. Like she'd thought many times before—they *all* had their issues—quirks—didn't they?

"Uh huh. I smell pizza, and it's Anne's recipe. Let's look at the old photos and remember how wonderful that family was. And just be thankful that we are all still here, and together, and so damned alive. And then I'll tell you of the time Elliot and I were both tapped by our superiors to go undercover, and he had to kiss me in the middle of a bar in Houston."

Mel gave a wicked grin. Gabby gawked. "Are you serious?" Gabby leaned forward eagerly. "You kissed him?"

"It was only for a moment, and I was more concerned with the gang surrounding us to focus on the feel of the man—to my regret."

"I bet he knows how to kiss really well," Brynna said. "He's older and more seasoned. I've always wanted to kiss an older man. At least once."

"He's thirty-six or seven, Brynna. Not exactly ancient," Mel said as the oven buzzed. "Then again, *you* are the youngest of us. That's probably way too old for you. Twenty-eight. That's probably as old as you should go. Just old enough to be more experienced than you, but not so much that he'd totally overwhelm you."

"The oldest guy I've ever kissed was twenty-two. And he wasn't very good at it." Brynna crinkled her nose and shook her head. "It sucked."

"He wasn't very good at being a *man*, Bryn. There's a difference." Mel looked at Gabby and smirked as she struggled to her feet. "He was a real prick. I put glue in his car locks."

"Mel! That's illegal!"

"It was water soluble. *If* he could get to it all. He deserved it for what he did to her."

"That was vandalism. She shouldn't have done it, but she did it because he hurt me." Brynna smiled at her older sister, how she felt for her right there on Brynna's face.

"Of course." Gabby's kitchen was right off the sitting area of the living room, and she could easily speak to her friends from the kitchen island. "And I won't tell a soul that a former detective with the TSP put glue in some jackass's car. I guess I'm a glue accessory after the fact."

"Gee, thanks. Make sure you're a sparkly accessory, at least. Tell you what, go tell the Chief of the Finley Creek TSP that I confess and he can cuff me however he wants. See what he says."

"Why would I talk to him again? I mean, I plan to give him copies of the pictures of his family, and that is it. Period. Nothing more between me and Elliot Marshall, Junior, at all. Certainly nothing like handcuffs."

"Probably not. I don't think you're the type he'd be interested in, to be honest." Mel started tearing up the lettuce Gabby handed her. "He prefers the temporary no-strings type, I think. The exact opposite of all of us. I think we're all safe from his clutches. Darn the luck. I bet he has good clutches… I've not been *clutched* in a year and a half." A fleeting brush of sadness went over Mel's face so quickly Gabby was almost certain she'd missed it.

"Ok, let's talk about something else, please. Like how was St. Louis?" Anything to turn the conversation from Elliot. *Anything*. "What did you find out?"

"It's not like I thought. If I take the job, I can do most of it from here. No relocating, thank goodness. Gretchen, the woman who owns the company, is really nice. And she believes in what she's doing. In what I would be doing. It'll be part-time, as needed, at first."

"I didn't want you to have to move. Carrie's so far away. I didn't want you to be, too." Brynna grabbed the drinks and plates from the cabinet. This was something they did a lot, just hanging out together. Gabby liked that they were just as comfortable in her apartment as she was in the home they shared with their father and two younger sisters.

Connections again.

"It was a huge factor, to be honest. But let's face it, disability after only six years with the TSP isn't much, especially since I was off the clock and out of state when this happened. I can't spend the rest of my life doing nothing. I can't even keep the house clean easily. Cooking is about the extent of my abilities right now—if I don't move around too much. But with Blessed Reunions I can do something that makes a difference. And the money will help."

Gabby understood. Mel sucked at *not* doing, didn't she? "What is Blessed Reunions exactly?"

"It's a company of what are basically licensed private investigators. They are contracted by people who are looking for lost loved ones. Like Carrie."

Gabby knew the story of Mel and Brynna's older half-sister. Carrie's mother had kept her a secret from their father until Mel was around eight. Then he'd tried to find the little girl but hadn't succeeded.

Brynna had actually found her while flipping through a computer forensics journal that Benny had given them while on their lunch break. The resemblance between Brynna and Carrie was strong enough for Brynna to wonder. To do a little digging until she had her answers.

"It's not right what was done to Carrie. Or my dad. Gretchen is the sister of Dan Reynolds, the man who helped save my father and Carrie's life when we first met. His daughters were kidnapped fifteen or sixteen years ago, too. Blessed Reunions helps reunite families, if possible. And provides counseling for families that can't reunite. And other services. I really want to be a part of this; if I can. Gretchen seems to think I can do a lot of the job remotely or by phone."

"So you're going to take it?"

"I'm seriously considering it. Leaning toward it, actually. We're still haggling details. I won't be doing much investigating, but I can use the phone and computers to do a great deal of the legwork for other investigators."

Gabby hugged her friend. She knew just how dark the days had gotten for Mel when she'd first been injured. "It sounds wonderful."

"I'm just glad you'll be able to do it from *home,* where you won't get hurt again. Or you can just stay home with us forever. I didn't like that you were considering leaving us."

Mel looked at her younger sister and smiled. "I know, Bryn, I know. That was one of the main issues for me, too."

"Ladies, pizza is ready." Gabby changed the subject quickly. Brynna hated any talk of her sisters leaving their childhood home. It was a discussion they'd all had before. Vehemently.

"Great. Let's eat, and I'll tell you about this really hot guy named Bertram that I met in St. Louis. He's from Houston originally and has a body that makes Elliot Marshall look like a stick boy. Talk about yum."

Yep. It was so…normal. Mel and Brynna were exactly what she needed tonight.

CHAPTER TEN.

* * *

GABBY got to the lab early and left a plastic container on Benny's desk with a note telling him what it was and that she appreciated him. Then she headed up the elevator toward the office she'd been in only once before. She was having a difficult time separating the idea of Sara's older brother Elliot from Division Chief Marshall—her boss. Even now, two days after she'd first seen him in the computer forensics lab.

It just seemed so weird to think of him that way.

Officer Journey was at her desk already, and it was neatly organized. Gabby didn't quite understand how the other woman functioned that way—organization was definitely not *her* strong suit. And Journey always looked so put together and beautiful. Sleek.

Gabby felt like a frumpy middle schooler most of the time. Just give her a pair of baggy overalls and a Beanie Baby and she was all set.

Journey looked up at her and smiled. "Good morning, Gabby. How can I help you today?"

"Uh…is Elliot, I mean Chief Marshall in? I have something for him. It's pizza. His mother's recipe. I had friends over last night, and they took half the leftovers, but there is so much I…" She didn't *mean* to ramble. It just always sort of…happened.

"Of course. I'll buzz him and let him know you're here."

"Thanks." Ok, she was really doing this. She'd give him his mother's pizza and then get back down to the Gabby-Cave and be perfectly fine.

It was just *Elliot,* after all. An older version of Slade, right? Old family friend. Old family friend.

Officer Journey opened the doors leading into the Division Chief's office. Gabby stepped in for the second time that week. Elliot sat behind his desk, wearing his dress greens.

Wow. That was her first thought.

He looked *really* good in his dress uniform. His desk was as ruthlessly organized as Officer Journey's and every inch of the room shouted *power* to her.

This wasn't exactly a chump change post; the head of Finley Creek TSP *had* serious juice behind them. Behind Elliot. The enormity of the position he held sank in. He practically ruled this little empire—and she was bringing him leftovers in a plastic container.

That made the gulf between them seem all the more...Grand Canyon-like. He stood and rounded the desk. He held his hand out to her. Gabby stopped walking. "El...Chief...I'm not sure what I'm supposed to call the guy I've known since I was eleven who now happens to be my boss. A pretty important one."

"In here, Elliot works just fine. Or El, like Chance does. Out there with the piranhas, probably better use Chief." He smiled as he said it and leaned back in his chair. She wasn't certain, but it almost looked like some of the tension that had been in his shoulders lessened a little. "You're in early today."

"I caught a ride with Jarrod again. He had the 8:30. I'm on at 9:30. I—uh—brought you something." She held out the container. "I got out one of your mom's cookbooks. One she was working on before she died. I made pizzas for my friends last night. Way too many leftovers. I made it just like she'd taught me, with garlic butter on the crust and everything. And she'd made notes that you really like mushrooms, so…anyway. I brought you some. I figured of everyone in the world; you'd like it. I brought some for Benny, too."

She sat it on the desk, feeling like a great big doofus when he just stared at her.

* * *

ELLIOT hated pizza. Correction—he hated all pizza except the kind his mother used to make. There had never been another pizza as good as hers. And there probably never would. Sometimes there were things he missed more than others.

The sight of his mother in the kitchen was one that would be burned into his memory for the rest of his days. The joy she'd taken from feeding all of them when he'd been a child, and then the pride when she'd turned her lifelong hobby into a successful career would be something he never forgot.

One of his main regrets had been that he'd never spent much time in the kitchen with her. She'd insisted he and his siblings learn the basics, but only Chance and Sara had enjoyed the process as well as the results.

He took the pizza the woman in front of him was holding out. He'd probably just toss it in the trash, but he couldn't refuse it. Or the memory card she held in her other hand.

"I know you've probably got tons of photos from Slade, but I didn't know if you had these. And I thought you'd like to have them. I made copies. And I've got your mom's last cookbook. It's her recipe for the pizza. I just…I'm sorry; I'm rambling again, aren't I? I'll leave you alone now. I've got tons of work waiting in the lab. I should probably—"

He didn't know how else to shut the woman up. He put a finger over her lips. Blue eyes widened behind thick lenses. She licked her lips unconsciously. Elliot's gut tightened. What would she do when a man touched her other places? Just how sensitive was she "Gabby, thank you."

"I should go. Downstairs. Get started. I can't keep you too long. I'm sure you—"

"Gab, honey…take a breath." Had she always just kept going whenever she had a conversation? Or was it something he'd done? She'd just been his baby sister's little friend, and he'd barely paid two teenage girls any attention. But he definitely knew she'd never chattered at him like this. Or was it something else? Was Gabby aware of him not as Sara's brother anymore, but as a man? The way, heaven help him, he was aware of her as a woman now?

He took a quick moment to study her. She didn't dress flashy, but the pale green sweater and light slacks made it clear that she was an attractive female. The eyes were gorgeous. Too bad she hid them behind the plastic-frame glasses. Her hair was long and pale, and she'd left it down today. It fell almost to her waist in golden waves that shown in the light. Made his fingers itch to touch.

She was a beautiful woman, wasn't she? Not a little girl anymore. His body stirred in a way it hadn't in a very long time. "Thank you, Gabby."

"Well, I should let you go. Let me know if you want copies of your mom's cookbook. I've had the original since…well…My stepfather—he brought it to me. Sara and I…well…we were helping your mom with it. She was writing one for young women just out on their own. She wanted us to test the recipes for her. She taught me how to cook; did you know that?"

"I hadn't realized."

"My mom was working a lot, and I spent a lot of time with yours. She was always happy to have Sara and me around when she was cooking."

There was something in her eyes, a shared moment of grief perhaps, that had him setting the pizza aside and wrapping his hand around her much smaller one. Small, warm, soft. His hand nearly swallowed hers. He'd always been partial to soft, feminine skin just like hers. Partial to delicate blondes, with large blue eyes and soft, pretty mouths.

Elliot clamped down on the urge to pull her closer and see if the lips were as soft as he imagined. He stepped back before he did just that.

"She loved having people there. Loved kids running in and out. I had quite a few friends who'd show up even when I wasn't home. Most of the time I found her in the kitchen with them, making cookies or brownies."

"She made absolutely perfect brownies. I still use that recipe, but I've never managed them exactly the same way she did." Big blue eyes turned serious. Fearful and sad. "Do you think they'll ever find the killers? Honestly? Ever learn the truth?"

He let go of her hand, and before he thought it through, he was running his fingers up her arm to the edge of her sweater. Her skin was the softest thing he'd ever touched. "I'll never stop looking. And Chance…"

"He calls sometimes. Asks me a bunch of questions that do nothing but confuse me for days, and then he hangs up. I wish I could help him more."

"My brother has let the search consume his entire life. I was almost that way. But when I was injured a few months ago I had time to think. I will still look, but I can't let it consume the rest of my life. Not anymore." For the first time, he put into words what he'd been feeling for a while.

"No. Your mom and dad would not have wanted that at all. They loved you all so much. And each other. I've never seen two people who loved each other more." She shook her head, sending blonde hair floating on the air around him. He got just a small hint of her shampoo. Flowers. Woman. *Gabby*. His gut tightened, over something so simple.

Attraction; it was there, wasn't it? Undeniable. But did she feel it, too? Something about her drew him, and it wasn't just her connection to his past that did it. It was *her*.

Whenever he'd met a woman that he could be interested in he'd wondered if she would be the one he'd love just the way his father had loved his mother. Until ten years ago, and he'd made the decision that he'd never be with a woman that way. That deeply.

He'd watched the video from the night his family was murdered.

This woman had recorded it. Had watched it in real time, knowing she would never be able to help them. He'd watched it after it was already done. He'd known the opportunity to help would never have been there, anyway.

Elliot would never forget how his father had looked at the moment his mother had been killed in front of him. The devastation on his father's face haunted him in his dreams still. He'd never looked at a woman with that much love or pain in his entire life.

Never would.

"No. Me, either. I don't think I ever will."

* * *

WHY did she find that so sad? He suddenly seemed so alone...She'd heard through the rumor mill that he'd spent some time in the Gulf area, working for one of the TSP posts there. She'd thought it was the Garrity post, one of the smaller ones in the system. Did he have friends there? People who cared about him? Did he still have friends in Finley Creek?

Why did the idea of him being so alone bother her so much? "You're welcome to come over tonight and take a look at the others I have. Or I can make copies. I'd be happy to cook dinner or something."

What was she *doing*?

She really hadn't just invited her new boss over to her apartment, had she? Gabby had a very short list of people she'd let in her personal space. Brynna, Jarrod, Mel. Her mother and Art and the kids, plus her stepsister whenever Lizzy was in town.

But Elliot Marshall. That was just crazy.

Wasn't it?

"I mean...since we've known each other for years, and such. As a welcome back dinner or something. It's ok if you say no." *Please say no, please say no, please say no*...She didn't want Elliot in her home, big and male and overwhelming like he was. But once the words were out there it wasn't like she could take them back, was it?

He stared at her for a long time, then smiled at her. A real smile, one that reached his eyes. "I…I would like that. I've not had some of my mother's brownies in too damn long."

Oh, crud. "Well…I work until five. Would seven work for you?"

"That would be perfect."

She settled more details, like the code needed to get past the security guard in the lobby of her building, then practically ran from his office.

CHAPTER ELEVEN.

* * *

BRYNNA was just getting settled in when Gabby flew through the door. "You're bright pink, Gabby. What did you do?"

"I think I asked the new chief on a date. I think. I'm not sure. It might not be. I don't even remember the last time I went on a date. What is a date, anyway?" Gabby practically squeaked as she paced around the small area that housed the main computers they worked with daily.

Brynna sat her pen down carefully and pushed her notebook away, before turning to face her more fully. "A date? A romantic event between two interested people? That kind of date? Or the 'let's set the time to remind us to get together for a specific purpose' kind of date?"

Gabby stopped pacing and looked at Brynna for a long moment. Brynna just looked back. Her friend still had her sunglasses on her face. She remained calm and relaxed as she waited for Gabby's answer. Did *anything* make her friend lose her cool? "A *date* date. The kind I am too embarrassed to think about. But it wasn't like that. I swear."

"Well, then how was it?"

Gabby checked the clock quickly. They had maybe five minutes before they had to clock in and get assignments from Benny. Their supervisor was already visible in the open door of his office.

"It was 'I found pictures of your family, would you like to come over and look at them?' followed by 'I can cook you some of your mother's brownies if you'd like to come for dinner.' Come to think of it, that doesn't sound so bad, does it?" Maybe it wasn't. Maybe they could just laugh, talk about the people they'd both loved, then that would be the end of it? Nothing more complicated than what she'd shared with Brynna and Mel the night before. Then she could stay in the annex with her computer, and he could go around ruling the Finley Creek TSP empire. No more thoughts of how beautiful he'd looked in his dress greens this morning.

Yeah, that would work. One dinner and then she'd stay far, far away from him. As soon as that stray idea hit her, she felt like a complete jerk. Like a hard-hearted, uncaring bitch. Not like the woman her mother—and Elliot's—had raised her to be.

Sara's face flashed in her mind, and Gabby remembered how the other girl had idolized her two oldest brothers. How she would have wanted Gabby to…to…to make a little *effort* where her big brother was concerned.

Yeah. Sara would have been the first one to jump in and make someone feel welcome. As would Sara's mother. They'd always had room in their hearts and lives for Gabby.

She owed it to them. They definitely wouldn't want Elliot to be so alone. And he'd been gone from Finley Creek for more than ten years; how close of connections could the guy have? Still, it was a big air-gulping moment, wasn't it?

Then again, maybe—like always—she was freaking out over nothing? Maybe this was just an opportunity to make another connection, another friend in the world? Why was she making such a big deal over it?

She somehow doubted he was going to gobble her up whole, or anything like that. It would be dinner and talking, and memories, and that was it. Perfectly normal and not freak-out-able. Seriously.

One day Gabby would have to get a grip on herself, wouldn't she?

"That doesn't sound too crazy to me. Who knows, maybe the guy would like a friend? He's been away from here for a really, really long time, hasn't he? And his brother is out there somewhere, right? I remember them. We stayed with Chief Marshall and his wife when my mom was having one of her surgeries. And lots of other times. They were nice to us."

Gabby understood. Brynna's mother had died from cancer several years ago and had been sick off and on for years before that; her father had been TSP for thirty years. He'd retired just as Gabby had hired in. He was another who'd made room for her in his family, somehow. Just because of her connection to Brynna and Mel.

She impulsively hugged her friend. "I love you. I don't say it enough because it feels weird, but I do. You and Mel and Jarrod and all of your family, too. I'd be completely nuts without you all."

"And we love you. But we should probably get to work. The Quincy case is pressing." A strict schedule, that was Brynna's way. Gabby, not so much, but she adapted because it mattered to her friend. "And it's 9:31."

"Yes, it is." A triple homicide that had started as a home invasion. She'd gotten ill just looking at the images stored on the suspect's smartphone.

Home invasions scared her more than any other case they dealt with. Benny was good about keeping her off those kinds of cases, but sometimes it was unavoidable.

Still, Gabby gave them the best she possibly could. She was a professional, and she prided herself on that. No matter how raw some of their cases left her feeling.

She was finally learning to just deal with things. Finally.

Just possibly, she'd be able to deal with Elliot Marshall, Junior, somehow, too.

CHAPTER TWELVE.

* * *

ANY day that started off with homemade pizza couldn't be a bad one, could it? At least, that's what Benny thought when he found the little note and container from one of his favorite girls in the middle of his desk.

Gabby was a real sweetheart, and he loved working with her and Brynna every single day. The two of them were good girls, just like his own three daughters, just as pretty, just as sweet, smart and kind. Benny's daughters were slightly younger than the two techs currently going through their pre-shift routine. *No one* messed with Gabby and Brynna's routine—at least not without consequences.

Benny had learned to adjust. They were talking about something, overanalyzing like they *always* did. He smiled. How many times had he sat in the living room of his house listening to his own trio of girls jabbering in much the same way?

His sons were older, and if he had his way, they'd be meeting Gabby and Brynna as soon as he could get the two girls *out* of the lab and into the real world somehow. His wife wanted grandchildren. These two would suit his boys nicely.

But Brynna and Gabby were remarkably unsocial at times.

He opened his office door to listen to them. He always got a kick out of their conversations. Between the two of them, their discussions went in some extremely unique directions.

Today's topic was the chief.

Benny's good mood evaporated almost immediately.

Marshall being back certainly complicated things for him. Made him feel on edge in a way he hadn't for years.

He listened to the girls, trying to figure out what was going on.

Benny didn't like the idea of Gabby getting with Marshall. Talking. Discussing the past.

Bringing up things that should be left alone and buried.

CHAPTER THIRTEEN.

* * *

THE day went quickly, and he wondered if it was the fact that once he got the lay of the land, so to speak, every TSP post was similar or if it had more to do with Gabby. He couldn't get her out of his head.

He hadn't been able to help himself; once he'd taken a peek in the plastic container and realized it *was* his mother's specialty pizza inside he'd had to head down to the breakroom and warm it up. The pizza had been perfect, and it had brought back good memories as well as the painful ones. Good ones that made him look forward to going through that final project of his mother's with the one person besides his brother who would understand what it meant.

It took him only a few moments to realize that it would most likely be just the two of them alone in her apartment. Laughing, looking at the good parts of the past. Sitting side by side. Close enough to touch. To watch her eyes darken when she looked up at him. When he leaned closer, brushed his lips against hers. He could lower her to the couch and…

He wasn't entirely certain how he felt about that. On one hand, he found her beautiful and intriguing, sexy in a lot of ways. On the other, he found her far too alluring for his own comfort. Nothing would ever come of it, and it was probably best to just stay as far from her as he could.

A woman like Gabby Kendall could confuse a man faster than anything. Could make him want things Elliot knew he couldn't have.

One dinner, then he'd stay far away from her. And he would make sure to keep his hands to himself.

CHAPTER FOURTEEN.

* * *

BENNY knew the threat the past meant to him. And he'd always been afraid something like this would come. It was why he had convinced the head of the IT department to transfer him the youngest, most inexperienced technician to Benny's department four years ago. Why he'd wanted Gabby where he could watch over her. Why he'd pulled her to day shift ahead of several other computer forensic technicians, who had more seniority. He'd wanted her close.

He'd just gotten too complacent over the last four years where she was concerned. He'd brooded about the Marshall Murders and Gabby's place in that crime all day. Worked himself up into a state of confusion and resignation.

If Gabby and Elliot Marshall started digging into the past, one of the mole holes they'd end up in would be *his.* He had no doubt about that. Benny had too much going on with his life to lose now. He couldn't let Gabby ruin what he'd built. But how was he to protect himself, his family, *and* her?

He cared about the two young women in his department—probably more than he did quite a few people with the TSP. But that didn't mean Benny didn't know the threat Gabby posed toward him.

All it took was her making a few simple connections, and everything he had would be lost. He didn't ever want to see a look of horror or disappointment in Nora and his children's eyes like had been there when his half-brother had been arrested all those years ago.

He wanted to be the hero for them that they had always thought that he was. Not some murdering bastard who killed little girls.

Little girls he'd known from the day they were born.

He'd never forgotten Sara or Slade Marshall. Those two kids sat on his shoulders and squeezed his heart almost every night. But he'd had no choice, and he'd accepted that long ago.

He had made his peace with what had happened and moved on. *Learned* from it.

Learned to watch his back better than he had.

He should have stayed away that night.

Gabby looked over and smiled at him. Such a beautiful, sweet-souled girl.

He'd been the one to look through Sara Marshall's webcam ten years ago and see her best friend. He'd recognized the girl. He and Elliot, Sr. had taken Sara and her best friend Gabby fishing six months before the murders. He'd found her charming, if a bit flighty back then. Harmless.

It had been Benny who had convinced the others to leave Gabby alone, that she probably wouldn't ever be able to identify them through the grainy webcam video anyway.

Because computers were his life—and because his own ass was just as much on the line as theirs, they had believed him.

When she'd applied to the TSP as a file clerk, he'd acted as a reference. When she'd wanted to transfer to his department, he'd welcomed her. Made it a cozy little haven for her. She was highly skilled at what she did, and the department benefited from having her, he couldn't deny that.

And what's more, he genuinely liked her.

He'd known Brynna her whole life, too. He'd been aggressive in getting her to his department three years earlier. Someone with her talent and skill was an asset any department would gladly possess.

They were nervous little creatures, though. Gabby and Brynna liked being isolated from the rest of the TSP, protected from the crowds.

They drew masculine attention—how could they not, as pretty as they were—but they didn't enjoy that. They'd rather hide. Benny indulged them. And when some of the guys got a bit too close to his girls, he'd step in. Protect.

Brynna was such a serious little thing, with big light brown eyes and long carrot red hair. She took everything so literally.

He listened to their conversation with half an ear. Gabby liked to chatter while she worked. Brynna definitely did not. There were a lot of "ums, and uh-huhs" from the slightly younger woman throughout their day. That was normal for them. His office was just close enough to their desks for him to hear most of what they said every day.

When he heard the talk shift to the Marshall murders, he sat up and paid closer attention. They rarely spoke of that, though he knew both had been impacted by it. By the loss of their friend Sara.

"So you don't mind if I look at the old video?" Brynna was asking. Benny's breath backed up. *He* most certainly did not want her looking at the zip drive in evidence.

He'd placed it there himself, and he knew exactly what it contained.

"No. But I don't want to look at it. Ever again," Gabby said. Benny had no difficulty imagining the look on her face. Gabby's face was as expressive as Brynna's wasn't. The two were opposites in a lot of ways, and exact copies of each other in still different ones.

He didn't want either of those girls digging around in that old file. Not for anything.

But how was he supposed to stop them?

He wanted to keep it quiet and buried for the rest of his life. And he for damned sure didn't want to make that note of fear creep into Gabby's voice. He hated it when she was afraid.

And then Brynna said something that made his blood run cold. "I'm thinking of running the video through Carrie's system. Seeing if there's anything on it the original investigators missed. And to see if our program works."

Brynna was talking about looking into the murders now.

Not Brynna. She didn't need to be involved in that shit in *any* way. Not with any of this.

Neither did Gabby, for that matter.

These two together? Would they be able to figure out who the men on the video were?

Bennett was the only one who'd gotten close enough to the camera that day. If he'd screwed up even once...

Brynna and Gabby *could* identify him. Could take what he'd done and pick it right apart. They were that good at what they did.

He coughed. And coughed some more as panic took hold of his throat. These girls could ruin him. End him.

And he wasn't the only man involved. If word got out to the wrong people, Gabby and Brynna would be as good as dead.

They rushed into his office, worry for *him* on their beautiful faces. Gabby put her hand on his shoulder. "Benny? Are you ok?"

Brynna grabbed a bottled water out of his mini-fridge and handed it to him. "You don't look good. I think you need to go home."

"I think you're right." He'd go home. And he'd try to figure out just what he was supposed to do now. Figure out how he was supposed to protect the people he loved the most.

CHAPTER FIFTEEN.

* * *

IT had been a particularly brutal day for Gabby's department, and she was jumpy by the time her shift ended—ninety minutes after she was supposed to clock out for the day. Benny had needed her to stay over since he'd left early. That extra hour had turned into ninety minutes, thanks to a last minute request from Guns and Gangs.

She had half an hour to take a taxi and get started on dinner before Elliot arrived.

The idea that Elliot was coming over was just another jumping bean down her spine.

She didn't know if she could do this. She'd never had on a man in her apartment except for Jarrod or Brynna's father. She'd been far too afraid to, honestly.

It all went back to the 'her apartment was her sanctuary' thing, didn't it?

Still, this was Elliot Marshall, head of the Finley Creek Texas State Police. If she couldn't trust a police chief, a man she'd known since before she had boobs, who could she trust?

Sobering thought.

She paid the cab driver and hurried into her building. She'd have to make sure the apartment was clean and that she had all the ingredients.

It was just dinner, Gab. Just dinner with an old friend. He wasn't going to eat her or turn into a troll, or a demon or anything else.

It wasn't a date or anything like that. It was dinner and conversation. Period. Between old family friends.

Maybe he needed it, too. Maybe he needed a reminder of what his family had been like from someone else's perspective.

Maybe she needed to call Mel and get some serious advice and fast. Get her head on straight, or something. She had her phone out and speed dial number three pressed with barely a thought. She'd just said hello when she arrived at her door.

Her *open* door. Her open and cracked door.

"Mel. My door's open. It's not supposed to be open!" She started to touch the door but stopped. Gabby knew better than to go into an unsafe situation. And this was definitely that. She flattened herself against the wall just outside her apartment and forced herself not to hyperventilate, or run screaming out into the night.

"Get out of the building and call it in. Don't look around, just go. Right now! Now, Gabby! Go! Get out! I'm on my way. I'm coming!"

CHAPTER SIXTEEN.

* * *

ELLIOT saw the Finley Creek city police cars—not TSP—the moment he pulled up outside Gabby's building. He parked and immediately went looking for the people in charge.

He flashed his credentials at the two officers and got the reverence and respect his position deserved. Texas State Police was higher on the jurisdictional hierarchy than city police. "Sir, there are two TSP detectives inside. We were just getting ready to interview neighbors."

"What happened? Was someone hurt?"

"B and E on the sixth floor. Apartment D."

"Six-D? Gabrielle Kendall? Gorgeous blonde with purple glasses? She's with the TSP."

"That's her."

"Have everything you find sent directly to the TSP, care of my office." He left the men and went inside. He didn't bother with the elevator. They'd said B-and-E, not assault. She was ok; she was ok. Elliot sped up. He needed to see her for himself.

Elliot found Gabby inside her apartment talking to two detectives he recognized from the second floor of the TSP. Evers and Callum, if he recalled correctly.

"Elliot!" She looked at him, and Elliot couldn't miss the panic in her eyes. She started to step toward him, and he saw just how pale she actually was. How she shivered. "You're here early. Thank goodness. I-I-I…"

Wild-eyed panic. Fear.

Damn it.

Hell with it, he needed to touch her. The thought of her scared and vulnerable pissed him off. And hurt him. What in hell had happened?

He barely looked at the trashed living room around him. He stepped over something—stuffing from an armchair, he thought—and put his hands on her shoulders. He turned her to face him. "Breathe, Gabby."

"I can't find Bug."

"Who?"

"My cat. He's not here. I can't find him."

No wonder. The living room and kitchen areas were damned near destroyed. Who? Why? "Honey, start at the beginning and tell me what happened."

"I came home and found my apartment like this. That's all I know. I went downstairs to the security guard, and he called it in. I stayed there until the local police came."

"Did you see anyone?"

"No." She swallowed and started shaking beneath his hands. "I noticed the door was open and it shouldn't have been. So I didn't go in, even to look for him. Bug had to have slipped out, Elliot. He's going to be really scared. He's an indoor cat."

"Inside an apartment building with doors that have to be buzzed open or opened with a code. We'll find the cat." The animal was the least of his worries. Whoever had done this to her apartment had taken one hell of a risk, and it was definitely targeted. Random breaking and entering wouldn't have done this kind of damage. Not like this. No random burglar had ever slashed an armchair in at least three dozen long slashes and then pulled the stuffing out into the floor. Not that he had ever seen, anyway.

No. That told him *rage.*

She had security in this building. No one should have been able to get into her apartment. Someone had to have that code. She'd given him the code that morning in his office and had told him that it changed on a monthly basis. It was a secured facility that she'd said her stepfather insisted she live in. Protected, as much as a young woman could be. Which could potentially limit their suspect pool, at least. He looked at her face again, and the depth of worry and fear had his gut clenching.

They'd find the sonofabitch who'd done this.

But first, they had to find the cat. Even if Elliot had to go door-to-door himself. He pulled her head to his chest and brushed a kiss over her blonde hair. "It'll be ok, baby. I promise. Even if I have to get the entire TSP post out, we'll figure this out."

Someone called her name from the door, and he turned to see the redhead who worked with Gabby in the forensics department. She stood just outside in the hall, holding a squirming and pissed off cat. Gabby looked at her friend and hiccupped.

"Bryn, you found him! Thank goodness."

"*He* found Mel. Ran right up to her like he always does. He was by the elevator. That big plant. I think he used it as a litter pan; *someone* is going to have to clean it out. It's gross. Can we come in or do we need to stay out here, Chief Marshall, sir?" She held the cat out away from her chest when he scratched at her arm with a back claw. "I *really* want to put him down now."

He couldn't remember her name. Had he heard it when he'd first entered the CF department a few days ago? "Call me Elliot when we're off the clock. No need for formality. Stay out there, though. Gabby, a cat carrier?"

She shook her head. "No."

Her friend had the solution. "I can put him in Jarrod's apartment. He won't mind. I have a key. For emergencies. This is an emergency."

"I forgot about Jarrod, where is he?" Gabby asked as another redheaded woman came up to the door. Elliot felt a small run of surprise. He knew the woman; had worked with her a few years earlier.

She hadn't been quite so thin three or four years ago—and hadn't been leaning on a crutch back then, either. "Melody? How—how are you?"

"Elliot, it's good to see you again. I heard through the grapevine you were taking Blankenbaker's place. I'm doing ok. As you can see, I had an argument with a .38. The .38 almost won. What happened here?" She looked at the two detectives expectantly. Elliot vaguely registered how the two men around his own age sucked in their guts and squared their shoulders when the woman focused on them. "Hey, boys. Long time, no see."

Mel had always had that impact on men of any age. It was the eyes and the hair. They'd laughed about it together before.

"I'll be back. I'm going to take him upstairs to Jarrod's," the other redhead said. Side by side they looked alike enough that he placed them as sisters, easily. Mel's hair was darker, but the similarities were strong.

It sank in then. Melody *Beck*. Kevin and Susan Beck's daughters. The Becks had been close friends of his parents for years. He'd probably known of the younger woman for her entire life. There had been one memorable Saturday when he'd babysat for the three younger ones. Most likely this friend of Gabby's was one of those girls, wasn't she?

That had been his one and only time ever agreeing to babysit for girls. They'd horrified him. Completely. Was this the one who'd locked him in the bathroom for two hours that day? The hair color was right—carroty. Only one had had hair that color. It probably was her, then. He'd been stuck in the Becks' bathroom until his father and hers had taken the door off the hinges to free him.

The connection to his past was pretty damned strong around there lately. She started to back out of the door; the cat tight in her arms.

"Wait. Detective Callum will escort you." It was entirely possible the person responsible for the damage to Gabby's apartment was still in the building. And he wasn't giving him another possible target in Kevin Beck's daughters. "Just in case."

She looked at the detective hesitantly. "Ok. Let's get going, then. He's scratching me and wants to be put down. Detective Foster lives on the eighth floor."

Callum looked at her appraisingly. Elliot had an idea what the man was thinking. The carrot hair didn't hide how pretty this Beck daughter was. "Yes, ma'am. You, uh, want me to carry him? I'd be glad to help."

"That's ok. I don't think Bug the Cat likes men very much. He only likes Gabby and me and Mel."

CHAPTER SEVENTEEN.

* * *

ELLIOT turned his attention to the other two women. Mel was in front of Gabby, speaking softly but firmly. Her free hand held Gabby's and Gabby was looking straight at her. Almost hyper-focused. Something about it struck him. It looked almost practiced. Like they'd been there before.

How close were they? He took a moment to study the two as they spoke. The younger sister returned within moments and settled next to Gabby on the couch. Melody had had to sit, regardless of the damage done to the furniture. He definitely wasn't used to seeing her so vulnerable.

Thankfully, the couch was undisturbed.

He couldn't say the same about the rest of the place. Or Gabby.

The panic had just kept growing in her eyes. He was honestly shocked she hadn't exploded by now.

Elliot felt like a fifth wheel while the Beck sisters tried to comfort Gabby.

Her panic and fear went deep. Traumatically deep, and Elliot totally understood it. For the first time, it started to sink in that what had happened to his family had greatly impacted her. Had shaped her into who she was now. *Still* influenced her every day of her life.

And what she was…was terrified. Who the hell had done this to her?

And how was he supposed to find them?

Elliot caught the look Mel sent him a few minutes later. She turned toward her sister. "Bryn, I'm going to talk to Elliot for a minute."

Brynna blinked at her sister, then nodded. "She's going to twig out again, isn't she?"

"Not if we don't let her. Help her get some clothes together for a few days." Mel's tone was firm. Elliot's curiosity rose. There was an undertone there that he didn't quite understand. "Go help her, Bryn. I think she needs it."

"Of course." She grabbed Gabby's hand and pulled her down the hallway, past Detective Evers.

Elliot waited until she was out of sight and looked back at Mel. "What do you want to say to me?"

"Outside. Just between the two of us."

It took her a moment to make her way out into the hall. When they were alone, he pulled the door shut behind them. "Ok. Spill."

"At least two dozen cops live in this apartment building, Elliot. Six or eight of them are with the TSP. Including two with Callum's department. One with Major Crimes. They'd have no difficulty getting the security code. Of getting in here. Something to keep in mind."

"I see."

"I don't quite think you do." Mel looked him straight in the eye and didn't sugar coat. Mel had always been straightforward, something he'd appreciated when they'd worked together before. "Gabby isn't the kind to make enemies. She barely leaves this apartment. She even has her groceries delivered. She doesn't drive, and the people she's closest to in this city are me, my sister, and Jarrod Foster. We get her out into the world as much as we can, but…that's it. She doesn't even speak to her neighbors."

That was more than he had expected. "Why?"

"Afraid. What happened to your family. What she saw. I have my theories and am convinced she has both anxiety issues and PTSD. Mild agoraphobia. This violation of her sanctuary is going to hurt her big time. We can take her home with us. We've done that before when she's had a tough time or two."

"No. If someone is targeting Gabby, I don't want your family in danger," Elliot said.

"Do *you* think this *is* related to the past?" Mel asked.

"I don't know. If it's not random, then what else could it be?"

"If it's not, there's a reason. I'm counting on you to find it. I'm a bit out of the game now. I wish…" Mel studied him for a minute. "This will hit her. *Hard.* Once it sinks in. If you need to, call us. We'll talk her down. We've done it before."

"She's lucky to have you as her friend."

"I don't think she's had very many of those in the last ten years. She's one of the most alone people I know. And we're just as lucky to have her. She's done wonders for Brynna as a friend. My sister's never had a *close* friend before Gabby. And she went with me to therapy when I was learning to walk again. Stuck by my side, no matter how snarly I got. My sisters are my sisters—but Gabby is my best friend. Take care of her, ok?"

"I'll do my best." How much taking care of did this woman do with Gabby?

"And one more thing—if you're not serious about her, you might want to cool down on the smoldering looks. Enough to melt a girl where it counts, if you know what I mean? Gabby hasn't caught on yet, but I'm not blind. Something to keep in mind." Mel grinned, and he remembered the woman she once was. It was nice to see she was still around in there, ready to yank on chains when needed.

"I'll keep that in mind."

CHAPTER EIGHTEEN.

* * *

GABBY wasn't ashamed to admit when she was scared. Especially with her two best friends. Now that Bug had been found she was starting to breathe again. Enough for the worry for the cat to be replaced by the fear for herself.

Her *home.* Someone had been in her home.

Gabby hugged Mel when the other woman held out her free arm once she'd returned from the hall where she'd been powwowing with Elliot.

"Do we have any idea who yet?" She needed names, faces before she even hope to think about what to do next.

"Elliot's talking with the detectives on duty," Mel said.

The TSP was dispatched to any call involving members of their branch of law enforcement; Gabby didn't know if it sucked to have two familiar faces in her living room or if it was a good thing. She knew the two men superficially, but that didn't matter. They'd still seen her underwear strewn all over her bedroom floor.

She doubted either of them had missed the tall dark-haired man who'd arrived moments after they had. Or the way he kept his hand on her back or her shoulder. How he kept her close.

She'd worry about that later. Gabby resisted the urge to cling to her friend like a total idiot.

Just having Mel there gave her a tiny boost of confidence. Mel was the kind of woman Gabby had always wanted to be. Strong, smart, funny...capable of just about anything. She was a few years older than Gabby, but the confidence she exuded didn't just come from age.

It came from ability. From the way people respected her friend. She and Brynna definitely didn't command the same kind of treatment.

Mel looked at the man behind Gabby. "Gabs, if you'd like, you can ride back to the house with us. The spare room is always open."

She'd slept over at the Beck house before. When Mel had first returned from St. Louis, Gabby and Brynna and Brynna's younger sister Jillian—a nursing student—had rotated staying with Mel in case she needed anything.

But this time... "Elliot's offered me his spare room."

Mel stared at her for a really long time, until Gabby was ready to squirm. "*Call* if you need anything, ok? Dad will be right there as quickly as he can. Probably with service pistol blazing."

Gabby smiled. She loved Mel's dad. He was one of those guys who adored his family and made no bones about it. And he'd made her welcome the first time she'd walked through the door.

He'd been the first TSP detective to take her statement ten years ago, and he'd been kind and patient. Protective. It had helped that she'd known him from the times they'd been at the Marshalls together. That memory would never leave her. No matter what happened. "I will. I..." Gabby sank onto the couch. "I'm not really sure what I'm supposed to do."

Mel and Brynna sat down on either side of her again. Their arms went around her—even Brynna, who rarely hugged anyone—and she clung right back. The tears fell fast.

It felt like her whole world had broken itself all around her again. She clung to the two people who mattered to her the most.

* * *

IT wasn't hard for anyone in the room to miss how close the three women were. He studied the faces of the detectives who'd answered the call. They were doing their best to be unobtrusive. He respected and appreciated their discretion. "The first moment you find something, I want to know about it."

"Yes, sir. Can you say for certain whether anything was taken?" the one on his left asked. Evers, Elliot thought. He spoke more often than his partner. His eyes went back to the trio on the couch.

"I'm not sure yet. We'll have to wait for Gabby to say one way or another and I think she's a bit overwhelmed." Mel was practically rocking Gabby *and* her younger sister. The strength of the connection between them was almost palpable. But…they *all* looked so damned vulnerable with the destruction of Gabby's home the backdrop.

"Yes, sir. We'll wait over here until she's ready."

"Thank you."

Elliot looked at the three women on the couch. He'd always liked and respected Melody. He'd even considered asking her out on a few occasions but had decided against it. She was the type of woman—much like

Gabby—that a man committed to. And Elliot hadn't been ready for that. He probably never would be.

He'd looked her up when he'd transferred to Finley Creek but had seen where she'd left the force. He hadn't decided if he was going to continue their friendship so hadn't taken the next step to contact her. Making casual friends wasn't something Elliot did much of.

She had her free arm around Gabby's shoulder and was reassuring her that the TSP would do everything possible and that she was safe. Mel was calm, reassuring, and firm.

Gabby didn't believe her; and who could blame her? She was panicking, frightened. Her safety had been violated, and after what she'd seen ten years ago, it was any wonder she hadn't fallen apart yet.

He knelt in front of the three women. Three pretty faces looked at him. "Gabby, you're safe. I'll see to that. You have my word. Get a bag together; we'll go to my duplex. We'll surround the damned building with TSP if we have to. You'll be safe, sweetheart. I promise."

He had caught the approval and speculation on Mel's face before she hid it quickly.

Gabby started to protest, but Mel cut her off. Deliberately. "You can't stay here. It's either with Elliot or Jarrod. Or us."

"And Jarrod's not home. He's making an arrest in that Quincy case," Brynna said. "You'd be alone, Gab. I say go home with the chief. You'll be safe there. At least you should be."

She hesitated, then nodded. "I guess. But what about Bug?"

"We'll get him and take him home with us." Elliot wasn't fond of cats, but he'd have a dozen brought into his apartment if that's what it took to erase the fear and panic in those big blue eyes. Anything.

CHAPTER NINETEEN.

* * *

BENNY felt like a total asshole. He hadn't *meant* to let all of his rage out on her apartment. He'd just been looking for some signs of what she'd been doing the night before. He'd overheard her and Brynna discussing journals and notes and the Marshall family. He'd only wanted to search her apartment, and maybe mess it up a little to frighten her. To remind Gabby of how vulnerable she still was.

Gabby really was a vulnerable little mix of anxiety, wasn't she? He spent half his work hours on some days keeping her from panicking over something inconsequential.

He knew how she felt about her home; how could he not?

It had been the situation he was angry with, not her. He'd needed to frighten her; he understood why. Gabby frightened meant Gabby retreating, hiding herself away, and not confronting anything.

That would buy him some time to *think* about what he was supposed to do now.

All of this was his brother's fault. If his brother hadn't pulled him into this shit twenty-four years ago, the events of ten years ago would not have happened.

The events of a few hours ago wouldn't have happened either.

It was all his brother's fault.

One choice twenty-four years ago had led to *this.*

And he didn't know what to do about it.

He just needed time to think.

Benny sat in his car, watching Evers and Callum as they talked to a few of Gabby's neighbors. No doubt they'd be checking security cameras soon. But Benny had thought about that.

It had been a simple matter for him to hack into the security companies digital files and blank out the system in Gabby's building for half an hour. Nothing he hadn't seen done before. One benefit of his position was access to the latest technology. He'd used that for personal means before.

Gabby came outside, carrying her cat against her chest, with the Beck sisters on either side of her.

No surprise. He'd expected them to show up and they had.

He ducked down farther in his seat when the older sister looked around the parking lot.

Mel was sharp as a tack and always had been. She'd been a damned fine police officer before the shooting. She'd been good, but Benny had been on the job since before Mel was born. He wasn't stupid.

He knew how to go undetected.

What concerned him most, though, was the tall dark-haired man walking behind them.

The idea that Elliot Marshall was taking an interest in Gabby—and Benny understood why the man *would*—had Benny's ulcer burning.

If the two started working together on what happened all those years ago, every layer of deception

Benny had put into place to protect those he loved would be rubbed away.

Exposed.

Benny would lose everything. He had five children and a beautiful wife who loved him.

He had so much to protect. To love. To cherish.

He couldn't let one bad choice all those years ago destroy everything he had now.

He waited until Marshall's car pulled out, then he followed, keeping a believable distance between them.

Benny wanted to know where the new chief was taking Gabby—just in case.

He parked his car in the apartment complex across the street from the chief's townhome, where he could have a clear vantage point of the place if they decided to leave.

Benny didn't know why he did it; he was certainly not planning on doing anything else he shouldn't that night.

He just wasn't ready to go home and face the bright smiles and pretty eyes of his daughters right then. Their faith and trust in him, their belief that he was *right* and *good* and working to make their world a safer place was more than he could deal with right then.

Gabby reminded him so much of his daughters.

If some bastard ever did something to deliberately terrify one of *his* girls the way Benny had set out to hurt Gabby, he'd rip them apart, wouldn't he?

What he'd done that afternoon was wrong, and Benny knew it.

He sat out in that parking lot for another four hours, until long after his girls were in bed.

What kind of bastard had he become?

CHAPTER TWENTY.

* * *

EVERY pair of panties and every bra she had had been sliced into ribbons. Just her undergarments.

A definite and deliberate *personal* threat. It sickened him.

As long as he lived, Elliot knew he would never forget how terrified she had been. How she had looked at him with pain and real fear in her blue eyes.

He could have a security detail assigned to watch her if he chose. Elliot knew he might be overreacting because of the emails she'd mentioned, but he'd rather overreact than have something happen to her.

Still, there were only a few pairs of eyes he absolutely trusted. He made a quick phone call when Gabby took a few minutes in his bathroom to freshen up. He got as satisfactory of an answer as he possibly could. When he disconnected she was just stepping out of the bathroom, wearing a soft t-shirt and cotton pajama pants with cats all over them. "Chance will be coming in tomorrow morning. He's going to look into this privately for me."

"Is that such a good idea? We don't know who did this to my apartment. It could have been random. You're the chief. People are going to talk about us. About this."

"Honey, someone did it deliberately. It wasn't random. And we both know that. I'd rather my brother be here to take a look into things, off the TSP books. In the meantime, you and I have to go about business as usual. Until we know more."

"I can't stay at your side forever, Elliot. You'd lose your job; I'd be in serious trouble for mine. And not to mention the rumors that are already flying since someone mentioned that I was alone in your office. I'm sure you don't want your name associated with me romantically, so that's something else we need to consider. It has to be embarrassing for you. Awkward for me. And some of the women at the TSP can be seriously catty where attractive men are concerned."

That hadn't even occurred to him, though it probably should have. Him being the boss and her a beautiful available woman? If she'd been a man they wouldn't have the gossip, but the fact that she was a beautiful woman? Rumors were a definite possibility. Speculation could kill someone's career real fast. "You've not got a boyfriend waiting in the wings who will be upset with you staying with me tonight?" A boyfriend who should be there, keeping her protected? If Gabby was *his,* he wouldn't leave her safety to some other man. No way in hell.

More blushing when she looked at him. Elliot wondered just how deep the flush went. How much of her skin was pink now? "No. Hardly. I don't date. At least, I haven't in about three years. Just didn't work out. He wanted someone a little less…*panicky*…over certain things. I don't know if you noticed, but I tend to have a few obsessive compulsive behaviors. I didn't use to. I mean not as bad. I had it as a kid, mildly. But after Sara and Slade…well, I tend to have an anxious…and rambling…personality. I'm sorry. I'm babbling again, aren't I? Just tell me 'Shut up, Gabby.' next time, okay?"

"I'm not going to tell you to shut up." Elliot grabbed her bag off the couch and put it next to the chair. He hadn't unpacked the spare room completely, but there was a bed in there. For the rare times his brother would visit. If Chance ever did. "I have a spare bedroom."

"Can't I sleep with you?"

His head jerked toward her. Her cheeks turned red, and her eyes widened.

"I'm *super* sorry. That came out totally wrong. You probably really don't want to sleep with me. Oh, wow. It keeps going, doesn't it? I…am shutting up now. Totally shutting up now." Her embarrassment hung on the air between them. The pink in her cheeks deepened.

He couldn't help it. Elliot laughed. She was too damned cute not to. Cute, definitely. There wasn't anything else that would describe her. Physically, she was stunning, but her personality made her *cute*.

Perhaps *sweet* was a better word. *Loveable.*

He'd never thought adorable was attractive before, but as he stared at her standing there with her hands over her cheeks, and her eyes wide and embarrassed, something clicked in his head.

Sleep with her? Curl around her body, press up against her through the night.

Hell yes, that was exactly what his body was telling him he wanted.

He'd just have to be an adult and not a horny teenager. That was all. The reasons ran through his head right after another. He was her boss, and she'd had a frightening evening, he was too old for her, she'd been his sister's best friend, and she was far too vulnerable, etc., etc. He told himself all of those things. It didn't matter.

Elliot had no business even thinking about what she'd look like under her clothes. Or under him.

No business at all.

"I'll be right next door. It has a connecting door between the two rooms. We can leave it open if that will make you feel safer." He stepped over toward her and pulled her hands down from her cheeks. "Hey, listen. *Nothing* is going to happen to you here. I promise. And you don't have to be embarrassed for being scared."

"Yeah. I'm going to hold you to that, Elliot. And if you mess up and I get killed, I'm going to haunt you. Every night. Probably at seven o'clock. Just as you're trying to eat dinner, I'll do something to remind you of me." The humor was her way, wasn't it, of dealing with the inevitable tension and nerves?

And she was nervous in his home.

Why? He took her hand and led her down the hall. Not toward his bed like he wanted, but toward the guest room.

"We can get something to eat as soon as you're settled in. The top two drawers are empty. There should be room for your stuff."

"Thank you. I really can't thank you enough." She sank down on the foot of his guest bed and looked up at him. He valiantly ignored the sight of her with a soft bed just waiting behind her. "If you hadn't been with me I'd still be at my apartment a blathering mess. Mel and Bryn would have found me in a puddle of blather, I swear. *They* were in my home. My home. They're coming for me, aren't they?"

Wet blue eyes blinked rapidly.

But what broke him was the tear that slid down her cheek.

Elliot scooped her up into his arms and held her while she cried.

CHAPTER TWENTY-ONE.

* * *

ELLIOT opened the door to the man knocking just after midnight. The guy on his porch was one he almost didn't recognize. His brother had changed in the ten years since their family's deaths. He'd hardened, and he'd turned toward hunting. Toward fighting. Toward tracking the lowest of men.

Elliot understood. The demons that drove him drove his brother, too. Only it had been because of an argument with Slade that had kept Chance from being there that night.

Chance had never told him exactly what it was they'd argued about. And Elliot had never asked. Just accepted that they both had their demons.

"I'm here. What the hell is going on?" Chance had a black bag thrown over his shoulder. It was all his brother carried.

"Someone has targeted Gabby Kendall. I need you to find the man responsible for me. Privately."

His brother stared at him then started into the duplex Elliot rented about a mile from the post. "You think it's the same people as before? I figured someone would come after her, eventually. They always promised they would. Kid's been living on borrowed time."

His brother's words were cold.

Uncaring.

"You knew she could be targeted and you've done nothing about it? She's terrified and vulnerable." A thought occurred to him and had him shifting to block his brother's entrance into the house. "Or is that what you're planning on?" He trusted his brother, didn't he? To always have his back—to do the right thing. Protecting Gabby was the right thing. He had no doubt about that. Did Chance? How far had his brother's demons driven him? Chance wasn't planning to eventually *use* Gabby as bait, was he?

"You think I'd throw *Sara's* best friend to the wolves? Hardly. Anyone else but her, maybe." Chance pushed past him and made his way through the front door and into the kitchen. Elliot followed.

"Then what exactly do you know about this?"

"Where is she? I assume you've made some arrangements to keep the girl safe?"

His brother was dressed more like an army ranger than a former Texas Ranger. Gray BDU pants and a black long-sleeved t-shirt and heavy boots made up his brother's entire outfit.

He looked dangerous, cold, and damned hard. Rough.

"She's here. Asleep in the spare bedroom."

"Putting you both in danger. Damn stupid, wouldn't you think? I'm sure there are safe houses she could go to. All it would take would be the Chief of the Finley Creek TSP making a simple phone call to arrange it."

"What else was I supposed to do? I wasn't letting her go through this alone. And I want the answers to whether this is related to our family. If it is, then she's definitely *my* responsibility."

"And the chance to catch the sons-of-bitches responsible isn't ninety percent of why you brought her here? Or is there more to it than that?"

Elliot opened the fridge and pulled out soda for each of them. His brother never touched alcohol. Something Elliot agreed on. "She's a sweet woman. Who doesn't deserve any of this."

"She's beautiful, too. I'm sure that doesn't hurt anything. The guy has a hard time resisting a woman who looks like her. I'm not blind. Considered it myself a few years ago. That why she's really here? You want her in your bed?" Chance looked at him, speculation in his eyes. "You'd be stupid to get messed up with a girl like her, though. She's too good for one of us."

That was something Elliot definitely agreed on. Gabby needed a stable guy without all the baggage. Someone who could see just how special she was. Someone who could give her a pretty house, pretty kids, and an absolutely pretty life. Elliot was not that man. "It's not like that. She's here until we figure out who trashed her place and we make sure she's safe there again."

"She'll have to go home sometime. Or this is going to mess shit up for you. Can't have one of your employees living with you in sin, you know. You ready for that? Or you plan to keep her here with you forever? You got a thing for her?"

"My interest right now is on finding the bastard responsible for the damage to her place. Nothing else." He leveled a look at his brother. "They sliced up her underwear, Chance. All of her underwear—none of her other clothes. Tell me what you think of that?"

"Doesn't sound random. She got a stalker who's going to come after you for bringing her here? Or is that something you're planning on? Standing between her and the bad guy? I think you're nuts, big brother. She's going to get her hooks into you for sure. And you'll never be able to shake a woman like her loose."

"Elliot?"

She was there, in the hallway. Looking beautiful and soft. Sexy.

Vulnerable…and mortified.

She'd heard him and his idiot brother, then, hadn't she? "Gabby, honey. I…"

Her chin went up, and pride flashed in blue eyes. "Hey, no need for explanations. I understand. And thou shalt not eavesdrop, right? Chance, I have no intentions of getting my hooks into your brother. I don't even *have* hooks anywhere. I'm afraid I'll poke myself or something. Mel and Brynna barely let me have kid scissors, after all."

So subdued. Her voice lacked the typical breezy, light Gabby tone. Her eyes weren't as bright as he was used to seeing, either. She'd definitely heard them, and it *had* hurt her.

He was the damned chief of police here; he could have arranged for her to have a safe house, to have a security detail assigned to her, or had her put up in a hotel with half the damned TSP post assigned to guard her if he wanted.

But he hadn't.

He'd brought her to his home.

What did that say about *his* expectations? He hadn't been thinking of possible career ramifications by having her in his own home; he'd only been thinking that she was scared and he'd wanted to protect her. Stand between her and whatever bad came her way. Did that say something about what he was feeling for her? It went beyond wanting to keep her safe, didn't it? It was *him,* wanting to protect *her.* Him not trusting anyone *else* to do the job. Because of her connection to his family? The connection between her and his family was tenuous at best now. This was about how *he* felt about *her.* Nothing more. "Gabby, sweetheart, you have to ignore my idiot brother here. He's allergic to women at times. I think he's a coward, actually. Afraid some decent woman will set her sights on him someday."

"I understand. I can still go to a hotel if you think that would be best. I know there's nothing *romantic* between us. Why would there be? Something like that between you and someone like me?"

Wow. Her eyes could stab a man straight in the gut, couldn't they? He ignored his brother's rude snort. He'd deal with Chance in a minute. "My focus *right now* has to be on keeping you safe. And damn it, that is exactly what I am going to do."

"Thank you. I do appreciate it. This isn't going to cause you problems being the division chief, will it?" Still so subdued. Did she believe him? He couldn't tell. She turned toward his brother, a wary look still on her face. "Chance, it's...well, can't really say it's *good* to see you again, but I'm glad you're looking well. I'm sure the two of you have lots to talk about. I'll just go back to the guestroom and let you do it. Good...uh...night."

"Good night, Gabby," Chance said. His tone had changed, softened. Elliot glanced at his brother's face.

There was a gleam of interest in his brother's eyes.

He got it. Gabby looked beautiful with her long blonde hair falling in waves down her back, her light pajamas hinting at the delicate feminine body beneath. He loved it when her hair was down. How it made a man want to wrap his hands in that gold mass and use it to hold her still while he kissed the hell out of her. No doubt Chance knew exactly what Elliot was thinking.

It was very clear to him—and probably his damned brother, as well—that Gabby Kendall was a damned attractive woman. One that would draw a man's attention from a thousand miles away.

She was beautiful, intriguing, and sexy as hell.

Damn it.

He waited until she was out of the room then glared at his brother. "Thanks, little brother. You don't have to look at her that way, either."

"Why not? She looked damned sexy just now. How can a man *not* look? No wedding ring. And she doesn't want to mess anything up for *you*. But I'm not TSP…"

"No. Don't even think it." Chance and Gabby? His brother was the last man any decent woman would need in her life. Chance wasn't the kind of guy who stuck around for anything. It was clear with just one look at him. Was everything Chance owned in that duffle bag? Elliot wouldn't be surprised.

"You want to think about it? Have you already?"

How was he supposed to answer that? "I'm not going to answer that."

"Coward. Until you make a claim on someone like her, you can't stop a guy from looking. Imagining just what is under those kitten covered pajamas."

"We need to focus on the task at hand. Like it or not I can't be there every second. Even at the TSP. And I want someone I know and trust on this. Just until I'm satisfied it's not connected to our family, at least. If it's something else, we'll let my people handle it following protocol."

"You have an entire police force at your disposal. Shouldn't they be able to handle finding a burglar?

Keeping your little hot stuff there safe? Isn't that kind of a perk of your position?"

"Her name is Gabby, Chance. Use it. She's safe at the TSP during the day. But I want you in the house at night. Dig around during the day for me. We have to sleep sometime. I need eyes. And you understand the stakes here. You're just as invested as I am if it's something from ten years ago."

"And then it's *our* fight. If it's the same bastards as before, I want them, El. And I'm going to do whatever I have to in order to get them."

"Maybe. But you are not using *her*." On that, he was absolutely serious.

"Why not? If they've already targeted her, why shouldn't we use that to our advantage?"

"Because..." His brother had a point, and if it was anyone else, he'd be the one suggesting it. But Gabby...Gabby was a part of Sara. The last one he still had, and one he didn't want to risk. And because of the way she'd looked when he'd first found her in her apartment. How vulnerable, how she'd looked at him like he could protect her from any asshole who'd ever looked at her sideways. How for a moment there, he'd felt like he could if she'd just smile at him again. "Because she was Sara's best friend. And I didn't protect Sara, the least I can do is protect her best friend. And...and she's *Gabby*. Sweet, funny, beautiful. There's something about her...I won't risk her in this."

Chance stared at him for a long moment. "So we find another way, then. One that doesn't put that pretty little ass in the line of fire."

"We find another way. I want her free from all of this, Chance. For ten years she's lived her life afraid. While *we've* been pissed and hunting, she's been afraid and hiding. Seriously afraid. And I hate that. Hate how she's been hurt."

"You're falling for her." Chance snorted. "Hell, I think you're past that point. You're totally gone. Might as well pack it in and call a minister. You're a goner."

"I just realized who she was a few days ago. Not even a week." No. He wasn't. Elliot was for damned sure not getting involved with a woman like Gabby. A woman like his mother, one made for families and cooking large Sunday dinners and snuggling on the couch. *That* kind of woman definitely wasn't for him. Just because Gabby wasn't the kind of woman he wanted in his life didn't mean he was going to let her face this alone.

"I know you, big brother. And I know you already have. She's got all the earmarks of the type you like but won't do anything about. It's the eyes, right? Or the body. Or the hair. A man looks at that hair and thinks of other places he wants to see it." Chance prowled around the kitchen, checking the windows. Then he did it a second time. Elliot wasn't surprised; his brother always had been like a caged wolf. He'd only gotten worse in the last ten years. "I don't know if it's a good thing or not. Don't do anything stupid. Women like her…they make a man stupid, vulnerable. Make him think of things that he shouldn't. Like the forever type of things. Houses, kids, dog. Mortgage. You ready to sign up for that shit, El? This here is a good start." Chance lifted the cat off the table where he had jumped up to investigate—he held the beast out significantly.

"Opinion or advice, whatever, noted. Now, shouldn't we discuss what you've been doing the last few months?" Elliot took the cat and put him on the floor.

"I followed a lead in Oklahoma. It didn't pan out. Ran down a kidnapper in St. Louis last week. The usual."

"You thinking of finding a job anytime soon? Or still freelancing?" His brother had private investigation licenses in at least three states that Elliot knew of. Chance would take on high-risk jobs for private clients and live off the proceeds for months at a time. Chance had always said his needs weren't much. Half the time Elliot feared his brother was sleeping in a car, or hotel, or on a park bench. The rest of the time he knew better. His brother had a home, somewhere. Elliot just didn't know where.

His brother wasn't homeless, but nothing he did was ever permanent. And hadn't been in ten years. For a moment, Elliot cursed the bastards from the past again—this time for what they'd done to his brother. Chance had been so different ten years ago.

So normal.

"I'm flush for a while. I'm not looking for permanent commitments until this is done."

"Obsession is never healthy, Chance."

"Maybe not. But they deserve justice. And I'm going to give it to them."

Elliot understood the drive; he was just starting to question the final cost. He didn't want anyone else in his life lost to the past. "Just don't let it keep you from living your own life. That would just piss them off; we both know that."

CHAPTER TWENTY-TWO.

* * *

GABBY tried not to let the embarrassment make her do anything too stupid. Like her going back out there and insisting they take her home. Or back to the TSP post and let her sleep there, surrounded by a wall of blue. Or rather dark green—TSP wore dark green uniforms to differentiate them from the city cops around here.

To hear Elliot and his brother discussing her that way? No wonder her cheeks were still burning. Hooks? She didn't want to *hook* Elliot!

"I won't think about it right now. I'm going to sleep. In this nice cozy bed. With two strong men out there to protect me, and two highly trained TSP officers outside to stand watch. I am *not* helpless, nor will I allow myself to be a wimpy mass of useless fear any longer. I am going to go to sleep, and that is final. And I won't think of Elliot Marshall, Jr. *that* way. Not like that. Hooks, my rear end."

Yeah, like that would work.

It was a long time before she slept.

She beat Elliot to the kitchen the next morning. Chance was there already, looking all gorgeous and broody as he sipped a cup of coffee.

He was the darkest of the brothers. Where Elliot's hair was a rich brown, Chance had almost black hair.

Chance just looked like a meaner, harder version of his older brother. Whereas Elliot looked like a hero-type, this one looked a little more like a villain.

She'd never really gone for the bad guy type, even though she knew Chance was good-at-heart.

He'd inherited his father's green eyes just like his brother, though. Deep and piercing, and enough to have her squirming and dribbling coffee down the front of her shirt.

She pulled the cotton away from her skin and fanned it back and forth, hoping to at least cool the hot liquid off. It was just a few spots, after all. Meaningless in the grander scheme of things. Besides, she spilled *something* on herself at least four times a week, didn't she?

She felt like a complete idiot when Elliot walked in and looked at her like she was…well…a complete idiot.

"Cloths are in the drawer there on the left."

"Thanks." Gabby turned away from him, knowing her cheeks had to be red—again. She'd been nothing but embarrassed since realizing *he* was the new police chief.

Well, at least she didn't need to wear make-up anymore. She had a permanent blush on her cheeks, now.

At least in his presence.

"I…I'm good. I'm on the schedule to be at work at nine. I don't know how you want to do this. I can just take some time off. Vacation time, comp time, big-chicken-needs-to-hide time. Find a hole and hide out in it for a while. I don't want to put you out. It probably wasn't the murderers anyway. I mean, what are the chances? It's not even the anniversary or anything. I can talk to Benny, tell him what's going on. Brynna's going up to St. Louis today to see her sister, but Benny can call one of the swing shifters in. I know he can."

"Gabby, you're rambling." Elliot dropped his hand to her shoulder and squeezed. So warm.

She looked up at him and tried to ignore his brother. It didn't work. He was more intimidating than Elliot could ever hope to be. And that was saying a lot. "That surprises you?"

"Not at all. You do it when you're nervous." He stepped closer, then reached behind her and pulled a hand towel from the drawer right behind her. He held it up level with her chest. "You don't have to be nervous here. And you're not going anywhere. I promised to keep you safe, and I meant every word. I've adjusted my schedule to fit yours, and I've spoken with your department head. Benny understands what's going on. Until this is settled, you'll be working the same hours as I am. And you are to go nowhere alone, outside of this building."

"Isn't that going to put a crimp in your style, for your…head of the TSP post stuff?"

"I've not been in this position long enough to have a style. Don't forget that. I don't do agendas, other than my own." He put his hands on both of her shoulders and turned her to face him. "My main goal is to keep you safe right now. Don't forget that. Journey can handle rescheduling if needed. We've deliberately kept my schedule light until Monday so that I can take a look at each department appropriately." He shocked the tar out of her when he leaned down and kissed her—right on the lips. Not a long embrace; just a quick enough brush for her to taste coffee on his lips. For him to comfort. Gabby just wanted to stay right where she was for a while. He pulled away. "It'll be ok, Gabby. I promise."

"Hey, I'll be ok. I'll just hide out with Benny. That'll work, won't it?" Gabby's hands climbed up around his neck like some puppeteer was controlling them with a string. She couldn't help herself. His slipped to her waist, and he held her. Close. Tight. Safe. Just as he had when she'd practically cried herself to sleep the night before. Long before Chance had shown up.

Chance coughed behind them, reminding her that they weren't alone in the kitchen.

And Chance was watching them.

CHAPTER TWENTY-THREE.

* * *

CHANCE watched the way his brother practically hovered over the girl. Elliot was definitely toast. Already gone over her. In less than a week. It didn't make a damned bit of sense to him. Yeah, she was pretty and sweet and smart and the kind of woman a guy wanted to keep forever.

But what was Elliot thinking? How could he even consider letting a girl like her get under his skin?

His brother was thirty-six now. Chance took a quick look around. The townhouse was nice. His brother had worked his ass off to move up the TSP ladder, and it was paying off. Elliot had a great job, decent place to live, and had just moved home after ten years away.

Maybe his brother was lonely? Maybe Elliot was looking for something *more* than just a damned townhouse and his career?

Elliot was the kind of man who'd be a good family man. His father certainly had been. His brother was good with kids, good with elderly ladies, a boy scout at times.

Hell, the picket fence lifestyle might be just what his brother needed. He could almost see that.

A girl like Gabby? She'd probably suit his brother just fine. Could Elliot be happy like that? Chance wasn't stupid—he knew his brother wasn't *happy* now. Not down deep. But then again, who was?

Chance leaned forward. *If* someone *was* after the girl, and he strongly suspected there was, he'd find them.

There wasn't a damned thing he wouldn't do to keep her safe.

Not just because it was the right thing to do, or because she was his sister's best friend, or because she was just too damned vulnerable to deal with this kind of thing—hell, he was going to do it for his brother.

Elliot shouldn't have to be alone just because they'd lost everyone *else* they'd loved. It wasn't right at all.

If Elliot wanted the girl permanently, he deserved the chance. Both Elliot *and* Gabby deserved to be happy.

CHAPTER TWENTY-FOUR.

* * *

SHE kept herself from freaking out somehow. Barely. Maybe, for the most part. It wasn't easy. Elliot stopped in to talk to Benny and check on her. Her supervisor looked at her with a worried expression and patted her on the shoulder.

"Don't worry, Chief Marshall, our Gabby will be taken care of. I can promise you that."

"Thanks, Benny. It's probably nothing, a random break-in, but with the security at her building so tight, we're not willing to take a chance on it being more than that."

"Of course," Benny said.

"Gabby, I'll try to make it to lunch around two-thirty. We'll eat together. If I can't, I'll message you. *You* do not leave this building. Understood?"

She didn't want him to go, but Gabby understood. There was no way she'd ever be able to have the Chief of Finley Creek TSP to herself completely. Elliot was as much his job as his father had been. It would consume his life almost completely for as long as he had the position. Sara had told her how it was with her own father. Elliot Sr. loved his family—but he'd loved his job, too. Every spare minute he had—which wasn't much—

had gone to his family. But Elliot had no family at home. The *job* was going to be his life, wasn't it?

The hours were longer than usual. Brynna had left for her trip. She'd had the meeting in St. Louis scheduled for three weeks in advance. They were talking about the software Brynna had developed. Lucas Industries wanted to back it for production, to be sold to law enforcement agencies around the world.

Gabby was so proud of the work her best friend had done on the project.

Plus, the trip got Brynna away from the commander of the Major Crimes Unit. The guy had given Brynna a very pricey flower arrangement and offered to take her to a very nice restaurant to thank her for her long hours on the Quincy case.

Brynna had accepted the flowers but declined the dinner invitation. Her friend was adamantly not looking for romance right now—even though she'd confessed to Gabby that she actually *liked* the MCU commander a great deal.

Brynna got really jumpy when commitment with a man was even hinted at.

Gabby half thought Brynna was afraid she couldn't do a relationship well, especially with a man more than ten years her senior.

She missed her friend. She and Brynna were on the schedule together ninety percent of the time and had been for at least the last eighteen months.

She was such a big weenie, wasn't she? Needing her bestie to hold her hand.

Gabby rolled her eyes and got back to work. Benny wanted her to get started on a dozen ATM cameras, to search out a common face. Hopefully, they'd be able to catch a push-and-grabber before lunch. The jerk had preyed on young mothers with babies in strollers. Grabbed their purses and bags and ran. He'd take the cards then dump the rest of the bags a block away.

Gabby wanted him found as fast as possible. Why would someone target someone with a baby? That was just…wrong. She tried to talk to Benny, but he had one of his moods on.

Sometimes he was approachable, other times he most definitely was not. It was best to just leave him alone when things got to him. She and Brynna had learned that lesson a while back.

But it made for a very long day.

* * *

ELLIOT'S day was busier than the previous few, for damned sure. Evers and Callum had a report on his desk fifteen minutes after they clocked in for the day.

The only thing they'd found about the break-in was that security videos were missing and one of her neighbors had reported seeing an average height white man walking on the floor who she didn't recognize.

They had no more than that. Everyone did agree with one thing—whoever was responsible had probably targeted her deliberately.

That had him distracted all day. Worried. Had him starting to head down to the Computer Forensics department and check on her himself over half a dozen times. He stopped himself every time. But it was hard.

Chance's taunting earlier had stuck in the back of his mind all day. Had him imagining things he probably shouldn't be.

Elliot pushed those thoughts aside and focused on budgetary meetings and promotion requests. Everything from Computer Forensics to Janitorial needed more bodies. Which meant more money. Which meant taking money from other departments…who also needed bodies. It was a vicious cycle, and one he hated to be in charge of. But it was a duty he'd signed up for when he took the job.

His first love was the patrol officers. They were the backbone of the TSP, the face the public saw. If he had his way he'd give a ten percent raise across the board, make comp-time more available, and add thirty percent more officers to the streets.

He definitely wasn't going to be able to do any of what he wanted, but he was able to approve ten more patrol officers, and move three who were ready to be promoted to detectives up the ladder.

It was a start. No doubt about it.

Journey took the paperwork with his signature to handle the next steps, but it left Elliot feeling like he was finally getting the Finley Creek ball rolling. Blankenbaker had been a good chief—his father had worked with him back when Elliot was a teenager—but over the last few years as Blankenbaker's wife started getting sick the chief's attention had started to shift.

Elliot couldn't blame him. When Blankenbaker had realized what was happening, he'd stepped down. It had been a tight ship before it had happened.

The mayor called for an update on the Tenth street crime reduction project Blankenbaker had started. Elliot thought it was a good start. He'd move bodies that way as soon as he could. Hopefully, an increased presence would equal a decrease in petty crime.

Officer Journey brought him the rest of his docket. "Here's what we've got for this afternoon, sir. A busy day."

"Hopefully a productive one." He took the top file from his assistant. "Call down to Computer Forensics. Tell Gabby it'll probably be two-thirty or two-forty-five before I'm free for lunch."

"Of course, sir. I'll let her know."

"And, get me Detective Evers, please. I need to speak with him about the break-in in Ms. Kendall's building last night."

"Yes, sir. Was anything taken? Was Ms. Kendall hurt?"

"No. But the vandalism was more than a simple burglary. It concerns me. I want to keep informed."

"Of course, sir."

He wanted to be out there searching for the assholes himself, and Elliot freely admitted that. But he couldn't exactly get his ass out there with the entire damned TSP post demanding his attention, could he?

CHAPTER TWENTY-FIVE.

* * *

GABBY made a point of staying right in the lab. People were talking about her and Elliot—and what had happened. Sometimes right in the room with her. It was almost like some of the women were coming to the Computer Forensics department *just* to see what she was doing with Elliot. A few men were curious, too. Benny finally stepped in and told the last bunch that if they didn't need anything to head back to their own departments. Gabby was mortified. She hated being the center of gossip, even if Elliot was used to it.

She didn't venture out until Journey called and said Elliot would be free for lunch soon. Even if it was up in his office. Well, Gabby was ok with that part. Better to hide out than deal with people staring at them both. He couldn't leave; he was waiting for an important phone call from the Superintendent of the entire TSP. She sat quietly while he finished the call, picking at the lunch she'd made for both of them that morning.

Elliot seemed to really like her cooking, at least. She could pay him back for all the trouble she'd caused him by feeding him anyway. Besides, she liked doing it for him.

Their lunch was inundated with call notifications and messages ringing his computer over and over again.

He finally told Journey to hold his calls to give him a decent lunch. Gabby definitely couldn't handle having that many people making demands on her like that.

But he did just fine.

When the calls were finally silenced for a few minutes he relaxed, right before her eyes. It was almost like there were two men inside of him—the Chief and Elliot. Was he happy that way? Gabby studied his eyes for a moment, trying to answers that question. Was he happy? She had no clue.

"Is it always like this? So…hectic?"

"Sometimes. A part of it is the newness of me being here. Different people are wanting to make the necessary connections to…get what they want from me. The mayor, for instance. Plus the governor's office calls regularly. I think that's just Marcus being a dick, but…it's still a time suck."

"Did you just refer to the governor of Texas as a dick time suck?"

"I sure did. He's always been that way." He smiled, flashing the dimples at her for just a moment. "He's my first cousin, Gabby. I'm not sure why I'm in this position, though. Unless it benefits our dear governor. I hate politics."

"I'm sure you've earned it. Garrity made lots of strides while you were there." Gabby felt her cheeks heat. "I looked it up."

"Did you? I hope you didn't see the worst of my reputation."

She strongly suspected he was a straight-arrow. Good, honorable. Always do the right thing. But how happy was he? "I don't think there was anything bad, Elliot. Did you like Garrity?"

He was quiet for a long while. She thought he wasn't going to answer. "It was small. Less than five hundred people in the town. I knew most of them. Garrity is a rural post, and that meant no city police. We covered the entire area."

"Do you think you'll miss it?"

"Garrity was the forgotten post of the TSP, Gab. No politics. I stink at politics." His smile was rueful as he held up a note with the governor's name on it.

"Yet you did just fine on the phone. I couldn't do it. You were actually *nice* but firm with the mayor. You got what you wanted, didn't you?"

"Yes. An increased TSP and city police presence down on Tenth Street and Bothe. There's been some gang activity down there that I don't like."

"You're responsible for everyone, aren't you?" Those shoulders were certainly broad—but were they strong enough to support the entire city? Gabby mentally shook herself for being so fanciful. Elliot would not have gotten as far as he had if he wasn't extremely good at what he did. He could do it.

"The entire region covered by Finley Creek. Forty-two thousand people. We average fifty-eight staff of the TSP per ten thousand civilians. Garrity had nine people for approximately five hundred civilians. Superintendent thought that was excessive. He cut it in half the month before I left."

"Ouch. I'm sorry."

"I understand his reasoning. But…they were my people. Two took transfers to Wichita Falls, another to Houston. I was offered this *after* I told the superintendent what I thought."

"You get cited for that?"

"He couldn't suspend me without making a PR fuss. Apparently, I'm well-liked by the citizens of Texas. One of my staff made a fuss to the papers a while back after a particular case I worked involving the FBI. Which the FBI confirmed. They claim I saved an agent's life—who is from Texas originally. Native daughter and all of that. Governor Deane and Superintendent Alvarez like publicity like that."

"And you don't."

"Not at all. Unless it furthers the TSP cause. Then parade me around like a damned monkey in a purple flame bikini."

She laughed. "That would definitely get publicity, wouldn't it?"

"It sure would." He grinned again, then sobered. "I'm going to be here until six, at least. I'll come down for you, ok?"

"Of course. It's whatever works best for you. You're the boss, after all."

"I may be the Division Chief, sweetheart. But I'm Elliot first. I have to be."

"I couldn't do it. I'm happy being hidden in the annex. It works for me. There's no serious pressure down there. I can't deal with pressure, at all."

He stared at her for a moment as she chased a mushroom around her salad with her fork. She knew the questions were inevitable. "Why the anxiety, Gabby? Is it because of ten years ago?"

"Hmmm. Part of it is genetics, but a lot of it *is* ten years ago, I think. And the emails that continued for years really did something up here." She pointed to her forehead. "Not good things; that's for sure. I've tried not to let it get to me. And I go stretches at a time without a problem. Then something will set it off. There was this one night in a movie theater parking lot, right before Mel got shot. It was around ten, a summer night. Beautiful out, really. Mel, Brynna, and I were coming outside and got catcalls from a bunch of guys behind us. We were perfectly safe, Elliot. A well-lit parking lot, plenty of people around. The guys were just being stupid jerks trying to impress each other. Us. I don't know. Mel even had her gun and badge on her, you know? And Jarrod was driving over from work to pick us up. We were safe. And I flipped out. Something about it set me off. It took twenty minutes—and Jarrod holding me—for me to calm down."

"I see. Medication doesn't help?"

"It can. When I'm on it. I'm not. I've always held the idea of a prescription in reserve; in case I get really uncontrollable. But it never comes to that."

"Therapy?"

"No, not recently, anyway. I function just fine on a day-to-day basis, Elliot. I just tend to worry about… I don't know…everything." She smiled at him, but she didn't mean it. "I'm not even sure what the worries are, half the time. Just that they are there. Mel said PTSD, and she would know. But…I haven't gone any further than that." Not yet, she just wasn't ready yet.

"Maybe you should." He finished his salad and wiped his mouth. "I did. After it happened. After seeing the video and the crime scene photos. I needed the extra help. I still see a counselor at times. Sometimes…sometimes there are decisions you have to make in this job that are just choosing the least damaging option. Lives are at stake. I've made calls that have cost men and women their lives. And I'll do it again. I can't handle that on my own, you understand? Not and be as effective as I want to be."

Gabby knew she stared. She'd never heard any man—especially one with as much power as a Division Chief—admit to needing mental health support. Even occasionally.

So many guys in her acquaintance just shrugged counseling off.

Not Elliot.

"I don't know. Maybe. When life around here gets back to normal." *If* it went back to normal. She couldn't escape the feeling that things would never be normal for her again.

"The department counselor is supposedly a good one. Might consider it. We pay her to be here, after all."

"I…I'll do it. Maybe it's time. And maybe we'll catch the killers eventually, too."

"We will. Even if it takes a thousand more days to do it. Ten thousand. I'll never stop. And neither will Chance."

She'd seen his brother wandering the TSP halls on her way up to Elliot's office. Chance had stopped whatever conversation he was having with a tall blond guy, and they'd both entered the elevator after her. Neither had said anything.

They'd just rode the elevator with her to Elliot's floor. Chance had touched her shoulder and gave her one of his super-intense-Chance looks and nodded. The blond guy had grinned at her but said nothing.

Another of Elliot's ever-loyal guard dogs was her best guess. "I saw Chance in the elevator. I'm not sure what he was doing. Probably scary-Chance things."

"He's looking into the apartment burglary for me. Special investigator. He's on the FC TSP books, but I'm not advertising that fact."

"Thanks, Elliot. I mean that. You didn't have to go to all this trouble for me, but I appreciate that you did."

"Gabby, I'm starting to think there's nothing I wouldn't do for you. All you have to do is ask."

CHAPTER TWENTY-SIX.

* * *

ELLIOT looked at his brother like Chance had grown two heads. Chance had shown up in his office five minutes before he was set to go downstairs to get Gabby for the end of the day. The news Chance dropped didn't exactly thrill him. "You sure you have to go now? Tonight?"

"No choice. The grand jury wants my testimony on a kidnapping with special circumstances case. The bastard hurt the victim bad, El. I've talked with Erickson. He's going to take over here for me on that little project of yours. Sit on you and Gabby until I get back. I'm going to head back to your place with you now, then take off. I'll drive up, give my testimony, and then get my ass back here as soon as I possibly can."

"Why not fly?"

"Have you taken a look outside lately? I doubt any planes will be going up anytime soon."

The thunder gave truth to his brother's words. The storms had rolled in an hour after lunch with Gabby and were predicted to be bad for a good third of the country. "Just be careful. I need you here."

"I know. I get you. I'm not happy about it, either. But this woman kidnapped—she's not any older than Gabby, El. Big blue eyes just like her. Her life was destroyed by what happened. I promised her I'd get the sonofabitch. I need to keep that promise."

Elliot understood. He didn't have to like it, but he understood. "Go. I have the entire TSP at my disposal. I'll handle this thing with Gabby. Grand juries are nothing to ignore. Stay safe."

"Watch your back. And Gabby's. I feel a little itchy—something is going to happen. And soon."

Elliot felt the same damned itch—and now his main backup was leaving for who knew how long. A lot could happen in a day or two, and they both knew it.

* * *

GABBY was completely exhausted when Elliot got her back to the house. "We'll grab dinner, Gabby. Then you can rest."

"I didn't sleep very well." She sighed as she said it, then bent down to pick up her cat. "I kept having nightmares."

"You're safe here."

"I know. I'm not worried, Elliot. Well, no more than usual. I can help with dinner."

"That would be appreciated."

So stilted, so formal. Was he regretting his offer for her to stay? Gabby would be the first to admit she wasn't very good at figuring out men and what motivated them. Not at all. "I should probably go home soon."

He looked at her, obviously startled. He shook his head. "No. I don't think that's a good idea. Give me a few more days to see if I can figure out who's behind the break-in."

Gabby wanted to stay right there where she was—how could she not? The thought of going back to her apartment scared her. She wasn't too proud to admit that. "People are talking about us. I tried to explain what happened, that you feel big-brotherly toward me, but I don't think they believed me."

"I don't care about gossip, sweetheart."

Gabby sat on his couch, and the cat curled up on her lap. She looked over at him. Elliot wore a dark blue suit that made his shoulders look twice as broad. Made *him* look strong and important and one of those men who women were just drawn to. That was probably behind some of the looks and questions, wasn't it? The way people had stared after they'd shared lunch in his office. "I don't like being the center of gossip, though."

"Gabby, I wasn't thinking about gossip when I took you home with me. I was thinking that I couldn't stand the thought of someone getting close enough to hurt you. And they'd already proven once that they could get past your building's security." He knelt down in front of her, his hands on either side of her knees. Gabby looked into his green eyes and her fingers itched to reach up and touch him. She settled for putting one hand on his shoulder and the other on his chest. Elliot's chest had just gotten better with age, hadn't it? "And despite what I didn't say last night with my idiot brother, my feelings for you are anything but brotherly."

"Really?" Gabby's eyes widened, and she knew she gawked at him like an idiot.

He smiled. "Yes, really. Stay here with me, sweetheart. Just for a few more days. Until Callum and Evers have a chance to figure out who it was. Whether there is any more danger. Screw the gossip-mongers. Only you and I need to worry about what's happening between us. No one else."

"I don't want you to lose your job."

"I won't. No matter what happens. And if I do, so what? I won't lie and say it won't hurt, but I've had other offers. Even the FBI, if I choose to. Let me keep you safe."

She nodded, unsure of what else to say. He smiled, then leaned forward, a look of intent in his eyes that she recognized.

His lips were on hers, and it was nothing like the kiss he'd given her that morning in front of his brother.

After setting her mouth and entire body on fire, he pulled away. "You make a man forget how to breathe, Gabby. You should come with a warning label. I think we need to focus on dinner. Do you like Italian?"

She nodded. It was official, he'd kissed her speechless, hadn't he?

So what was she supposed to do about it?

CHAPTER TWENTY-SEVEN.

* * *

THE phone rang and rang and rang. Finally, an angry voice answered. Nausea rose in his throat, but he forced the words out. "We have a problem. One of my techs, Kevin Beck's daughter—she's been digging."

And he couldn't call her off. That would just bring unwanted attention his way.

"Deal with her."

"I can't. She's too close to me. Someone will look into anything that happens to her." And the thought of anything hurting that sweet little Brynna maddened him. "I—I don't want the girl hurt."

"You won't have a choice. If she's anything like her father—"

"Her friend is going around with Elliot Marshall." He had told no one about Gabby or her apartment. He figured he could handle her and any minimal threat she'd presented. But Brynna with a computer and *that* video—she was far more threatening at the moment. "If anything happens *right now* he'll be all over it."

"We should have found him and his brother ten years ago and eliminated any problem from that quarter."

He knew arguing was useless. If the man on the other end of the call thought it had to be done, he'd wipe the entire Beck family off of the map. And this time, he wouldn't leave witnesses or family still alive. Kevin Beck and every daughter he had would be targeted and removed quickly. Even the man's granddaughter in St. Louis. Because he had done it before.

He sickened Benny.

"Where is she?"

Benny bowed his head and said a quick prayer for his damned soul. "Brynna's on her way to St. Louis. She has a copy of the original video from the Marshall incident." He gave the rest of what he knew just as the familiar sound of his middle daughter's little car—he needed to replace the fan belt soon—pulled into his drive.

Alyssia's *'Hi Dad!'* and smile reminded him of what was ultimately important.

If Brynna threatened the security he'd always provided for his family, then he had to stop her, didn't he?

No matter how much it hurt him.

He made it through the rest of the evening but excused himself to the garage he'd converted into a computer lab twenty years earlier. He'd been dedicated to his field for his entire career. He'd taken it seriously long before the money was there to fund the lab that was now his solace.

He booted up his laptop and hit a few buttons. He didn't know why he did it. There wasn't much point in it any longer, was there?

Brynna's laptop sat next to him. He was supposed to be upgrading it, *adding* protection. Brynna was so frightened of someone spying on her digitally. She trusted *him* to keep her safe.

She *trusted* him.

Benny closed his eyes as light brown eyes and a slightly crooked smile flashed into his mind. He opened

Brynna's laptop and waited until the familiar wallpaper popped. Brynna, Gabby, and Melody smiled back at him. They looked young, sweet, and beautiful.

Trusting.

Once again, he'd betrayed that trust like the monster he was.

Benny grabbed his laptop and threw it against the wall. He watched it shatter.

He collapsed on the floor. And wept.

For his Brynna.

CHAPTER TWENTY-EIGHT.

* * *

HE hated grand juries, but Chance made it through. The sick sonofabitch who'd hurt his own niece because he could was going down. It was just a matter of time. The ADA was damned good at what he did, and Chance respected how hard the guy was working.

There were a few lawyers—more than a few—that he could say the exact opposite. He was tired from the drive up; the storm had added an additional two hours to his drive time and testifying always pissed him off some.

He wasn't looking forward to driving back to Finley Creek, but he was itching to get back to his brother. Something was stirring overhead, and it wasn't the blanket of storms covering pretty much all of Tornado Alley. It was more than that.

He stepped out of the courthouse and headed to Coby's deli three blocks up and two over. He was starved, and his testimony had lasted until almost five. He'd called a contact of his in the St. Louis field office and set up a meeting with an agent who'd worked with Art Kendall back on his family's case. He wanted to make this trip as useful as possible. Then maybe he wouldn't feel so damned guilty for leaving his brother in the lurch.

Elliot was taking this threat to Gabby seriously. Chance wasn't entirely convinced the apartment was related to what happened ten years ago. But he could see it making sense. As deeply as his brother felt for the girl, he could also understand Elliot's hovering.

Gabby remained a lynchpin for a lot of the case, still. If someone wanted to make sure *nothing* else was found, taking her—and him and his brother—out would be one way to do it. If they did it in a way that didn't draw suspicion.

All they had to do was make it out that Gabby had pissed someone off in her work with the TSP or make it out that *Elliot* had—and they could take them all out. Even Chance, if he was there with them when it happened. It would be just another chapter in the Marshall Murder saga. Elliot and Gabby being together just made targeting them all that much easier.

Collateral damage. Chance was convinced fully that that was what Sara, Slade, and his mother had been.

Collateral for his father's job.

He just hoped Elliot got that. There was a blonde bundle of collateral counting on his brother to keep her safe.

His brother must have balls of steel. Chance knew he'd never put himself in such a position. Elliot was different, though. Elliot was the optimist of their little family. Damn it; he hoped his brother and Gabby figured things out between them soon. They both were entitled to some happiness now. Didn't the damned fates realize they deserved that?

He ate, idly watching the crowd exit the FBI buildings just down the street from Coby's. They look just like he'd expect of a bunch of feebs.

Chance had two hours before he had to meet his contact.

He hadn't told Elliot, but he had a line on a guy who'd heard rumors of a corrupt asshole—possibly in the Texas governor's office.

Chance doubted it was Gov. Marcus Deane. His cousin was a politician to the core—but not a crooked one. At least he didn't think so. Nothing would surprise him anymore, though. Not anymore.

He grabbed his bag and left a hefty tip on the table for the waitress—she was cute and good at her job, so he was more than generous—and headed out. His contact worked just across the street from the fancy building with the words PAVAD looming over the entrance.

He snorted. Everyone had heard of PAVAD, hadn't they? Chance admitted to a sense of professional curiosity, but hell, PAVAD—all traditional law enforcement agencies—were no longer the path for him.

Chance liked it that way. He liked the freedom of the life he had built. No sense in changing what wasn't broken.

His meeting with the feeb went well; it wasn't as informative as he'd have liked—but it was a start. He had a few lines of inquiry to check out that he hadn't had before.

Rain poured overhead as he made his way across the parking garage shared between the PAVAD: FBI and St. Louis Field Office buildings. He'd had to get a visitor pass and practically give a blood and urine *and* DNA sample before he'd been allowed in the lower level just to park.

The rain and thunder were magnified in the concrete structure and made it nearly impossible for him to hear anything.

"Mr. Marshall?"

He almost missed her words. But he sensed her. Chance turned toward the woman who'd come up behind him. He hadn't carried a weapon into the FBI offices—that would be kind of stupid of him—but his first instinct was to go for the gun now locked in the glove compartment of his rental.

The girl next to his rental car didn't look like much of a threat—but that didn't mean shit, did it?

He studied her—five-foot-eight or so, one hundred twenty pounds. Red hair. He'd have remembered the red hair if they'd met before. It was so…carrot. Soft looking, long, shiny—but definitely carrot.

He couldn't see her eyes; she had them covered with big sunglasses. In an enclosed parking garage. How did she see with those things on? Was she trying to hide behind them? Deliberately?

"Are you Chance Marshall? I think you are. You look just like Elliot does. Like your dad did before. Except your hair is a lot darker."

"Who the hell are you?" It was the mention of his father that threw him off. She would have been a young kid back when his father was alive. Was this woman even twenty-one? She didn't look it.

"You probably won't remember me. You dumped pancake batter on my head when I was six, and you were sixteen, I think. Your mom made you wash my hair. I screamed at you then. *Do* you remember me? I'm one of Kevin Beck's daughters. And I need you to take me home with you. Now. Tonight."

CHAPTER TWENTY-NINE.

* * *

THE next evening, Elliot had one major concern—how long could he keep his hands off his houseguest? She'd brushed against him when they'd been making dinner together, and Elliot still couldn't get the scent of warm woman and flowers out of his head, out of his lungs.

Gabby didn't seem aware of the impact she was having on him, not at all. Was she completely innocent of the effect she had a man? On him? He'd had a hell of a difficult time stopping when he'd kissed her the night before. His hands had trembled, and every instinct he had was shouting at him to scoop her up and keep her in his bed for as long as it took for her to realize just what he was feeling—and where she belonged.

He'd never felt like such a caveman with a woman before. So why her?

Elliot had known he was giving in from the moment he'd kissed her in his kitchen, four feet from his damned brother.

Elliot had thought about her almost every minute they'd been apart at the TSP. He'd wondered, and he'd worried.

They hadn't been able to eat lunch together, but Journey had offered to spend her own lunch break with Gabby. He'd appreciated it.

When six o'clock had rolled around, he'd made his way down to the CF lab and waited while she finished her end of shift routine.

Elliot had felt like a damned high schooler waiting for his freshman girlfriend to get out of gym class or something. The sly looks sent his way when people thought he wasn't looking didn't help.

Gabby had looked up at him when he'd walked in with sweetness and relief in her big blue eyes. Elliot had felt the worry slip away right there.

He didn't doubt that every damned person who worked in the Finley Creek TSP knew exactly where Gabby Kendall was spending the night. He knew the kind of speculation that was on their minds. But what was he going to do about it? She hadn't said anything about it yet, but he suspected she'd bear the brunt of it. No matter what he said or did—she was younger, lower on the totem pole, and with far less power than he had. How was he supposed to protect her?

He looked at her where she sat, tapping on her tablet, messaging one of her friends. She actually wasn't fidgeting as much as she had earlier, and he took the moment to study her. Her hair wasn't pulled up or braided; it waved over her shoulders and reached almost to her waist. Soft and beautiful and just tempting him to bury his fingers in the gold and pull her to him. He'd spent most of the evening before in his bed, thinking of doing just that. He couldn't recall ever wanting a woman more. He'd pull her toward him and lean down…

To taste the soft pink bottom lip she was chewing on with his tongue. He'd start with that, then guide her back on the couch and take it from there.

She must have felt him staring. Gabby looked up at him from the bluest eyes he had ever seen. The glasses she wore made them look even bigger. Bluer. She wet her lips. "Elliot? What's wrong? You're kind of staring."

Wrong? Nothing was wrong, except he was sitting there thinking about Gabby in a way she probably wouldn't like. And what would come of it, anyway? He wouldn't be offering any woman a future anytime soon. Even if he was so inclined.

His dad had practically lived for every breath his mother had taken. Once, Elliot had liked that. Had respected his father for the love he'd had for Elliot's mother.

But…letting a woman into your heart like that and then possibly losing that woman? Elliot had lost so many people he loved already. He flat out didn't *want* to love a woman. Even Gabby. Especially Gabby.

He hadn't been a celibate over the last decade, but the affairs he'd had in those years had been with women who were as focused on their careers as he was, and who hadn't wanted anything permanent, either.

One look at Gabby and a smart man knew she was the permanent kind. And he should stay far, far away. At least…keep the part of him that wanted to strip her naked and push her back on the soft couch and show her how much he wanted her as far away from her as he could. For his own sanity, at least.

"Elliot? Are you ok?" She reached a hand out toward him—a soft feminine hand that he wanted to touch. Needed to. He wrapped his hand around hers. It was the *need* he felt for her that did it. Made the ultimate choice for him.

"What? I'm fine."

"You're staring, remember?" Red tinted her cheeks, and he felt like an ass for embarrassing her. "Do I have something on my face?" She licked her lips again and almost had him grabbing her right then and there.

He shifted and tried to unobtrusively fix his pants so that she couldn't see what it was she had done to him. What he had done to himself with the thoughts of her he shouldn't have had.

"Elliot?" She wasn't going to let him brush this aside, was she? "What is it?"

She leaned closer, licked her lips and looked up at him again. That was all it took for him to lose control. "It's…it's….damn it. It's this…" He pounced. He couldn't think of a better word for it. He had his hands under her arms and had her off the couch in a quarter of a second flat. The tablet fell to the floor. Elliot lifted until her chest was flush against his own. Blue eyes widened, and her hands landed on his shoulders. But she didn't pull away. "It's the perfume you're wearing…"

"I don't wear perfume. Soap. Shampoo, maybe." She whispered the words. He felt her breath across his face. "I'm sorry, is it bothering you? I usually use a different brand. I mean…I grabbed the wrong bottle at the store last time, and I didn't want to exchange it."

"Gabby, just stop talking for a minute, will you?" He'd made her nervous, hadn't he? Why else was she babbling about shampoo, of all things?

"What are you doing?" She scrunched her eyes shut then opened them quickly. "I mean, I kind of figured what you are trying to do, but I'm not sure *why* you want to do it with me. I mean…I'm just me. I know you kissed me before but…I didn't think you'd want to—"

Elliot kissed her. It was the only way he knew would stop the babbling.

And it was what he'd wanted all along.

* * *

WOW. That was the first thought Gabby had after Elliot pressed his lips against hers. He tasted like coffee again, and it surprised her that she liked it. She had never liked coffee. But maybe it was *Elliot* she liked instead?

He was a really good kisser. At least...he was a better kisser than any of the handful of guys she'd kissed in the last ten years. Her fingers dug into his shoulders through the blue cotton and she clung to him. He had really great shoulders.

It took her a long moment to realize her feet weren't touching the ground. He'd lifted her off the floor, and she could feel every bit of him pressed against her.

Elliot was absolutely perfect. What was she supposed to think about that?

Gabby didn't have a clue. All she could do was kiss him back and hold on for the ride.

What had caused this shift? Today hadn't been any different than yesterday, really. They'd both worked, came back to his place, made dinner. Just like the evening before. It hadn't been awkward at all. She'd *liked* it. Just as much as when she'd spend the evenings with Jarrod. More. The attraction between her and Jarrod wasn't nearly as strong as the pull she felt for Elliot. But...she'd thought she'd done a good job of *ignoring* it.

It was a really good ride. Much better than the brush of a kiss in the kitchen that morning. *That* was almost platonic compared to this.

Elliot kissed her like he meant it. And Gabby wanted him to. She wanted him to mean it, wanted more than just this friendly type of stasis they'd ended up in. She wanted to know he felt what she was.

Gabby just wasn't very good at going for what she wanted, *especially* with men. Especially when the risk was as great as it was right then.

When he lowered her back down to the floor, she didn't want to step away. But she did.

He was staring down at her with those eyes of his that made her all gooey inside.

For once she was at a total loss of words.

What was she supposed to do now?

* * *

HE looked down at the woman in front of him and knew this was exactly what he'd been waiting for from the moment he'd realized who the pretty girl in computer forensics was. He wanted her in front of him, vulnerable, sexy, and focused completely on him. Her eyes were wide, her cheeks flushed. She was beautiful, perfect. She made him feel something again—did she realize that? "Gabby. Damn it, baby; you have two seconds to tell me this is not something you want…I can't guarantee it would be any more than this. I've not been serious about someone in over ten years. I don't think I can be anymore. But…I want to be with you."

Why did he feel like he was lying through his teeth? He couldn't see just one night with her. It would have to be more. Far more than just one night.

He tangled his fingers in her hair and tilted her head back and stared into blue eyes while he waited for her to make the choice.

"Elliot…" She licked her lips, and he almost died right there. "Elliot…I think I'd like that very much. No matter what happens. We don't have to promise each other anything. We both know we're not guaranteed tomorrows, or…or anything else…So yes, I think…I think I'd like to be with you, too."

Elliot scooped her off of her feet and carried her toward the bedroom at the end of the hall.

CHAPTER THIRTY.

* * *

WHAT was she doing? Gabby had never taken such a risk in her entire life. It was crazy. She was crazy. She was going to wake up and realize she was in the middle of a full-scale mushroom-induced delusion, wasn't she?

Why else would she be standing in front of Elliot waiting for him to do something—anything—other than stand there staring at her? She thought she had a pretty decent body—they were just breasts, after all. Most women had them—some bigger, some smaller. She was just…not used to standing in front of a man, knowing they were about to take each other's clothes off and have sex. Make love. Whatever they called it.

"I've never seen anything more beautiful." He touched her cheek with a single finger. That had her shivering more than if he'd just grabbed her. His words were soft, almost reverent.

Heat flamed in her cheeks. She'd always been so shy in the bedroom—maybe the main reason there hadn't been all that many bedroom scenes in her life. This seemed so much *more* than all those others, didn't it? "Elliot—"

"Don't say anything. Just let me look at you for a minute. Until I catch my breath—you're perfect, Gabby."

Had he really just said that? Gabby had never heard anything that hot in her entire life. At least—not directed at her. "No, I'm not. I'm just…me. Gabby."

"That's what I said." He smiled as he leaned down and brushed his lips against hers. Gabby stretched up on tiptoe, her arms going around his neck. Elliot had some seriously broad shoulders, didn't he? He put his hands around her waist and slid them underneath the edge of her sweater. With a quick move that had her squealing softly, he pulled the soft material right over her head.

His hands went to her hair next. He buried his fingers in it and used it to pull her closer. "Your hair is one of my favorite things about you—at least physically. I've dreamed of it spread out over my pillow. Dreamed of you, naked, with this hair around you. Did you know that? I was sitting at my desk, in a meeting with the mayor, and I thought about your hair today."

Gabby's cheeks flamed. "Uh…"

"I know. That's how I knew I was never going to escape you." He laughed softly, then slipped a finger behind the button of her trousers. "Let's take these off, baby."

She pulled in a breath and nodded. Had she ever had a man undress her like this before? She'd had exactly two relationships since she'd graduated high school—not quite tons of experience, was it?—and they'd been with nice, unassuming guys who were as quirky as she was.

Elliot blew them all out the water. Gabby stood in front of him wearing nothing but her lilac bra and matching panties. He stared down at her with eyes that were faintly burning. She shifted when he didn't look away or touch her or do *anything* for the longest time. "Elliot?"

"Just let me look at you..." But he wasn't just looking. His hand traced the edge of her bra, then ghosted over her nipple. Gabby felt her body's immediate reaction. He smiled. "You are beautiful, sweetheart. I wish you saw what I see when I look at you."

Oh, boy. Why did every part of her melt when he looked at her just like that? Gabby tried to hide her nerves by reaching for *him*. She ran her fingers over the buttons on his shirt, slipping each one free until his undershirt was revealed. She pushed the open shirt off his shoulders; it fell to the floor. He pulled the white undershirt over his head, and it followed the other to the floor.

Elliot's chest had just gotten better with age. Gabby's fingers curled with the need to touch. And then she realized she didn't have to hold herself back anymore. What they were doing kind of gave her an open invitation to touch all that warm muscle, didn't it?

He had scars. Jagged ones that told her just how close *he* had come to dying at some point. She ran one hand over them. He shivered. "What happened here?"

"Too close to a bullet for comfort." He leaned down and kissed her right shoulder. "You have freckles here."

"A few." She shivered at the feel of his lips on her skin.

"I've always loved freckles." His fingers slid the clasp on the front open, and lilac silk trailed down her arms. Gabby struggled not to raise her arms to cover herself. This slow exploration was far different from the hurried fumbling in the dark she'd experienced before.

But she didn't want to be passive. She wanted to be a part of whatever was going to happen between them. "Elliot? I—"

What was she supposed to say? That whatever they were about to do meant more to her than any ever had before? That *he* meant more to her. But for the first time, Gabby couldn't find any words. Not for this. All she could do was feel.

Elliot scooped her up and held her for a long moment. Gabby felt her skin pressed against his. His scent surrounded her, warm male and spice. She rested her head against his shoulder, nervous. More nervous than *she* had ever been before in her life. And wasn't that saying something?

He laughed. "Nervous?"

"Yeah." She tightened her arm around his neck. "I've not exactly done a lot of *this,* you know."

He lowered her to the bed and slipped out of his pants. "And that's what makes this matter as much as it does."

Gabby reached up for him and then he was there. Everywhere. Kissing her, reassuring her—showing her how to touch him the way it really mattered. Showing her how *she* loved to be touched, too.

Elliot was a natural leader, wasn't he? Why should making love be any different? Gabby was content to follow wherever he guided her.

And she did. Until something changed between them and *she* became just as frantic. Her hands pulled at him, stroked him, her lips told him exactly what she felt for him.

Until they were both wrapped around each other, unable to tell where one began and the other ended.

CHAPTER THIRTY-ONE.

* * *

ELLIOT heard the pounding on the door and jerked out of bed. He didn't want to wake the woman next to him, but it was too late. Gabby sat up, stark naked, and looked around wildly. He handed her the purple glasses he'd placed on the bedside table earlier.

"Someone's at the door. Get dressed." He was already reaching for his pants.

"Something's happened. It has to have." The fear in her tone had him pausing and looking at her for a moment.

"No panicking, sweetheart. Not until we know what's going on."

Elliot had been in this world long enough to know that. When someone pounded on the chief of the TSP's door at six in the morning something was going on that wasn't going to be all that good.

He refused to let fear take hold. But he wasn't an idiot.

Whoever was at that door was about to deliver bad news.

And the only person he could lose—besides the one next to him—was his brother. It was hard not to let his own fear overwhelm him.

He made it to the front door, weapon in hand—he wasn't stupid—because he hadn't forgotten why Gabby was there, in time to hear someone cursing on the other side. He checked who it was.

Foster.

With Mel Beck at his side. A pale, frightened Mel Beck.

He threw the door open quickly. "Mel? What's happened?"

"Have you heard from your brother?"

That was the last thing he'd expected from Mel.

He stepped back to give her room to get inside the narrow hallway. His porch was damned slippery in the rain. Foster helped her over the step impatiently by lifting her into the entryway. Mel didn't protest his high-handedness—which told Elliot exactly how upset she was. "No. Why?"

"I got a message hours ago on my phone, but I'd already gone to bed. Brynna was getting a ride from St. Louis with your brother. They were driving back together tonight."

"Seriously?" Thunder and lightning cracked and burned overhead. What the hell had Chance been thinking?

"Yes. Seriously. And the Oklahoma police called about an hour ago."

Elliot tensed. "What's happened?"

Gabby had made it to the living room. Mel held out a hand to her. Gabby immediately hugged her friend. "Mel, what's going on? Why have you been crying? What's happened? Brynna?"

Elliot's attention focused on Mel's face. It was true—there were tear tracks on her pale cheeks, not rain. "Mel…are they alive? Just tell me."

“We don’t know.” Foster’s tone was harsh. Elliot looked at him. There was fear in the man’s eyes, wasn’t there? Any doubts about the depth of his feelings for the three women flew out the window. The guy cared. It was in how he looked at the two women. “Your brother’s rental car was found ran off the road. Passenger side impact. Another truck was abandoned at the same spot. It had been reported stolen two days ago.”

“Brynna? Jarrod, where’s Brynna? Where is *she?*”

Elliot knew his brother well enough to know Chance would have been the one driving. Which meant…Brynna Beck would have been on the side hit. “Foster, tell us what you know. Fast.”

“Brynna’s bag was found about a hundred feet away. Her laptop was missing, but her phone was there. Her tablet. There was blood on the bag. And on the passenger window—where we think Brynna was pulled from the vehicle.” Mel’s words were harsh. “After that, we don’t know.”

“So Chance could have pulled her out and taken her to the hospital?” The hope in Gabby’s voice hurt him. Elliot wrapped his fingers in her still tangled hair. She wore only her pajama pants and his t-shirt with Garrity TSP Softball League printed on the front.

“The nearest hospitals are this side of the Oklahoma-Texas border,” Mel said. She sank into the nearest chair. “The police have checked. Jilly called and checked, as well. Ariella and Lacy are driving her to the hospitals now, with photos of both Chance and Brynna just in case.”

“Did anyone see the crash?” Elliot asked, refusing to let panic take hold until he knew more.

"Oklahoma police have checked the four houses within two miles. No one saw or heard a thing. They're out there somewhere."

"The driver of the other vehicle?" A two-car crash involved more than one driver. That was just a damned given. "What about them?"

"We don't know. A contact with the Oklahoma police told me there were signs there were more than two people there." Foster put his hand on Mel's shoulder. "Said it was possible there was foul play, especially with the truck having been stolen."

"Why was Brynna riding back with Chance in the first place?" Gabby asked. "I talked to her online and got a text from her around six. She didn't say anything about coming home."

"I've called Carrie. She and Sebastian are driving to Oklahoma now. But it will take them a while—they were closer to here than St. Louis when it happened. Carrie said Brynna had told her that she had something to do that she couldn't wait on. Said she needed the first ride home she could find. Sebastian offered to drive her in the morning, but she said Brynna was upset about something. I don't even know how she found your brother."

"I think I told her. He was up there talking to a grand jury about a kidnapping," Gabby said slowly. "I told Brynna he had been here and was headed up there."

"Brynna could have met up with him near there," Mel said. "It makes sense."

Elliot looked at her questioningly. "How?"

"We have connections with the FBI in St. Louis. Our sister, Carrie. But we don't know what happened next."

Elliot could hear the fear in her tone. He felt it himself. “Chance is damned good at what he does. He’s capable of keeping them both safe.”

“Then where is he?” Gabby asked. Elliot looked down at her. “And where’s Brynna?”

Elliot tightened his arms around her. “I don’t know, baby. But we’ll find them. Somehow.”

CHAPTER THIRTY-TWO.

* * *

GABBY stepped away from Elliot and sat down near Mel. "So what do we do next? To find them?" They *had* to find them, had to.

Thunder shook the house, and Gabby shivered. Storms. That's what it was. Brynna and Chance were probably in a gas station freezer somewhere waiting out the worst of the storms. That's probably all it was. Scary, but believable. Logical. Smart. What two intelligent people like Brynna and Chance would do. No doubt about it.

"We wait." Jarrod's words were harsh, and Gabby looked at him. He was pale, and it was obvious he was worried. "We don't know that anything more than a traffic accident happened. And with the storms covering the region, we can't get in there. The Oklahoma police are doing what they can, but their focus has to be on keeping on top of the damned weather. They've already had reports of an F4 on the scale. Less than a mile from where the rental car was found. And that's just the first wave. More shit's headed their way."

"Brynna's terrified of storms," Gabby whispered, hurting for what her friend must be feeling.

"They may be holed up somewhere," Elliot said. "Waiting it out." He grabbed his cell phone and hit a button. “My brother carries burn phones. He gives me a new number every so many months.”

They waited while he dialed. Gabby’s eyes welled when he shook his head. “It’s going straight to voice mail. But if they’re out waiting a storm that’s not surprising.”

“I can’t stand *this*.” Mel pulled herself off the couch. Gabby watched her friend pace as much as she was able to. “Brynna…Brynna is practically defenseless. And what if she’s hurt out there? She wouldn’t be able to find herself help. I know she wouldn’t. We’ve *always* been there to do it for her—*I’ve* always done it for her. Why didn’t she call Dad, or just wait until Seb could drive her? What was so important she had to risk this? We both know she watches the weather just like any other of her obsessions. Twenty percent chance of rain and she won’t step outside half the time. It’s *Brynna* we’re talking about.”

Gabby’s eyes watered, and this time, she lost the battle with the tears. “I don’t know.”

Jarrod pulled Mel close. “Stop it, you two. Right now. It’s no one’s fault, not even yours, Super Mel. It was a car accident. And I’d say most likely Marshall figured the weather was about to go to hell and back and he dragged your sister off somewhere to wait it out. He wouldn’t have thought to grab her computer. *We* know how attached she is to it, but he wouldn’t have. He’s resourceful, I think. We’ll find her.”

“As soon as the storm breaks, we’ll get some TSP helicopters in the air. We’ll be sending some to assist with the storms, anyway. We’ll find them. I promise.” Elliot’s hand was warm on Gabby’s back. She leaned into him.

Could he keep that promise, no matter what? Gabby just hoped he could.

She looked at him again, and that's when she saw it. When it sank in. His brother, the only family he had left. It had to be just as terrifying for Elliot as it was for Mel, wasn't it?

Yet he was holding himself together, being strong. Taking charge in his quiet *Elliot-can-handle-the-world* way. Her heart hurt for him, and she just wanted to hold *him*. To make him see that he didn't have to be alone anymore. That he had *her*.

Not that she wasn't a quivering mess of freaked-outedness most of the time. She still wanted to be there for him.

Not just because of what they'd just done in his bedroom. Several times. Every time she'd turn to him or him to her it had somehow ended up with kissing, holding. Touching. *Loving*.

She wasn't stupid—you couldn't fall in love in a matter of days. The connection was there. The room in her heart. She couldn't tell him that—he'd said no strings, no commitments and she'd agreed to it. That didn't mean she wasn't feeling it.

"So what do we do now?"

"I need to get back to the house for Syd. I had a friend stay with her while I came over here to see what you may have heard. Syd was still sleeping when we found out what was going on. I'm going to have to tell her that Brynna is missing."

"We'll find her, Mel. I know we will. And Brynna won't do anything stupid. She's too smart for that. She's probably in a closet or basement somewhere telling Chance all about tornado statistics and the Wichita Falls outbreak in 1963 or 64, whenever it was. Or that Easter outbreak she freaks out over every year. Or any other in the past one hundred years." Gabby's breath hiccupped on the last. She could imagine her best friend doing exactly that. There had been a time or two when Gabby had crowded into the Beck family basement during severe weather. Brynna had filled everyone's heads with horrors during those times.

Mel and Brynna had argued horribly the last time that had happened. Snipping and snapping at each other. Like the sisters they were. Jilly had finally gotten between them and told them *enough was enough out of them.*

The next-to-youngest Beck sister was very quiet, but when she snapped *she snapped.*

They were a real family. They loved one another. And this had to be tearing all of them apart, too. Mel was going to be alone with a frightened seventeen-year-old girl to deal with. Gabby winced, remembering her own traumas at that age. She stood. She wasn't going to let her friend deal with that alone. Not if she could help. And it was better if they were all in one place while they decided what to do. It was either the Beck house—or the TSP, wasn't it? "I'm going to grab my things and put on some other clothes. We'll go back with you, Mel. Be there when we *all* find out what is going on, together."

* * *

ELLIOT refused to let worry fill him, make him useless. Chance had been in tough situations before. His brother had nine lives; Elliot had been convinced of that before.

The most logical explanation was that Chance and Brynna were waiting out the storm after a minor traffic accident. He refused to think about the blood, or the left laptop—which he didn't see as too much of a problem.

People left all sorts of things behind when disoriented after an accident.

The fact that Chance could have pulled an unconscious woman from the passenger side was a really big possibility. But he didn't mention it. The women were already terrified. His eyes met Foster's. The other man knew what the real odds were, though. Elliot had no doubt about that. Mel and Gabby knew, too, but they were clinging to hope. He couldn't blame them for that.

Odds were his brother and Brynna had run into some criminal element in a stolen vehicle. And to hide their crimes, they'd hurt his brother and Mel's younger sister.

Or Chance and Brynna were running from those criminals.

Gabby hurried down the hall, and Elliot followed. He'd grab his own clothes and his weapon.

He wasn't going to stop until he had his brother back and safe.

As well as Brynna Beck.

CHAPTER THIRTY-THREE.

* * *

THE Beck house was grim when Gabby and Elliot arrived there. Elliot tried his damnedest not to imagine what had happened to his brother. Tried to reassure himself that Chance was a survivor, was well-trained, and wasn't stupid.

His brother could take care of himself.

He wasn't so certain Chance could take care of the woman with him, though. Gabby had told him quite a bit about her best friend. How would she handle being out there? Was she already hurt?

Kevin Beck was pale, and the fear on the man's face would stay with Elliot forever. He'd pulled in a moment or two after Gabby and Elliot. "Any word?"

Elliot hesitated. As the head of the TSP post, it was logical he'd have the information they needed, wasn't it? "Nothing yet. We've contacted the FBI to have their forensics team process, since it's over the state lines and originated possibly in Missouri. But it's going to take them some time. This storm hit everywhere from Finley Creek up to the middle of Indiana. It's going to be bad. Resources are already spread thin."

"And my baby's out there in the middle of it all. Damn it all. Let me make a call. I have some contacts at the FBI. Brynna's sister and her friends. They're the best. I...trust them. Maybe they can help." There was a wild desperation in the man's eyes. Gabby hugged him, and Beck let her for a moment.

"We'll find them. Brynna's resourceful, you know? She always surprises me. Usually when people least expect it. And Chance is pretty fierce. They'll be ok."

Elliot hoped she believed her own words. He took a moment to look around the home. He'd been there before—when he was a child and teenager. His father and Beck had been partners and friends long before his family was killed.

Beck may have been Slade's godfather—Elliot couldn't remember. He did remember that the Beck children had all been significantly younger than him and Chance—so they hadn't known them well. At least his brother wasn't a total stranger to Brynna Beck, was he?

Framed photos dominated the walls—filled with images of beautiful redheaded women who had started off as beautiful redheaded children. There was a recent portrait that had Beck's five daughters surrounding a happy dark-haired baby girl held tightly in her grandfather's arms.

One of Mel, Brynna, and Gabby on the beach, arms around each other and smiling. Mel and another redhead holding guitars. That other redhead, a brunette, and a blonde dancing on the stage. A teenager wearing a prom dress and grinning. Kevin Beck's family. Photo after photo after photo. Beautiful. Every last one of them.

Family. They loved each other deeply. Like he had loved his own.

What was that girl going through out there?

Or were they going to be too late? Was Brynna, was Chance...were they both dead? Elliot pushed that fear aside.

The most likely explanation was that the storms had pushed them into finding shelter and they couldn't contact anyone yet. He'd seen worse happen in severe Texas weather.

He refused to let himself think of the bodies of the dead he'd seen after such weather. His brother was smarter than that.

He'd keep himself and Brynna safe.

"I think the FBI would be a good idea." Hell, what would it hurt to *try*?

"That's good, right?" Gabby asked. "Maybe…the FBI could start on their end, and we can start down here, and we can find them somehow between us?" He heard the panic next. She'd lost her best friend—and was about to possibly lose another. What would that do to her?

He refused to think about what would happen if he lost his only remaining brother, as well. "*If* the FBI can even take the case—*if* there is a case, which I am hoping there isn't. Chance will call as soon as they can. I have no doubts of that. We may be grasping at straws here. They may just be waiting out the storm."

CHAPTER THIRTY-FOUR.

* * *

SHE couldn't freak. She couldn't. Freaking would *not* get Brynna back any quicker. Gabby told herself this over and over again as the hours progressed with no word. The storm lessened, but the rain didn't go away. And wasn't going to for a while. They faced the real threat of floods next; it was supposed to storm again, too. It was like Mother Nature herself didn't want them getting anywhere near Chance and Brynna right then.

It didn't help Gabby's nerves at all. Every time the thunder boomed overhead she'd jump out of her skin and wonder if Brynna was alive to hear it.

Gabby was losing it, wasn't she? Especially when the fear swarmed in and surrounded her like rabid pissed off bees. She was allergic to bees—they'd always terrified her. Probably as much as storms frightened Brynna.

She couldn't get her friend out of her head. The fear. Nothing was as bad as the fear…the idea that Brynna was out there alone somewhere. Yes, Chance was with her. But…what if he wasn't? What if something had happened to him and Brynna was out there with no one? Elliot's brother could take care of himself; she had no doubt about that.

But Brynna?

If she was out there by herself…

She told herself Brynna was a highly competent adult. Probably more so than Gabby, right? Logic guided Brynna in absolutely *everything*. If there was a problem, she'd look for the logical solution. She could take care of herself, no matter what other people seemed to think.

But lost in a raging thunderstorm in a place she wasn't all that familiar with *after* a car accident? That sounded like hell for Brynna.

For Gabby, too.

* * *

GABBY felt like a bystander in everything as the day just kept going with *nothing* definitive. Every search party that went out was diverted by assisting storm victims. Jilly's best friends Ariella and Lacy had taken her to every hospital in a three-hour radius of the car crash. They'd found nothing. There'd been one woman who resembled Brynna—but she'd been cut by glass when a branch had flown through her living room window.

That was the closest they'd found anyone matching Brynna's description. The let-down had been terrible for all of them.

Kevin's contacts at the FBI were going to be there as soon as they could, but it was taking longer than expected to get them mobilized. But he was trying.

He was on his own phone, calling every person he knew who owed him a favor between St. Louis and the Mexican border. They were bringing in their own version of the troops—slowly.

It was going to take hours to search the Texas side of the border where Brynna and Chance might be.

Elliot was talking to the governor of Oklahoma *and* the Texas governor, trying to get the two to allow Finley Creek helicopters to assist in an aerial search for storm victims. The two governors were willing, but like the Oklahoma governor had said—what they wanted versus what Mother Nature was going to allow weren't necessarily the same things.

But both governors had promised to get Elliot whatever he needed as soon as the weather cleared enough to help.

Elliot handled TSP business—even though it was Saturday—from the kitchen at the Beck house. Gabby kept herself busy with making sure everyone had food and drinks and pens and papers and cell phones and anything else they needed.

She'd helped herself to Mel's laptop and got into the system to the TSP computers remotely. It was entirely possible that one of Brynna's old cases had come back to haunt her.

But she didn't think that was it.

She thought it was most likely something *Chance* had brought with him. He was up there on a kidnapping case, after all.

What if he'd collared the wrong guy and the real kidnapper had come after him and grabbed Brynna as revenge?

It was as likely as anything else they'd considered, wasn't it?

Gabby closed her eyes and pulled in a breath. *Think, Gab. Breathe, Gab. Don't be stupid, Gab.* It was most likely the storm. Most likely they were in the car accident, and both drivers had to abandon their cars and outrun the storm. Maybe Chance or the other drivers had pulled Brynna out of the car in a hurry and gotten her to safety because her door wouldn't open with a large truck jammed into it and a tornado was coming? Maybe the drivers of both vehicles were just trying to outrun the storm? Why were they panicking over that? Were they just hearing horses and automatically thinking zebras or something?

That was possible. But where did they go after? And why hadn't they been found by now?

Warm hands wrapped around her from behind. She knew who it was. Elliot hadn't let her out of his sight for more than a few minutes at a time since they'd gotten to the Becks'. His face was pale and the strain was tight around his eyes. "Anything?"

"No. Governor Deane has issued a state of emergency for the area. We've already had three confirmed deaths—and no tornado came through Texas. Just straight line winds. Oklahoma was hit far worse. And they say more is coming."

"We're not going to be able to get anyone out there, are we?"

"I've tried. But I can't justify sending people out to look for my brother when there are so many others who need TSP help right now in this state. In this area."

"But—"

"I'm not any happier about it. But I understand it." He pulled her closer. Gabby turned in his arms and wrapped hers around his waist. She forgot everyone in the room with them, forgot the fears.

Did anyone else see how tightly *he* was holding himself together? Or was it just her? Were they seeing him as the leader of the Finley Creek TSP and depending on him to have the answers? Did anyone see how terrified he had to be for his own brother? Gabby's arms tightened around him.

"We'll find them, Elliot. I know we will." She rested her head against his chest for a long moment, taking reassurance from the steady *thump-thump* of his heart beneath her ear.

"I hope so."

"In the meantime, you do what you have to do. I'm here when you need me." As long as he needed her.

Just exactly how she was starting to feel for him hit her like a dump truck full of bricks.

Gabby busied herself by googling every article she could find on the areas near the car crash that had been hit by the storms. She wanted to find *something* that might give searchers an idea of where to look. She checked geographical charts, weather patterns, flood patterns, social media posts, bloggers, user comments on weather station updates—anything to point to a possible direction. Or any mention of a redheaded woman and a man looking like Elliot's brother. Even the hospitals yielded her nothing more than what they already had.

Nothing. Nada. Zip. Zilch.

She didn't find much of anything.

The biggest questions everyone had were whether the crash was accidental, whether something from Chance's work had caused them to be attacked, and whether Brynna's software designs had led to the results.

They were still waiting for forensics on the vehicles involved. The weather had washed a lot of it away, but there were skid marks. Marks that said someone *accelerated* toward Chance's SUV. Deliberately striking it, striking Brynna's side. Had it been? Had someone aimed right at her friend? It had been late; was Brynna sleeping in the car while Chance drove? Had she watched the vehicle come for them? Had she *known* at that moment she was going to get hit? Like Sara had known she was going to die that day?

Gabby didn't want to go there; but how could she not?

She googled Chance's name, just to see what would come up, whether his name was listed anywhere in conjunction with crimes.

The first result shocked the heck out of her. It was about Chance…and Brynna. She clicked on the link and read it out loud.

She was alone in Brynna's room, where all the *good* computer equipment was located. She had spent many hours with Brynna's computers while just hanging out with her best friends. Mel would join them and read or write or even knit while they did whatever they did on Brynna's system. "*Autistic Girl and Former Texas Ranger lost in the Wilderness. Sources say Foul-Play Suspected.* Seriously? *Marshall Murders Have New Developments: Son Missing.*"

She read, learning nothing informative, but getting hugely embarrassed for her friend. Each article seemed wilder than the first. What would Brynna think, seeing some of the things mentioned in the articles? The sites speculated that Brynna and Chance had been together that late at night because of a romantic rendezvous that had been interrupted by crazy kidnappers—who were using Brynna to force Chance to confess to the murders of his family.

Of course, *that* one was from *The Snotty Garlic,* a snarky supposed news site that she and Brynna liked to joke over. What would Brynna think, knowing she'd made the *Garlic*?

Gabby missed her friend so much the ache in her chest was almost real. She clicked to a few other blogs and news hosts. Just to see what the world—at least the internet world—was saying.

It was mostly just reports of them missing. There was some speculation about why. Brynna was mildly famous among software developers for some of her work with her oldest sister, and that was mentioned. Some speculated *that* software had led to her current situation.

Gabby didn't know how she thought about that. It was obvious to her that *Chance* had been the real target. If they had been targeted at all. Why would someone go after Brynna?

That barely made sense at all.

CHAPTER THIRTY-FIVE.

* * *

HOURS passed with nothing to show for them. Gabby found herself back in Brynna's room as the storms picked up again. Elliot was busy downstairs—he'd set up a mobile TSP command post in the Beck family dining room, and was juggling his duties as division chief from there. No one said a word to challenge him. He was definitely in charge, commanding, used to getting things *done.*

Journey and a few others had also joined the crowd at the Becks.

Another reason she was practically hiding in Brynna's room. She circled back around to one of the black hat websites she'd sometimes used in her work for Computer Forensics. There was chatter that it *was* Brynna's software.

Gabby read deeper.

There was always the possibility, wasn't there? Brynna's software was for exclusive *law enforcement* usage. And it was far above cutting edge. There were bound to be jealous programmers and developers out there. Not to mention companies who would want it on the commercial market side of things. Had one of them done this? Taken Brynna to get her software, and *Chance* was the collateral?

Or maybe Brynna had found something on one of her cases that led to this? She and Gabby didn't work *all* their cases together. Sometimes she or Brynna was tapped by different departments; it just depended on the workload. Like Benny had moved Brynna exclusively to the Quincy case. Brynna had worked with Jarrod and the Commander of Major Crimes closely on that one. Maybe someone had discovered her work on that case, and was angry about it? Brynna was good at keeping herself out of the limelight on their cases—she and Gabby both let Benny be the face of the CF department. Gabby had testified twice in four years with CF. Brynna probably twice that, but still enough to count on one hand.

It was rare they were associated directly with any of the TSP cases. But the possibility existed, didn't it?

Maybe that had something to do with it?

There were too many possibilities for Gabby to think straight. She wasn't *good* at this part of things. It was Benny who would help fill in the motive for her and Brynna while they focused on the technical. The digital and the programming.

That was all they were really good at.

Along with Brynna's skills in developing new ways to use programs in their field. And with the other things Brynna had in the works.

Gabby helped her with some of those projects, and when Brynna inevitably sold something big—which they both knew would happen—Gabby would get a commission, as well.

Brynna's sister Carrie was in on it, too. They all stood to make a huge chunk of money. Gabby's and Carrie's was substantially smaller, but Brynna's…

If someone wanted to stop that software from being used, stopping Brynna would be a good place to start.

It was an angle she doubted anyone else had considered.

Gabby shut the laptop down. She needed to talk to Elliot. Brynna's laptop that was missing was a personal one. *They* had no idea of what was actually on it. She did.

It was *hers,* after all. Brynna had needed it for her pet project—and Benny had been upgrading Brynna's with a different virus software he'd written specifically for Brynna and Gabby's use.

* * *

ELLIOT looked up when Gabby walked into the dining room. "I've thought of something."

He nodded. Elliot had his phone at his ear, and she waited patiently for him to finish the call. He disconnected the phone and looked at her. "What did you find?"

"I did some digging," Gabby said as Mel and the rest of her family stopped what they were doing to look at her. "Internet chatter is everything from one of his private investigations to a competitor wanting her software. She's getting a lot of attention for it right now anyway. More than I would have thought. Nothing really significant on where they may be, though. I isolated two or three general areas that they could have found shelter in, but I don't have a clue what to do next." She handed him her notepad. "If it is her software, I don't have a clue where we should look next."

"Who is planning to buy it?"

"Probably Lucas Industries, out of St. Louis. The Lucas Tech branch. He's a family connection," Mel said.

"But there are other competitors of his out there. Tenaro Corp. and Barratt-Handley come to mind."

"Has anyone talked to him?"

"I did. Brynna and Carrie were out there the afternoon she disappeared. He said nothing unusual happened."

"Gabby, do you think you can get us a list of who else would want that software?" Elliot asked. "That might give us another direction to look in."

"Off the top of my head the number one other company—they're in direct competition with LI, is Barratt-Handley. One of their divisions," Gabby said. "I'll write down all that I can think of."

At least it was something. She wasn't just going to sit back and do nothing while her friend was out there.

CHAPTER THIRTY-SIX.

* * *

THE two days that had passed with no word on Brynna had been two of the worst in Benny's life. A part of him just wished it would end. That Brynna would be found and tucked back safely in her frilly little bedroom in the house she'd grown up in. With *her* father to watch over her, as it should be.

The other part of him just wanted answers. Even if they were in the form of her body.

He would never have expected Brynna to be with that Marshall boy. The former Texas Ranger was enough to give a rattlesnake night terrors. And he was somehow mixed up with sweet, innocent, naïve little Brynna? Unless she *had* found something on that video, found out his little secret, and had told Marshall exactly what it was?

He wouldn't put it past Brynna to be just that skilled.

Or was it something else? Marshall's brother had turned to Brynna's best friend rather quickly. Maybe his brother was involved with Brynna. Maybe they'd been involved all along?

What in the hell was Brynna thinking? A man like Chance Marshall would use a woman like Brynna and break her heart without a care.

She had to know that way lay only heartache?

Once they found her, he was going to tell her exactly that.

If they found her alive.

Why did it matter if she was with Marshall? Eliminating *him* would only serve Benny's purpose overall, wouldn't it? One less set of eyes on the past.

Just like getting rid of Marshall's older brother—and Gabby.

But *Benny* couldn't—wouldn't make that call. Not yet.

He couldn't hurt Gabby now. Sending men after Brynna had damned near destroyed what was left of Benny's rotting soul.

Gabby.

She beat Benny to the lab, and it was no surprise to see the damned chief with her. He probably thought the safest place in the world for that girl was the TSP building.

Benny bit back a bitter laugh. If Marshall only knew...

Benny promised Marshall he'd keep their Gabby safe and protected.

She looked horrible and more guilt soaked into his heart. Benny hugged her when her emotions got to her. Like he'd always done when something would upset her.

Half the time he was convinced she was just as much his daughter as Allana, Alyssia, and Addilyn. Her *and* Brynna.

Brynna.

Damn it. Benny felt like his damned heart was being torn right out of his chest. Would they ever find her? What would he do if they did?

CHAPTER THIRTY-SEVEN.

* * *

"ANY news about Brynna, sir?" Officer Journey asked as he checked his messages and prayed at least one of them would be about his brother on the third morning after Chance and Brynna disappeared.

The only thing even partially Chance-related was from Gov. Deane wanting an update. He and Chance weren't exactly the friendliest of cousins, but they weren't exactly enemies, either. Hell, Marcus and his two younger brothers were family. Elliot thought the governor truly did care about what had happened to him. He still didn't like the asshole, though.

"Not yet." It had been a full three days, plus several hours, since the last time anyone had seen or spoken to his brother or Brynna. Elliot was refusing to give up hope, but that wasn't like his brother at all. Chance would have to know the girl's family would be worried sick about her. He would have contacted *someone* if he'd been able. Something had happened out there. And it had been bad. And Elliot was stuck on his ass, twiddling his thumbs. The futility of it wasn't lost on him. "We're still looking. We'll find them."

"Of course we will. I've trimmed your schedule for today as much as I possibly could. Just in case." She was good at what she did—and she protected his time and interests like a rabid lion at times. He was very appreciative of Magda Journey.

Gabby was waved into his office at lunch time by Journey with a much more relaxed and welcoming expression from his assistant than anyone else had gotten. Journey liked Gabby, then. Good. It would make things a bit easier.

"Gabby, honey, I was looking forward to getting out of here and to you."

She looked uncertain for a moment. "I'm sorry… "

"I am glad you're here." He stood and rounded the desk. Held his hands out to her. He didn't give a damn if there were a million cameras in his office, or if the place was bugged or if there were a billion pairs of eyes pressed up to the window watching them. He wanted to hold her. Kiss her. Remind himself that *she* was safe. "Come here, sweetheart. Let me hold you."

As soon as the words left his mouth, she was in his arms. And Elliot felt rocked to his very core. How many millions of times had he heard his father talk to his mother in that same tone? With those same words?

How many times had his mother looked at his father just like Gabby had looked at him before she'd flown into his arms?

It was already happening to him, wasn't it? He was losing himself in Gabby, wasn't he?

* * *

SHE smelled him. Felt him. Gabby wrapped her arms around his waist and held him for a moment. "Benny left again. And it was too quiet down there by myself. I did some googling."

He pulled back and sat on the edge of his desk. She stood in between his knees and fiddled with the brown tie he wore. “Did you know some of the more idiotic news sites are still speculating that Brynna and Chance are romantically involved? Isn’t that silly?”

He laughed. That was a bit far-fetched. “Yes. While your friend is a seriously beautiful woman, I don’t think she’s my brother’s type. She’s too...normal. Strange as that sounds. She has ties, roots, a family. A home and a job. She’s...*normal*.”

“And Chance isn’t. I get that. There was something else. I’m still looking at all the competitors for her software. Most of them are getting ready for a big tech summit down in Mexico, though.”

“I don’t know that it is the software.” While it was a definite possible motive, Elliot had a feeling that it wasn’t the right one. That it was something *more* going on. But he’d given the information to McKellen in Major Crimes. The other man was following that angle.

“Elliot, I’m talking at least a two million dollar software design we’ve been working on. Mostly Brynna’s work, so she’d get the lion’s share of it. That’s why she was in St. Louis in the first place.”

“And Chance was there last minute. He had no plans to go up there. The ADA called him out of the blue.”

“But Brynna had plans. Our entire department knew about it three weeks ago.”

“Making it a hell of a lot more likely *she* was the target. The Oklahoma forensics confirmed the blood on the window was hers, baby. And that there was a third vehicle involved.”

She hoped she was wrong. Hoped they were just hiding from the storms. It wasn’t likely that they’d have had no contact, though. Hope was definitely dwindling for all of them.

Gabby had to face the very strong possibility that…

Her best friend…was dead.

* * *

ELLIOT saw the realization in her eyes and felt the defeat in her shoulders and back. "*Don't.* Don't let yourself think it. We'll find them. We'll get the answers. She could have hit her head or busted her lip or nose, and the blood got on the car that way. It's actually pretty likely. I'm not stopping until we have them."

"That's what Art said after Sara…and he still doesn't have them. He *quit* before he could find those answers." She whispered the words.

"I'm never going to quit on my brother. Or on your friend. I promise you that. *I'll* find them, Gabby. I swear."

"How much longer can we look, though?" Gabby asked the question in his mind. Elliot stroked her back, then tangled his hand in the hair she'd left down. He'd held her through the past two nights while she'd tossed and turned. While her worries had chased through her dreams.

He'd only felt that useless once in his life before.

The fear of losing his brother was almost debilitating. But Elliot had forced himself to go on. When all he really wanted was to put Gabby someplace he'd know she was completely safe and get out there and search for Chance himself. He knew if their roles were reversed his brother would never stop looking. Elliot barely felt like he'd looked at all.

He couldn't. He had every eye on him right now. Watching him, wondering if he'd put personal business above the TSP. And he would in a heartbeat if he thought it would accomplish what he wanted, but right then the TSP was *his* best tool for finding Chance.

Chance's life couldn't be put above any other. It just didn't work that way. No matter how much he may have wanted it to.

Serve and protect the ones they found when they found them. And hope Brynna and Chance were the ones they found. *That* was all he could do.

He'd never felt more useless in the past ten years.

CHAPTER THIRTY-EIGHT.

* * *

BRYNNA'S last confirmed sighting had been in the St. Louis FBI parking garage. A special emailed video clip had come to Gabby's attention that first evening. They'd watched Brynna confront Chance and practically force her way into his brother's rental car. Chance's expression had been absolutely priceless. Elliot had choked back a laugh when his brother had tried to pull Brynna from the front seat, and she'd held on to the seatbelt and grinned at Chance's frustration. Then held on even tighter. Chance had eventually given up. Defeated by a carrot-topped twenty-four-year-old computer geek.

His laugh had died almost before it had begun when he focused on the pics of the SUV after the collision next.

Because Brynna Beck *had* been pulled out of that vehicle, after all.

He did every damned thing he could think of to mobilize his people. But it only got him so far. Oklahoma officials were willing to trade favors, but it was slow in coming.

And gained them very little. Two more tornado producing thunderstorms had rolled through Oklahoma and Texas over the last three days, hindering everything.

Two possible vehicular assault victims were a lower priority.

The contrast between the media perception of his brother and the younger woman had the more salacious sites going nuts with speculation. He did take comfort that the coverage was getting their faces in front of the public. Maybe it would get them remembered at just the right time to do some good.

He just wanted to find them. Not only for himself, but for the other people who loved them. His cousin Tobias had called him—expressing his own worry. He'd even sent six ranch hands to aid Elliot in the search. He'd sent them with Erickson to assist recovery efforts in the general area.

Hopefully, someone would find them—and soon.

He'd barely been able to look Gabby in the eyes. As the hours passed with no progress, she'd gotten more and bleaker. Frightened and hurting.

He had no idea how to help her. Mel had burst into the TSP building that second day; she'd marched—as much as she was able—right past Officer Journey, demanding that she be a part of everything. There had been some protests—many right to her face and Elliot's, but most had welcomed her with a great deal of respect.

Mel had been one of the best and the Finley Creek TSP apparently still knew it.

Mel had set up shop in Computer Forensics, watching over Gabby like a hawk. No one could budge her.

It had been almost sixty-five hours since Brynna and his brother had left the FBI parking garage. Time was quickly running out. If they hadn't found them by now—odds were high that they were dead. That seventy-two-hour mark was fast approaching.

He was starting to lose hope. Journey tapped on his door and opened it shortly after he'd convinced Gabby and Mel to go to the breakroom for something besides soda and potato chips. He'd pulled Evers and Callum to accompany them—he'd taken a look at the detectives' personnel jackets. He'd respected what he saw.

"Journey?"

"Still nothing, sir. I'm sorry."

"I'm running out of ideas."

"Mel said something about making phone calls and pulling favors from some high-up friends in St. Louis."

"I don't know what they'd be able to do—part of the problem are the damned storms. More eyes out there—no guarantee it would be Brynna and Chance found." Most of the search teams kept getting diverted by storm victims. Priority of life meant they had to help whenever they found someone in distress—and that was the way it should be. He'd do that himself—if he was out there.

Damn it; he *needed* to be out there. Searching. For his brother *and* Gabby's best friend.

He wasn't so great at being his brother's keeper, was he?

"You're doing the best you can. With both your brother and this job."

"Let's be honest. You've done more to run this place this past week than I have." He'd been at the post mere days.

"It's called a honeymoon period. Let me have your back, Chief Marshall. We'll get you and Ms. Kendall through this—no matter what happen—"

"Thank you. I mean that." Elliot looked at the woman he was fast growing fond of. "I won't forget."

"Of course. You're welcome, sir. Why don't you join Ms. Kendall in the cafeteria? She's not the only one who needs to eat."

* * *

ELLIOT was conscious of the eyes on him as he entered the cafeteria. Mel and Gabby were surrounded by detectives and staff. Gabby had a wild look he accurately identified, utter panic, from the press of the crowd. Mel held center court, answering questions about her sister.

"Chief Marshall—any word?" McKellen, the commander of Major Crimes, asked. The worry in his eyes was genuine. He had feelings for Brynna, didn't he? Elliot felt a rush of sympathy for the man. Did Brynna know?

"Nothing yet—"

"Chief! Chief!" Officer Journey ran—actually ran—into the cafeteria. "Turn the TV to Channel 7 now."

Someone immediately obeyed. Everyone crowded around under the television bracketed in the upper corner of the room.

"Elliot, *look*." Gabby moved closer to the TV and to his side. The small crowd parted to let her through. It was hard to miss what she meant.

The ribbon on the screen screamed. Alive! Autistic Woman & Texas Ranger Found!

Elliot saw the breaking video—his brother carrying an obviously injured and bloody Brynna into a hospital. Chance held her tight, his emotions visible even in the grainy video. Elliot felt an answering pull in his own gut. Was the girl alive? Had Chance gotten her there too late? What had happened to them? How had she been hurt?

Thank God his brother was alive. Elliot's breath shuddered out, and he almost lost the rope he had around his own emotions. He'd convinced himself that all they'd be finding of Chance and Brynna were their bodies. He'd been *prepared* for that. He'd just been holding himself together until that happened for Gabby's sake. The rest of the Beck family's.

But now…

Now they needed to get there and make sure the same could be said for Mel's sister.

CHAPTER THIRTY-NINE.

* * *

GABBY had to force herself to breathe. Elliot and Journey mobilized quickly. Evers and McKellen hopped into the radio cars to lead the procession to the hospital where Mel's sister Jilly worked. Mel had her cell to her ear, calling her father and sisters.

Brynna was alive in that video. She was alive then. Chance had been carrying her—and they'd both been covered with blood. She was alive—but hurt. How bad? How bad was Brynna hurt? Gabby really tried to keep the panic away. Brynna had been *alive.* Odds were that she still was, right? She was at the best hospital in the city. Getting the care she needed.

Just like Slade had been.

She tried not to think about that.

She'd been so filled with hope when she'd first learned Slade hadn't died immediately. When he had…

Devastation on top of cruel hope.

"She's alive. She's alive." Gabby didn't realize she was the one saying it until Elliot wrapped his hand around hers as he drove.

"She is, sweetheart. She is." Gabby held his hand and clung.

Mel was on her phone, giving her own version of orders to her youngest sister and the crowd that was still at her house.

Gabby closed her eyes—finally letting her fears break free.

They'd found Brynna. Gabby could *breathe* again. Mostly. She needed to see her friend before *both* lungs worked again, though.

Elliot parked near the front entrance. Half a dozen radio cars pulled in beside and behind them. Gabby found herself encircled by a wall of TSP green as Evers procured a wheelchair to get Mel across the parking lot and inside the ER faster.

An armed escort was definitely surreal to Gabby. She was used to being the forgotten of the TSP, after all. Elliot, however, was not fazed by the crowd. He did have a tight hold on her fingers as he pulled her along behind him. Gabby clung just as tightly.

A petite blonde in a sleek business suit met them at the entrance. She looked familiar to Gabby, but she couldn't figure out why. "Chief Marshall, sir. I'm Finley Coulter. We've set up a private conference room for your use. If you'll follow me?"

"Thank you." Gabby watched Elliot shake the petite blonde's hand. "My brother and Brynna Beck?"

"We'll speak privately. Once we have her next of kin's permission."

"That would be me." Mel pulled herself from the wheelchair. The people surrounding them parted to give her room to get to the front of the crowd.

The blonde looked at Mel closely. "Are you Mel? Jilly's on her way in now. I spoke with her personally. She's a friend. I've met Brynna a few times. I know waiting is difficult. I don't believe we've ever met, but I've been to your home several times."

"Of course." Mel shook the woman's hand next. "*Fin.* Jilly's mentioned you."

"How did the security video from here get to Channel 7?" Elliot asked.

"When did he bring Brynna in?" Mel asked. "How long has she been back there alone?"

"Mr. Marshall brought her in about half an hour ago. He's been with her as much as he could since."

"And the video?" Elliot asked again.

"Leaked, Chief Marshall. We're working to find the breach. It may even be a cell phone video from a patient in the ER. We're doing what we can." Journey was there, with the answers Elliot wanted. Gabby was impressed.

"My brother? Ms. Beck?" Elliot said once they were in the conference room.

The blonde—Gabby had forgotten her name already, though she was sure she'd met her before—looked at Mel for permission.

"Go on. We're all family here," Mel said. She held her hand out for Gabby's. They clung to one another as much as possible.

"I've confirmed that she's still in surgery. I will get another update for you."

"Thanks," Mel said. "Brynna…She hates hospitals. But Jilly insists this is the best."

"Jilly's one of *our* best. We'll do everything we can to take care of Brynna. I'll make it my personal mission to make this as easy for her as we can. Why don't you get comfortable in the conference room? I'll see what I can find out."

Mel sat back down in the wheelchair. Elliot pushed her to the conference room down the hall. Gabby knew her friend hated the chair—but it was faster, and less strain on Mel. Mel didn't complain. She never did.

It was a cushy little conference room, a small round table surrounded by expensive looking chairs, the couch, and a full coffee and pastry bar.

None of it mattered. Brynna was what mattered.

Gabby forced herself to focus on her breathing. On the fact that it was broad daylight, they were in a secure place, and Brynna was getting the help she needed.

Elliot barked some orders at Journey and Evers, but Gabby didn't catch them all. He'd handle things, wouldn't he? She looked up at him. He was definitely good at being in charge, wasn't he? Then they were alone in the conference room with Mel, just waiting…

He stopped pacing near the head of the conference table and looked at her and Mel. He stared at her for a long moment then came to her. He knelt in front of both of them. "We've got them, sweetheart. Mel, we have them *back*. I'm not stopping until I have all the answers. Those answers are out there."

"Hell, Elliot—you're one of the few people I'd trust to do just that." Mel patted him on the cheek and let her hand linger. It sank in then—Mel respected Elliot, a great deal. Liked him. That mattered to Gabby for some reason. The connections. "I'll stick here. You go check on your brother. Make sure he's ok. I have a feeling we Becks may owe him a big one for this."

He looked over at Gabby and something passed through his eyes, an emotion she couldn't quite identify. His hand wrapped around the one Mel still held. They were connected; she drew a little more breath in. "I don't want to leave Gabby alone right now. Chance will find me as soon as he's able."

"Elliot, he's your brother." And she—better than anyone else in the room—knew what that meant to him, and how worried he had been. How his hands shook when he didn't think she was watching.

"I know. But he'll *find* me quicker if I stay put, won't he? I'm staying here until we know about Brynna."

He held his arms open, and Gabby practically dove at him. She pulled in a deep breath.

Finally, she could breathe again.

CHAPTER FORTY.

* * *

BENNY didn't know whether to curse or give thanks.

Brynna wasn't dead. At least not yet. What had happened to her out there? To Marshall?

He wished *that* sonofabitch was dead. It would be one less hunting on Benny's trail, after all.

The entire building seemed to be in a flurry. Most everyone liked Brynna, and none had wanted to see her harmed.

Benny had gone almost sick worrying about what those men might have done to Brynna out there. He had his opinions on one of them—the guy liked helpless young women. Brynna would be his preferred victim as it was. Add that she could potentially send them all to prison…it would be a wonder if Chuck didn't focus entirely on making certain Brynna went out of this world in the most painful way possible.

Benny had vomited at least a dozen times just thinking about it. But he hadn't dared make a connection with his contact. Better not to have himself tied to them, just in case.

The damned boogeyman was closer to the people in this building than they ever would suspect, wasn't he?

What if it had been one of his girls out there like Brynna? She and his Alyssia were about the same age.

They had the same sort of innocence about them. Alyssia wouldn't have had a clue what to do if lost in the woods with a real hard ass like Chance Marshall.

His blood froze just thinking about it.

Not to mention Chuck and the others. If they had been after one of Benny's daughters, he'd go insane trying to stop them. He would rip the bastards apart.

He knew exactly how Kevin must have felt. The fear as only a father of daughters could know.

Was Brynna going to live?

He texted Detective Foster for an update. How much did Brynna and Marshall know? There had been at least three men after Brynna—how had Marshall managed to keep them both alive this long?

And what in hell was Benny supposed to do now?

CHAPTER FORTY-ONE.

* * *

ELLIOT'S brother found them five minutes later. Chance came in, a wild look in his green eyes. Elliot studied him for a moment—Chance's clothes were covered with blood and dirt. One sleeve was completely missing. Chance's face was bruised and nearly as dirty. Elliot had been in the game long enough to recognize signs of an altercation.

And a serious one at that. His brother had practically had the shit beaten out of him, hadn't he?

Elliot grabbed his arm. He blocked Chance from the women on the couch. They didn't need to see Brynna's blood so line of sight. Didn't need to see what had been done to his brother and speculate about how they would find Brynna when they finally saw her.

Gabby and Mel didn't need to see that blood and know it was Brynna's. "Come on. Hallway."

"Brynna's condition first." Chance's words were harsh. "I—I need to know how she is. They won't let me back in there with her anymore."

The conference room door opened. Elliot stepped aside to let the rest of the Becks file in. There was one he didn't recognize. He assumed it was the sister from St. Louis Gabby had mentioned.

There was a dark-haired man about Elliot's own age following behind her, though. One he recognized. The man held out his hand toward Elliot. "Chief Marshall, sorry we're meeting again under the circumstances."

"Agent Lorcan, I didn't realize you were a Beck connection."

"My wife is the eldest daughter. We got in late last night and stayed with Syd for most of the day." Elliot knew the wife's story then. Gabby had told him how the eldest Beck daughter had been kidnapped when she was nine.

He'd worked with Sebastian Lorcan on a stalking case back in Garrity. It was a small world at the top of the TSP food chain sometimes. "How are Paige and Al and the rest?" he asked of the agents he'd worked with in the past.

"Just fine."

"All this is just great, but how is *Brynna*?" His brother's words broke into the conversation. "Tell me…how is she? The blood…?"

Dr. Coulter stepped into the room in time to catch Chance's question. "Mr. Marshall, I told you. Next-of-kin. It's up to them to give out the information. Not me."

"I'm her father," Kevin said. "How's my daughter? You can share with all of us here."

"She's still in surgery. There was some damage from the knife, but it was mostly superficial. The biggest concern was the bleeding. She did have to have a transfusion. And to combat infection, they've put her on strong antibiotics. She's responding well. Very well, actually. She'll be out for a few hours—most likely until morning. I've pulled some strings. I can't get just anyone back there to sit *with* her, but Jilly is cleared since she routinely works the surgery floor here. I thought it might be best for Brynna not to wake up in the hospital without a familiar face nearby."

Brynna's slightly younger sister nodded around her tears. "Of course. Thank you. Fin, I owe you one."

"No thanks necessary. I owe Bryn a few myself."

Chance turned and walked out of the conference room. Elliot followed his brother. They had a lot to talk about.

* * *

ELLIOT nodded at Erickson when he passed the man in the hall. Erickson had assigned himself as Elliot's guard dog since he'd strolled into the TSP the morning Chance had left for St. Louis. The other man followed him and Chance down the hall—two yards behind the ever present Magda Journey, who'd been waiting just outside the conference room.

He trusted Agent Lorcan—otherwise, he wouldn't have left Gabby in there alone. He strongly suspected the other man was armed and willing to do what was necessary to protect his family, and Gabby.

Chance left the conference room. Elliot followed. Their boot steps echoed on the tile floor. Chance walked straight out of the hospital into the pouring rain.

Elliot's detail sped up their steps. He didn't care. He was there for his brother. Chance stayed silent for the longest time.

"Chance?"

His brother spun around, a wild look in his eyes. Elliot tensed. "She's going to be ok. She's not going to die."

"That's what they say."

Chance looked up into the rain. He stepped back under the awning. Elliot followed. "You'll need my shirt. Damn it. It's got DNA. You'll need it with someone like that sonofabitch. Can't let it get any more degraded than it has."

Elliot's attention sharpened. "What happened out there?"

His brother pulled his shirt over his head and thrust it into Elliot's hands. He balled it up and tossed it back behind him. Journey caught it like he knew she would. She'd see to it that it got to the right place. Elliot looked at his brother again, *needing* to get a good look at the damage. For his own piece of mind.

His brother had bruises all over his chest.

"Chance. Tell me." At that moment, he didn't give a damn if he caught the guys. He was just glad to still have his brother standing right there in front of him instead of rotting in the dirt just like Slade.

Elliot looked at Journey and jerked his head back toward the hospital. They needed privacy for a minute, didn't they?

He grabbed his brother and jerked him closer. "Don't scare me like that ever again."

"Get off of it, Elliot. I'm alive."

"Almost three days, Chance. While I thought my brother was dead. I get a hug, whether you like it or not." He didn't want to cling, but…he hadn't let himself think of what could have happened.

"Sorry. Sonsofbitches didn't make it easy. We had to rabbit out of there fast. We holed up in an old camp storm shelter just south of the Oklahoma border. Just waited out the storm mostly. Barratt and his friends caught us again on the way out."

"Barratt? Houghton—the billionaire's son?"

"No. The billionaire himself. She got away from him while I was otherwise occupied." His brother flexed his bruised and cut hands, the move telling Elliot exactly how Chance had been occupied. "You'll have to ask her…when she wakes up."

"He the one who stabbed her?"

"No. Another big bastard. I don't know his name. But I'm going to find him. For her. She'll never feel safe as long as they're out there." Chance had a wild look in his eyes Elliot finally understood. "I made her a promise that I would keep her safe, Elliot. And I'm going to keep it."

"We'll get them. Do you know why they were on your tail? Were they? Or did you stumble into something? Possibly the grand jury issue? Were you followed?" Every scenario possible, he'd run through his mind over the past seventy-something hours. Only Chance and Brynna could give him the right one now.

"They weren't after me, El. They went for *her* first thing. Her laptop. They wanted what she had. What she knew. And they wanted her."

"Which was?" They'd entertained the possibility that it had been centered on Brynna, but the odds hadn't been all that great that it was.

"She ran the video taken ten years ago through some video software program she's designed. And found something. Something new. This is about her. And it's about Gabby. And it's about us."

Elliot had considered it, but because it hadn't been likely, he'd discounted it. But with the break-in at Gabby's, and now this…"What was it?"

"She didn't know. She was coming back to have Gabby—and Russell—take a look."

"No. Not Russell. And this goes no further than you and I. No one outside of the inner circle." Elliot said slowly as dominoes started to fall into place in his thoughts. "You, me, Gabby, the Becks, Erickson. That's it. We can tap Journey and Foster if needed. No one else."

"Why?"

"Because Brynna is isolated, practically sheltered as much as Gabby. *More* than Gabby in a lot of ways. *If* someone was after *that* girl—they were Texas State Police, Chance. It was the only way they learned of *her*. Most of her work has Russell's name on it. She never even testifies before the grand jury."

Chance grabbed Elliot's shirt front and pulled him closer. The rage and madness in his brother's eyes shocked him at the intensity. "Then *you* find the rat on your ship, big brother. *Before* I do. Because I plan to kill him when I do. They *touched* her, El. And that one guy—he wasn't just going to kill her. He was going to *force* her first, *rape* her. She'll always have the memory of that threat. Of his hands on her body. He's going to pay for that. You get my drift? *Him*—I'm going to find and rip apart with my bare hands. One cell at a time. Just for her."

Elliot looked at his younger brother and…he understood.

CHAPTER FORTY-TWO.

* * *

JILLY texted them a photo of Brynna sleeping. Gabby stared at it for a while before she practically dove onto the couch next to Mel. She hugged Gabby, and they cried together for a while, with Mel's youngest sister Syd caught between them. Their Dad was pacing around the room. Gabby knew Kevin wanted to be in there with her; but with Jilly back there, they had to be satisfied. It was the best they could do. And it mattered. They had proof she was going to be ok. That they had her back where she belonged. The worst of the nightmare was over.

Kevin practically jumped Elliot when he came back in twenty minutes later. "What do you know?"

Elliot looked at the dark-haired man Gabby knew was Mel's brother-in-law. He'd told Kevin earlier that he'd worked with Elliot before. The respect was there; she hadn't missed it. "No further than this room, Lorcan."

"Of course. Syd, I need you to go outside with Officer Journey." The teenager obeyed her brother-in-law. That left Mel and Brynna's father, older sister, and brother-in-law. And Gabby.

The door opened again. Chance stepped in, without his t-shirt. Gabby gasped when she saw the bruises covering Elliot's brother.

Elliot shrugged out of his outer shirt and tossed it toward him. Chance slipped into and buttoned it quickly.

"What do you know, El?" Mel asked. Her gaze was direct—and determined.

"What happened to Brynna? To Brynna?" Carrie asked.

Gabby watched Chance's face when he looked at the oldest Beck daughter. Brynna's half-sister looked more like her than any of the others; she was a little curvier, and the hair was a darker shade of red and styled differently. But the resemblance was strong. He stared at her for a moment like it hurt him to look at her. Chance pulled his gaze away. "Three men, two vehicles. They ambushed us at the stop sign. They hit on her side, enough to stun us both. Superficial injuries, bruises. They didn't want to kill her right away. They dragged her from the vehicle—they wanted *her* and her laptop." He paused and his glare deepened as he looked at Brynna's sisters again. "They got the laptop. We escaped. Ran. Holed up in a storm shelter for a few days. When we came out, we were surrounded."

"Then what happened?" Kevin asked. Gabby had to admire how he was holding himself together.

"We managed to get away again, but she was stabbed. We made it to the interstate. A trucker from Indiana picked us up there and brought us here. She wanted…the hospital where her sister works." Chance prowled around as he spoke; Gabby hadn't ever seen him that upset before.

Except once. Chance finally stopped moving near his brother.

"Chance, you think you can write down everything you remember?" Elliot asked, his hand on his brother's shoulder.

"Yeah. I can do that. Elliot, you find our rat. Remember."

"What's going on? Elliot?" Gabby asked. Something had passed between the brothers. "What rat?"

"If someone was after *Brynna*, there would be only one way they'd even know about her," Mel said, slowly. "Through the TSP. You think someone at the TSP did this, don't you?"

"But what did they want from her?" Kevin asked. "Is it case related?"

Brynna's oldest sister stood up and grabbed her own bag. She pulled out a memory card and handed it to Gabby. "She was working on this at my house. When…when…word came that Brynna hadn't made it home, and as upset as she'd been, I duplicated her files off my hard drives. I have a backup system in place that keeps everything for thirty days. My systems are as secure as possible. PAVAD insured that. I didn't look at it; not without permission. But everything she did on *my* system is right there."

"Thanks, Carrie." Gabby looked at the memory card. "I know she was working on something for Major Crimes, but I think she finished that up before she left. Jarrod made the arrest. And she was playing around with that video software we were developing. Said she was going to run some things through your stuff."

"She did. But she has private access to my servers. I wasn't able to be in there with her; I got called in to help find a missing ten-year-old." She paused for a moment and looked up at her husband. "When Sebastian and I got back home, Brynna was upset and worried. We tried to get her to let us help, but she wanted to get home. To get home."

Did anyone else see Chance flinch whenever Carrie talked? Or was it just Gabby's imagination?

"I texted her for a while. I may have mentioned Chance was also in St. Louis."

"And that's when—and *how*—she found me," Chance said.

"She was determined to get home, and she would have made other arrangements. This still would have—could have—happened. She still would have been in their sights. Possibly with someone who couldn't help her." Brynna's brother-in-law said. "You kept her alive."

"Did she tell you what she found that upset her?" Mel asked.

Chance hesitated. "She was working on the video from ten years ago. The one of our family. She'd found something, but even she wasn't sure what it was. She wanted Russell to look at it to see if he could spot it. She didn't want to show it to Gabby again if she didn't have to."

"It was enough to upset her pretty significantly, though. And that's not like her at all," Carrie's husband said. "Not Brynna."

Gabby had met Carrie a few times when she'd visited Texas, but most of their contact had been through video chat. She'd only seen pictures of the husband. *Brynna* thought her brother-in-law hung the moon. She'd said he really loved her sister and niece a great deal. "So why didn't she say something?"

"I think she wanted to bring it straight to Russell and Elliot," Chance said. "She didn't trust it over the phone—or the internet. She would barely talk about it with me. She said it was for Elliot's eyes only first. I'm not sure what she'd found or done was completely legal. She got jumpy when I asked her. Or she was afraid someone else might hack into her stuff. Scared."

"No. She wouldn't have said anything without permission, even with family. She always follows TSP protocols if she's working on something for CF. We both do. Brynna's a bit paranoid about technological spying. We do it all the time in our job. She is afraid someone could get into *her* stuff too easily." Gabby thought for a moment, about everything she knew Brynna had been working on recently. Everything she knew Brynna would have thought to do with old video through her sister's more sophisticated computer setup. "But… guys…Brynna had *my* spare laptop with her in St. Louis. She and Benny were updating hers with some serious upgrades. The laptop they took was mine."

Elliot's hand wrapped around her arm, and he turned her slightly. "Do you think that's significant?"

"I don't know. Brynna and I run pretty much the same systems on our personal laptops. They're the ones we play with—" She looked at Carrie, suspecting Brynna's older sister was the same way. "We code on them; we develop software. We game on them. Everything. When Benny couldn't get Brynna's finished in time for her before her shift ended, she took mine. It had the software we've been working on. We built the laptops together out of spare parts a few years ago."

"Is it possible someone was after that software design instead of what she found on that old video?" Kevin asked. "I know Bryn said it's pretty high tech."

"It is," Sebastian said. "And it'll be in high demand, once it's released. Everyone who worked on it will net a nice payout. Most of that money is Brynna's."

"Eighty percent. We're keeping a careful watch on the project. Ten percent for Carrie, ten for me." But it wasn't about the money. It was about the technological advances in their field. They'd found a way to make the forensic video software *better* all around. And they'd been working on it for two years. "But it's just the three of us. Me, Brynna, and Carrie. We certainly haven't mentioned it to anyone outside of this room. Jarrod and Benny. That's it."

"How much money are we talking about here?" Elliot asked. "Could that possibly be a motive?"

"Estimation of it's worth is over one point five million, conservatively. I'm expecting it to be more like two. Just for the basic prototype. We've also made some optional upgrades that could push it closer to three million," Carrie said. "But…it's a private deal, with Lucas Industries out of St. Louis. He's a family connection. We've kept this under wraps for as long as I've known Brynna. She's been working on it for years—long before I got involved. Very few people know about it."

"I'm telling you all, it wasn't about that program she wrote," Chance said again. "It's about what she found on the video. Of the night our family was killed. She ran it through as a test. She found something, and I think someone else knew it. Knew exactly what she found and what she was working on."

"That's next to impossible. Unless one of us or all of us, were hacked. Spyware to see what she was working on? Is that possible? That a sophisticated enough spyware was used to get past all of our checkpoints. Including Carrie's?" Gabby asked. "I don't know how anyone would even be able to do that. I mean…of course there are ways. Nothing is completely secure. But…"

Brynna's oldest sister looked at her husband. "We can have PAVAD look into that angle. If it touched *my* system, we'd get permission. I know we will."

"I've already got Brynna's laptop back from Benny. He gave it back to me today," Gabby said. "We'll take a closer look at it. Maybe…we can find something we overlooked on hers; that may lead to whatever is on mine, as well."

CHAPTER FORTY-THREE.

* * *

CHANCE waited until he saw her younger sister walk out of the private room Brynna was now in. He understood the need to keep people out of the recovery ward, but…he needed to see her. One more time. Before he left. Just to make sure.

He was going hunting, and nothing was going to stop him from finding his prey. He owed her, and he'd made her a promise. Chance always kept his promises to the people who mattered.

Security at the hospital was pretty damned tight—but the guy watching Brynna's room was one he recognized. "Erickson."

"Marshall. You know I'm not supposed to let anyone but that pretty sister of hers in, right?"

"Then just turn your damn head. I'm only going to be a minute or so."

"Unh huh. I'll give you five; then I'm running you out. I'll look like a hero to the sister, and maybe she'll let me take her out for…coffee. Her scrubs have kittens on them. I've always liked kittens."

"Sure." Chance had known the other man for a decade. Erickson had gotten Elliot through the shit right after the funerals. The two had been partners, and Chance appreciated how the man had stuck by his brother's side while they'd dealt with everything. "And no corrupting the sister. She's too good for you."

Erickson had been there when they'd pulled the plug on Slade.

"I need to see her for myself, Gunnar. She…she saved my ass out there, and look what that got her." He needed to touch her one more time. Convince himself she was alive and breathing.

"She's a fighter, then. It has to be the red hair. I'll keep an eye on her tonight, Chance. I guarantee it. You have my word."

There were very few men he'd trust with that. Erickson was one of them. "Thanks."

"Anytime."

Chance stepped into the room. She was dressed in a yellow hospital gown that he knew immediately she wouldn't like. Yellow was not a Brynna-approved color; she'd told him that during one of their endless conversations in the cellar.

They had an oxygen tube on her, and an IV ran into her left hand. There were a few monitors nearby that hummed and beeped steadily.

He didn't look at them. He looked at her. She was pale, and her hair needed to be combed. The blanket was tucked tight around her; probably her sister's doing.

Her chest rose evenly.

She was safe. Alive. Protected.

He walked closer. Chance brushed a hand down her free arm, feeling the soft, soft skin that he'd loved kissing and touching. He just stood there next to her for the longest time. Feeling *her*. She was real. Safe. *Alive.*

He lifted her hand from the blanket and kissed the palm just once before he turned and walked out of the room.

Chance had some hunting to do, didn't he?

He walked right past the redheaded sister standing in the hall next to Erickson, watching him with a hesitant look on her face. She looked at him, with surprise in the eyes just like her sister's.

Eyes that made him feel like a total slug.

Eyes that reminded him of everything that had almost been lost forever.

CHAPTER FORTY-FOUR.

* * *

ELLIOT brought Gabby to the hospital early the next morning. She hadn't wanted to leave the night before, but it had made the most sense. Brynna was expected to make a full recovery. It would take her a few weeks to feel one hundred percent, but she was going to be fine, and back to work within two weeks—at the most. It was hard to believe.

Gabby had talked about nothing else from the time they'd rolled out of bed. Elliot had a time keeping up with her.

He had no clue where his brother had ended up, but he suspected Chance had left the hospital sometime the night before. If he had—his brother was in pursuit of the assholes who'd ambushed them.

In pursuit of Handley Barratt.

Elliot was going to start with Barratt, as soon as he had Gabby someplace guarded and safe. Other than her apartment being vandalized, they had no proof of any threat to Gabby specifically. But he wasn't taking any chances. Foster was relieving Erickson on Brynna's security detail, and he had no doubt Mel and her father would also be at the hospital. Gabby would be safe there, with Kevin to guard her. Elliot suspected Lorcan would be prowling around the hospital, keeping his wife's family safe, as well. People he could trust to keep Gabby safe, too. There weren't many he could say that about in the TSP anymore.

He had to figure out who in the three hundred plus people in his organization could have arranged the attack on Brynna—and why.

Now that he had his brother back, Elliot had some hunting of his own to do.

CHAPTER FORTY-FIVE.

* * *

ELLIOT left her with Brynna and stepped out into the hall with Jarrod. Gabby had asked him what the next steps need to be. They had to find out who had targeted Brynna and why. She didn't have a clue how to do that. She and Elliot had spent several hours after they left the hospital the night before going over the laptop she'd picked up from Benny.

There had been no signs that she could find of *anything* on Brynna's laptop that shouldn't have been there. But that didn't mean that the one Brynna had taken with her was clean.

Had someone found a way to infect her laptop? To spy on her? How long had they been watching? Were they watching Brynna, as well? That made a sort of sense. Maybe everyone in the Computer Forensics department was under surveillance?

She discounted that thought. To do that on a large scale would be a massive undertaking.

She hadn't accessed the files from Sara's murder even once since she'd started working with the TSP. Brynna obviously had, though.

What did it all mean?

Gabby waited for her friend to wake up, keeping herself occupied with the phone Officer Journey had passed her when she'd spoken with Elliot outside his home. She'd met them outside with a security detail—complete with car, which was a nice and unexpected little perk—and a list of Elliot's pressing itinerary. He was able to do a lot of it virtually, with his laptop and cell.

But she wasn't fooling herself. He'd have to return to the TSP sometime today. He had an entire post to run. He had been away from it for too long. Elliot couldn't afford to jeopardize his career by neglecting his duties any longer.

Brynna finally woke with a little cry. Gabby leaned over her. "Bryn? It's ok; I'm here."

Brynna frowned up at her and tried to sit up. She cried out, then settled back against the pillows. "Gabby, this really happened, didn't it?"

Her eyes filled. Gabby grabbed the tissues and handed them to Brynna. "It did. We were totally scared, by the way. I tried to tell Mel—who kept blubbering like crazy—that you were superwoman and would be just fine, but she didn't really believe me. Ok, so I was the blubbery one—no surprise, right? How do you feel? Do you need anything?"

"Where's Chance?" Brynna asked. "Is he ok? Did they hurt him, too? Where is he?"

"Bruises. I saw them on his chest. He has a nice one, but his chest isn't as good as Elliot's, though."

"No, it's better."

"So you saw it naked? What did you two do in that shelter all that time?"

Definitely the *wrong* question to ask. Brynna's crying tripled. "Oh, Gab…I've done something completely and utterly stupid here."

"Dear Gravy, Bryn. Did you and Chance….?" It explained a few things, didn't it? Why he was so…so…intense when he talked about Brynna. "Oh, Bryn…"

"I know." She wiped her eyes, then took a breath. Pulled herself together right before Gabby's eyes. "We both agreed it didn't mean anything. And no strings. *I* don't want strings with a man like him, either. Nothing could come of it, and I'm too young. Too young."

But the pain in her words was hard for Gabby to miss.

And she got it—those Marshall men made a woman do things she probably shouldn't even think about. With no promises of what tomorrow would bring.

Brynna seemed to understand that. "I shouldn't feel like this for him, Gab. I shouldn't. It doesn't make sense."

But she did. Gabby knew exactly how she felt. "Oh, Bryn. I understand. Believe me, I do."

At that moment, if that frog Chance Marshall had been right there in front of her she would have slugged him.

What had he been thinking?

She would forever be grateful that he kept her friend safe out there, but he hadn't needed to break Brynna's heart in the process, had he?

Someone stepped through the door and Gabby looked up.

Everything Mel felt was right there on her face as she looked at her sister for the first time. "Brynna. Thank God. You really scared us, kid."

Brynna looked up at Gabby and then over at her sister. "I'm ok, Mel. I'm ok, ok. I promise. You don't have to worry about me now. I'm ok."

Mel limped closer to the bed and then placed her crutch on the air conditioning unit beneath the window. Then she was on the bed right next to Gabby, and the three women were clinging to each other—as carefully as they could with Brynna's injuries between them. Gabby just held on.

These two were her normal. As close to her as Sara had been all those years ago. Thank God Brynna was alive.

Brynna pulled away after a while. She didn't like to be touched all that much; it surprised Gabby she'd touched her and Mel as long as she had. "I found something in the video."

"Chance told us," Mel said. "What was it?"

"I need to talk to Benny about it."

Gabby shook her head. "Elliot doesn't want you to. He wants to keep it off the TSP radar. Until we know…He thinks there might be someone at the TSP involved. He doesn't want any of this discussed with *anyone* outside of your family, him and Chance, and his friend Erickson. He wants to keep you out of it now, too."

Brynna sniffed. "It's my job. And you're my friend. Sara was my friend, too. And her brothers...her parents...Chance needs…I can show you. I can help. I will. I *need* to. It's not finished. It's not finished."

"It is for you," Mel's tone was harsh. "I want you to go back to St. Louis with Carrie when you get out of here. Stay with her. At least until we find out what's going on."

"I don't think I can do that." Brynna lifted her chin. Her eyes were still wet, but she didn't look as desolate as she had when Mel had first walked in. "I'm a part of this now. And I'm going to see it through to the end. I know the name of one of the men who did this. And I can find him. If Chance hasn't gotten there first."

Gabby and Mel stared at her. Brynna's eyes filled again.

"I think you need to start at the beginning," Brynna's sister said. "Who was it that took you?"

"Handley Barratt."

Gabby's eyes widened, and she knew she stared at her friend like a stupid fish. "The guy with all the money?"

"I recognized him from that benefit we went to with Ariella and Luc last July. You remember the one?" Mel and Jarrod had dared her and Brynna to go to support their friend Ariella, who was active for the charity that was based on preventing violence against women. Ariella's brother, the richest guy in St. Louis, was a big supporter of Ariella's project.

She and Brynna had attended together, wearing beautiful dresses and sitting with Ariella and her brother. Handley Barratt had been there with his son, but they hadn't sat anywhere near them.

"You're sure? Absolutely sure?" Mel asked, slowly. She'd paled, and her hand gripped the blanket between them. "Handley Barratt from Barratt-Handley Enterprises? The older man…not Hough—the son?"

Gabby got it. To accuse someone like Barratt was going to be world changing.

"He took me away from the other man, the one who was going to—Handley Barratt took me away, and he told me to run, to hide from the other men. But I went back for Chance. I couldn't leave him. I got close enough to see the California shaped mole on Handley Barratt's neck. It was *him,* and Ch-Chance knows it, too. Just...find him and ask him. Don't let Chance go after him alone, Mel. Promise me. Don't let him go alone."

Brynna's face crumbled and Gabby wrapped her arms around her friend again. Mel looked at her with a question in her light brown eyes.

“Brynna has deep feelings—*seriously* deep—for Chance Marshall.”

Mel closed her eyes and winced. “I see.” She opened her eyes and then laid a comforting hand over her sister’s. “It’ll be ok, Bryn. I promise. It gets easier with time. You’ll get past this. Just trust me, I know. And one day you’ll wake up and be able to breathe without him again.”

CHAPTER FORTY-SIX.

* * *

ELLIOT could hear Brynna crying quietly. He peered in the door and looked at the women on the hospital bed.

Gabby was holding Brynna's hand and repeating reassurances. "It'll be ok, Brynna. You're safe."

"He's leaving, Mel. I know he is. We agreed on no strings, but…" Brynna clung to Gabby and Mel. Elliot stepped away, not wanting to intrude on her pain. "He doesn't want to be with me."

Her words sunk in. *He.* Chance?

His brother and Brynna together—maybe it wasn't surprising after all, considering what they'd gone through together. Emotions would have been high; they had been trapped for hours together. Did it surprise him at all, considering how he and Gabby had grown close over the past few days? And *they* hadn't been trapped in a damned cellar.

Chance cared about the woman in that hospital bed. Elliot knew it to his bones. Probably just as much as Elliot cared about Gabby.

So where the hell was his brother? Why wasn't his brother in there with his woman, holding her? Reassuring her that he'd keep the bad guys far away from her forever?

Elliot nodded at Foster then told him quietly that he was going to find his brother.

He found Chance in the cafeteria, sitting next to the ice machine, nursing a cup of coffee and glaring at everyone. "Here you are. I wondered."

"I waited with her until she wasn't alone. Until Foster called Erickson to let him know, he was on his way in. I didn't want to be caught in her room. Her sister had to go back to work at six this morning."

"Were you in there with Jillian?"

"No. I stayed in the empty room next door, in case Brynna needed me. Or Erickson needed a bathroom break. About that. He must have a bladder the size of Texas, that guy. Never left his post even once. Don't think Brynna's sister knew I was in there, though. I'd like to keep it that way."

"How did you know Gabby and I were here?"

"Called the nurse's station. Asked if a guy that looked like me with a blonde woman had come in yet."

"I see."

"They think it's romantic." Chance's derision wasn't hard to miss. "Nothing romantic about running from a bunch of killers during tornados. She could have died out there."

"It was a good story, I guess. Why are you down here instead of up there *with* her? I think she needs you to be."

"Stay out of it, El. It's between us." His brother's face was closed off completely. But this was the one person in the world Elliot knew best of all. Chance was all tied in knots. Over a woman he thought he couldn't have. *Shouldn't* have. Elliot knew just how his brother felt. "I nearly got her killed."

"From what I've heard, you kept her alive long enough to survive."

"Barely."

"Tell me—who was it that was attacked? You or her? Our theory is that Gabby's laptop was bugged—it was hers that Brynna had with her, did you know that? *Gabby's*. And Brynna ended up finding something the killer didn't like."

"He held a knife to her, El. Did you see the blood where he cut her? Do you know how scared she looked when he had his *hands* on her?" Fury was tightly held in his brother's voice. Had it been Gabby, Elliot knew he would have felt the same. Elliot finally understood it, the look that had been in his father's eyes when Elliot's mother had died right in front of him. That look was in Chance's eyes right now. "She was looking at me with those eyes of hers, silently *begging* for me to help her. For a minute there she turned into Sara. And I couldn't do a damned thing. I didn't even realize she was bleeding until we'd been walking for hours that first morning. She could have bled to death right there behind me."

Elliot understood what his brother *wasn't* saying.

A woman like Brynna, like Gabby too, made men like them feel guilty for not being able to make their world a perfect place. "She's alive. And with Gabby and Mel now. The brother-in-law is from the FBI. He's going to look into a few things on his end for me. Off the books. He's good at what he does. I've worked with him before."

"She mentioned him. Talked about her niece. She really loves that kid. Her family. She has a *family* who loves her. They don't deserve to be brought into this. I'm going to find the bastards responsible before that can happen. Before they can hurt her again."

Chance stood. He tossed his coffee cup into the trashcan. He turned back to Elliot. "You keep her safe for me, Elliot. Promise me that. No matter what. You keep Brynna safe."

"You're going."

"Hell yes. I'm not what she needs. I'm the last thing *that* woman needs in her life."

"She's up there crying over you." And Elliot had no doubt that his brother was hurting just as much, but the anger was masking it. For right now.

"She'll get over it. It was the situation; it filled her with ideas she didn't have any business thinking. I'm not like *you!* I'm not like Dad. I'm not the staying kind. And I never will be."

Elliot didn't doubt that his brother wasn't the kind to stay—but that didn't mean his brother wasn't the kind to love, did it?

"How do you feel about her? Honestly."

"Don't ask me that." A wild panic he would never have expected entered the eyes so much like their father's. "I love you, Elliot. Don't forget that. No matter what happens. But I won't talk about her again."

"I won't. And it's returned. Chance, don't go after these guys by yourself. Promise me that."

"I can't do that. You go after Handley Barratt. Brynna can tell you more about him and what he said to her. The rest of those bastards are *mine*."

And then his brother turned and just walked away.

CHAPTER FORTY-SEVEN.

* * *

ELLIOT headed back to the TSP. Life stopped for nothing, it seemed. He did what he had to do to get a search warrant to serve to one of the wealthiest, most influential men in Texas. It was going to be a royal cluster—all the evidence they had was Brynna's witness statement—collaborated by his brother's, Brynna's lover. It was weak, and everyone knew it.

The state attorney general was dead set against any steps to arrest Barratt. He'd summed up every possible result of even trying without some seriously strong evidence. They didn't have that, even forensics. The storm had destroyed every hope for that. No, they would have to get Handley Barratt some other way.

Elliot forced himself to calm down after disconnecting his conference call with the state attorney general. He'd always respected Carson Nolan—he still did, even though the other man couldn't help him now.

He *had* gotten a promise that once he had something solid, he could go after Barratt with both barrels.

He just had to get that something solid first.

His assistant buzzed to let him know his brother and Sebastian Lorcan waited outside his office, around eleven.

Elliot was relieved to see his brother hadn't taken off, after all.

"Figured you'd want to speak with people at Barratt-Handley today," Chance said. "I'm going with you."

"Who is with Brynna right now?" Elliot had put an officer on her at all times, but he suspected the family had pulled together to see she had a little extra protection in the room with her. And Gabby. He doubted she was leaving her friend's side.

"Mel and Kevin, as well as Carrie, are in the room with her," Lorcan said, settling into the chair across from the desk. He was a tall man with a calm manner—and a razor-sharp mind. They'd worked together before, and he'd found the man to be damned good at what he did. "They're all three armed."

"Plus there's a man of mine walking the halls." Chance prowled around the room, stopping at the photo of their father in his full service uniform. "She's safe. *They* are safe."

"I'm sending the head of Major Crimes to Barratt-Handley Enterprises. Attorney General pointed out that I can't go myself." Elliot understood, of course. But the fact that he was being sidelined in his own life pissed him off.

"You sure he's trustworthy?" Chance asked.

"He's only been in Finley Creek a year—and he's got a thing for Brynna." Elliot watched his brother's eyes narrow at that. "I trust him about as much as I do anyone else in this damned building. But I can't go myself. I'm sending Foster with him."

"Jarrod's clean," Lorcan said. "I've known him for a while now. There's nothing he won't do for Brynna or Mel. Or the rest of the Becks, either, for that matter."

Chance was still prowling. "So this is it. We can just *ask questions* to find the assholes that hurt her?"

"We can't pound the answers out of anyone who knows Barratt." No matter how much Elliot wanted that, they had to play by the rules. "We need something solid."

Chance's two-word response was harsh, but not unexpected. "I know. But it's what we have to do."

"I'll ride along with Foster. Maybe I can work up a profile," Lorcan said. "Look, I know exactly what you are both feeling right now. I watched Carrie *dive* off a four-story building to escape a serial killer who held a grudge against the father Carrie hadn't even met. The ache, the fear—I still have nightmares about her face as she looked at me. I knew she was going over. You just have to fall back on your training and experience. Your instinct. You'll figure this out."

Elliot appreciated the guy's attempt—and he wondered how Lorcan had handled watching his woman go over the edge of a building like that. Thankfully she'd survived.

Until they had the threat against them all stopped, he wouldn't breathe easily. No doubt Chance felt the same—*his* woman was lying in a hospital bed with stitches holding her together, after all.

"Barratt-Handley Enterprises and Handley Barratt—that's where we go from here."

CHAPTER FORTY-EIGHT.

* * *

HOUGHTON Barratt was in his office when his secretary buzzed to let him know that the head of the Finley Creek TSP Major Crimes unit was in their building, looking for Houghton's father.

Houghton had been looking for the man himself for three days. His father flew all over the world for their business dealings, but this was the first time he hadn't had so much as an email from his dad since they'd met for dinner between meetings three days ago.

Dread filled him. Had they found his father somewhere? Was he hurt?

He had tried his father's personal assistant, but she hadn't heard from his father either. And she was worried. He knew she cared about his father—more than just cared, if Houghton was honest. She'd loved his father for two decades now.

Not that his father ever returned that affection.

If Josephine was worried, there was probably something going on, wasn't there?

He'd filled out a police report that morning with the Texas State Police. And he'd put out private feelers with his own people, himself.

He stood when three men entered his office.

"Houghton Barratt?" a tall dark-haired man asked.

"Yes. I understand you're here about my father. Have you found him yet?" Houghton had years of experience at keeping his demeanor under control. To not let how he felt about anything show. It served him well now. The men introduced themselves quickly. FBI and TSP Major Crimes? What was going on here?

Commander McKellen shook his head. "No. We haven't. Mr. Barratt, have you been following the news reports about the missing Texas Ranger?"

"And the autistic girl? I haven't been following it, but I've seen some. What does that have to do with me?" He was confused. How did that have to do with the missing person's report? His father?

"That's what brought us here, today," the man from the FBI said.

"Can someone tell me what's going on? Is my father alive?" He refused to feel fear until he had the information he needed. It was just Houghton's way. His father was his only immediate relative left. And the two of them had always been close. They were family—a small one, but a family nonetheless. The two dozen cousins he had spread over Texas were family, but his father was the center of his world.

At least until he found the woman he wanted to spend the rest of his life with.

"Mr. Barratt, your father's been named a person of interest in the kidnapping and assault of Brynna Beck and Chance Marshall. Do you know where he is?" the head of Major Crimes asked.

"No, I do not. And I'll tell you this—you're wrong. My father didn't hurt anyone. And if you have any more questions, you'll need to speak with the Barratt family attorneys. We employ the law firm located on the first floor of this building; my cousin Alex is on retainer."

Houghton wasn't the type of man to leap to conclusions or make rash decisions. His first priority was finding his father. No matter what.

"Brynna Beck identified your father as one of the men who assaulted her. She's in the hospital," Agent Lorcan said. "We need to find him. To figure this out. It'll be easier for him, with less damage, if he comes forward. You need to make that clear to him."

"Agent Lorcan, if I knew where he was, I wouldn't have filed a missing person's report hours ago—would I?" Not a damned bit of what they said made any sense. His father wouldn't attack some woman, not for anything. His dad had raised Houghton to believe in helping your neighbor, not hurting them.

Why would this woman lie about his father?

Was she just another crazy out there? A gold-digger? Perhaps a former lover? Some of his father's past liaisons had turned spiteful. Or greedy. But this was the first time the FBI had ever ended up involved. Something was definitely going on, wasn't it?

What the hell had his father gotten involved in?

"Mr. Barratt, we understand that this can be upsetting to you. But we need to find him before someone else does," McKellen said.

"Like I said, our attorneys are on the first floor." Houghton had some research to do. He was going to find out everything he could about a woman named Brynna Beck. *Everything.*

CHAPTER FORTY-NINE.

* * *

MEL stayed with Brynna at the hospital practically the whole day. Gabby didn't know if that was because Mel didn't trust the guard detail Elliot had on Brynna around the clock or because she was just as frightened as Gabby was.

Probably the latter.

Elliot had to go back to work after he took Gabby to see Brynna that first day, and she went with him on the second morning. She'd not wanted to leave her friend, but someone had to cover their department. Benny needed the help, and it was going to have to be her. He'd given her an extra day with Brynna, anyway.

No matter how much she didn't want to leave Brynna. How afraid she was. *Life* didn't get to stop when bad things happened. You just had to keep going.

Gabby knew *that* for the truth, didn't she? Elliot was nervous of leaving her downstairs. Benny had promised to take care of Gabby.

She appreciated it. But she couldn't let fear keep her from doing her job, or living or life, or anything like that.

She could do this. She had to learn to take care of herself.

It seemed like everyone wanted to stop by and see how Brynna was. Gabby spent most of her work day fielding questions.

There had only been a few snide comments about her and Elliot. She thought she handled them well. All she'd admitted to was that her apartment had been vandalized and was a possible target for whoever had attacked Brynna and left it at that and Elliot—a friend she'd had since childhood—had offered her his spare room until they caught the vandals, and got the mess cleaned up.

Most people seemed to think that because she was with Elliot, and Brynna had disappeared with his brother, that it had something to do with the Marshall murders.

She couldn't lie about that. It *did* have something to do with the Marshall murders.

She just couldn't figure out what. Brynna would have to help figure out that part.

After her shift was over, she waited for Elliot in the reception area. He had ordered an officer to fetch his car, and they waited at the front entrance. Elliot kept her just inside the doors, where she was moderately safer.

He was taking the idea of a threat to them all very seriously. Gabby was just trying to appear like she could handle it.

"The house or the hospital first?" he asked after they were both in the SUV she recognized as his.

There was no real question was there? "Brynna. I need to see that she's ok. And I think we need to talk to her about the video. I didn't want to ask this morning. She was too upset. But there was something on it. She'll tell you, though. Maybe it will give us a place to start."

"Major Crimes interviewed Handley Barratt's son this afternoon."

"What did they learn?"

Elliot shook his head. "Not much. Guy said his father has been missing for more than a week. He's slick and damned evasive, according to Lorcan. He's not going to be much help."

"Do you think he's involved?"

"I don't know. He was hiding something, planning something. McKellen and Lorcan both agreed on that. I'd bet my non-existent billions on it."

She shivered. "How are we going to figure this out, Elliot? I don't know what I'm supposed to be doing here. At all. I have the memory card that Brynna's sister gave me. But I didn't want to run it through the TSP system."

"Can you run what's on the zip drive at the hospital? Safely?"

"I don't know. Safer than anywhere else, I think, with a few tweaks to the hospital's Wi-Fi for security purposes. And we can ask her what she found. But..." She looked out the window at everything rushing by. "But I don't *want* to look at that video again."

"I don't either."

"We're going to have to, though, aren't we?"

CHAPTER FIFTY.

* * *

THEY picked up his brother in the lobby. Chance had split his time between prowling the hall outside the Computer Forensics department and the evidence room located one floor up. Gabby knew he was going through everything he could find on the murder of his family. Hopefully, there would be something to connect his father with Handley Barratt. Something to at least give them direction.

From the stormy expression on his face, his search had turned up nothing.

Chance drove, even though it was Elliot's SUV. No one spoke much; Chance's obvious frustration kept Gabby's mouth shut for once. Elliot looked at his brother for a long time before saying anything. "We need to talk to Brynna about what she found on that laptop."

Chance nodded. "She wouldn't tell me much. Said she had to talk to her boss first since it was *evidence*. Damned stubborn female."

"She's a stickler for protocol. She never wants a case to get tossed because of something she did. We both are that way. We are good at our jobs," Gabby said in her friend's defense.

Chance looked at her in the mirror. "I know. I gave up pushing her after the first *twelve* hours of her saying nothing about it."

"But she'll tell Elliot."

"That's why I'm coming along for this."

"Have you been to see her since she woke up?" Gabby asked softly. How did this man feel about her best friend?

His hands tightened on the wheel. "No. I've been busy."

"I see." She didn't. Not really. Whatever they'd *promised* each other in that storm shelter, Brynna felt for him. Deeply. The least he could do was be there for her when she was in the hospital. She liked Chance, but…Brynna was her best friend. First loyalty was to her. "Mel called and said she's doing ok. Even though she's absolutely terrified of hospitals and germs. They're trying to keep her as distracted as possible. But she's starting to fight them, wanting to go home. Moving around more than she should. If she gets really worked up, they're afraid she'll pull out the stitches. Mel said she already popped two."

"She's staying in the hospital until they say she's better. Even if I have to tie her to the damned bed." Chance's words came out so low Gabby could barely hear him. Almost as if he was talking to himself. But if they'd made no promises to each other, why did he seem to care so much?

"Mel and her dad can handle her, though. They've been doing it her whole life. Brynna has people who love her and will get her through this." She didn't like to see *him* hurting, either. And Gabby strongly suspected he was. Why? Did he care that much about Brynna, too? If he did, why wasn't he *with* her right now?

Chance Marshall was one man she was never going to understand all the way. Rather like his brother.

She didn't think she would ever fully understand Elliot.

But…she and Elliot hadn't made any more promises to each other than Brynna and Chance had, had they? Maybe once this *thing* with the Marshall murders was finished and life got back to somewhat normal, she and Elliot would find they didn't have anything *real* between them, either? Maybe it would be her crying her heart out for a Marshall man?

Maybe this was just an interlude in time, with all their emotions churning between them? Maybe the sex had been inevitable? But doomed to not be repeated long term?

How did she feel about that? Damn it—what had they both done to themselves? Why hadn't these questions hit her before now?

Gabby sat back against the seat and thought about that for the remainder of the short drive between the Finley Creek TSP and the Finley General Hospital. She had no more answers for herself than she did for Brynna.

CHAPTER FIFTY-ONE.

* * *

ELLIOT was the first in the room and was in time to see how Brynna's eyes flared and filled with love the moment his idiot brother walked in right behind him. Then a shutter came down, and she looked away. When she looked back at them, no hint of how she felt was on her face. The relief at seeing Gabby was there, though.

"Gabs."

"Hey, Bryn. I hear you're giving Jilly and the rest of the nurses gray hair."

"Hardly. I'm on my best behavior. This is my new friend, Handley Bear here. From Jarrod." Brynna sat the stuffed animal beside her on the bed. "I even ate the *yellow* Jell-O Jilly forced on me."

"Yellow is not going to poison you, Bryn," Mel said from the corner of the room where she sat with a notebook. "I promise. And are you *really* going to name that damned thing that? Rather morbid, don't you think?"

"Yellow tastes like lemon. Lemon as in Lysol. Why would I eat that?" Brynna grimaced, then shot her older sister a look filled with sisterly malice. "And *yes.* That *is* the bear's name."

Mel laughed and looked at Gabby and the two men. “She's even more *Brynna* than usual today. I think she’s bored.”

“*Mel* wouldn’t give me a laptop.” Brynna’s hostility at that was hard to miss.

“You needed to rest,” her sister said. “Not work—of any kind.”

“But…they took my laptop—sorry, Gabs, it was yours—and I’ve not been on a computer in *days*.”

“Tough, toots.”

“Gabby. Make her see reason. Please, I’m going crazy here!”

“No way. I’m too smart to get between the two of you when you start bickering.”

Two redheads turned toward Gabby and glared out of nearly identical eyes. “We do not *bicker*,” they said in unison.

Gabby giggled, and Elliot smiled to hear such a carefree sound from her after the last week. “You do, too. Remember the time you got so mad at each other Jilly dumped a gallon of Gatorade on both of your heads to shut you up?”

“Rather hard to forget,” Mel said.

Brynna shuddered. “*Yellow* Gatorade. It was horrible.”

Mel turned toward the two men. “Brynna screamed and screamed and screamed. It took Jilly, Gabby, and me and a water hose to get her calmed down before someone called in a noise disturbance. *Another* noise disturbance. Our house has a bit of a reputation on our block.”

“I still haven’t forgiven you three for that hose. It was freezing.”

"Hey, at least it was summer, and we were outside." Mel reached over and squeezed her sister's hand. Brynna turned her palm up and squeezed back.

"It scared off Jilly's boyfriend, though. Apparently, he thought *she* was the normal one of us and *me* the crazy one. Until she dumped the drink on us and started yelling. Boy, did he learn. He knocked over the mailbox when he drove off like that." Brynna pulled her hand away from her sister. "I'm never going to like *yellow,* though."

"Well, I brought you a present, Bryn." Gabby pulled her bag up on the bed near her friend's feet. "And we all know you didn't like the guy and were trying to scare him off with that whole crazy autistic fit act. I grabbed this out of my closet and took it to Elliot's with me after the break-in. It's my old one, but…I backed everything up to it after we made that breakthrough three months ago. It doesn't have our recent changes yet. But I have this, and I have your regular one. I think we can figure out what was lost from my laptop and from Carrie."

Brynna practically squealed with delight. "Finally! Someone here who *understands* me. Give. Give. Give."

Mel sighed and made a face at Gabby. "Enabler. I had a bet going with Jilly and Carrie about how long we could keep her fingers off a keyboard."

"So who won?"

"Carrie, of course. She predicted twenty-four hours from time of admittance. Jilly had her at a full week—she's the family optimist, after all. I was hoping she'd hold out until tomorrow. I had a hundred riding on it."

Brynna sighed as she booted up the laptop. "See how they treat me? My very own sisters. I think I'm going to move up to St. Louis with Carrie. Apparently, *she* understands me."

"Can we get down to business here?" Chance asked. Elliot looked at his brother in surprise. All he had done since walking into the room was try not to look like he was staring at the redhead on the hospital bed. And failing miserably.

The glint of humor in Brynna's eyes and her happiness over the laptop faded quickly. Elliot wanted to kick his idiot brother for his careless words.

Brynna wouldn't even *look* at Chance, would she? Elliot hoped the two of them figured out what was between them before something happened and they lost each other forever.

Gabby shifted in the chair she'd pulled up next to the bed, bumping the hand he hadn't realized he'd placed on her shoulder. When had that happened? Was he so drawn to her that he had to touch her, even when he wasn't aware of it?

He wasn't alone. He had Gabby now, didn't he? But for how long? How did he know that she wouldn't say thanks for the protection and then go her own way?

Wasn't that what he was expecting? Or did *he* want something more with her? Something more long-term, permanent?

"So what are you three doing here?" Mel asked, bluntly. "What's happening?"

"We need to know what Brynna found on that video that sent her heading back to Texas so quickly." Chance moved between Gabby's chair and the top of the bed. He was less than a foot from where Brynna rested, yet he held his body completely rigid.

Was his brother afraid he'd touch the girl and betray just exactly how he felt for her?

Elliot had news for his brother if he didn't already know it. Chance's feelings were as plain as day for him to see.

Or maybe it was because Elliot was inundated with his own similar emotions where Gabby was concerned.

Brynna shivered and looked over at Gabby. "Gabs? Do you want to be here while I tell them? Show them? Show them?"

Gabby pulled in a deep breath. "Do I want to be here? Heck no. But it's no more painful for me than it is for Elliot or Chance. If—if what happened that night has caused all of this. Has gotten *you* hurt, too, then I'll be the first one to watch it. A million times over if I have to. I have lost one best friend because of these people—" Gabby's breath hiccupped. "I can't lose another."

Brynna was quiet for a moment. "I'm ok, Gabs. I promise. I promise. I am *ok*. So are you. So is Mel. We are all ok now."

"Then we can do this," Mel said as she shifted her own chair closer to the bed. She leaned toward her sister as Gabby leaned toward Brynna from the opposite side. These three women were connected at that moment, unintentionally shutting him and Chance out. "We'll do it together."

Brynna pulled in a shuddering breath, then winced. Her hand went to her side. Chance cursed and put his hands on her shoulders. She leaned back against him for a moment then he guided her back against the pillow. "Damn it, Brynna, don't hurt yourself."

"The number one reason we didn't want you to have a laptop, goof. We didn't want you sitting up for too long," Mel said, pulling a pillow from the closet and putting it beneath the laptop to get it at a better angle.

"I have to sit up sometime. I can't lay down forever. I need to get home and back to work. Back to my *life*."

"Brynna, what was on the video?" Gabby asked.

Brynna looked at the laptop for a moment, like she saw something that wasn't there. "There was layering that shouldn't have been in there in one of the frames. So I ran it through Carrie's system. Hers is better than ours, Gab. A lot better. And then I split the video and looked closer."

"What did you find?"

"*Someone* had been erased from the video. Meticulously. Frame by frame. It must have taken days of work to do. And access to the TSP files a *long* time ago."

"Who?" Elliot asked.

"I don't know. I tried to find a shadow, but couldn't. But…whoever did it has some serious skill. If I wasn't working on Carrie's 70-inch monitor, I wouldn't have noticed the first frame. I think someone erased the *fifth* man. But all I could figure out was that he was taller than Slade and heavier."

"That was enough to get you ran off the road?" Mel asked. "If there was nothing identifiable, why would it matter?"

"I don't know. I also don't know *how* they knew. Unless Gabby's laptop had spyware on it that *we* didn't find. And that's stretching it. Someone had to have serious access to even get it on one of our laptops. Plus to get it past Carrie's? That takes skill. And resources. Lots of them." Brynna pulled the blanket tighter around her shoulders. Chance's hands were there to help, but Elliot didn't miss the way his idiot brother glared down at her.

When Brynna looked up at him, there was a hesitation in her face. And love. So much love. Why didn't his brother see it?

Or did he? Was that what had his brother so damned scared? Did she even realize that she still leaned into his brother, that Chance had shifted enough that he was behind her on the bed, holding her up? That her head was resting on his brother's shoulder?

Damn the bastards who'd hurt them all—because of them Chance was about to throw away probably the best thing to ever happen to him.

Elliot's gut tightened when he looked down at Gabby. Decision made.

He wasn't going to be making the same damned mistake. When they left the hospital, he was taking her somewhere and telling her, *showing her,* exactly how he felt about her.

Taking the time they had together and making the most of every moment. Together.

"Maybe it wasn't just what was found on her laptop," Chance said. "Maybe they were just not wanting someone looking at the files at all."

"But by harming her, that was bound to draw attention to what she was working on," Elliot said. "And it was Gabby's laptop. How do we know they didn't somehow track the laptop to find you?"

"Is that even possible?" Mel asked. "I mean, that quickly?"

"I don't think it would have been necessary," Brynna said, shifting uncomfortably. "They probably traced my phone."

"But why did they focus on you? Instead of Gabby?"

"Because I had Gabby's laptop and had signed out a zip drive that had the videos from that night on it. *My* name was right there on the evidence log. Anyone at the TSP could have seen it. Could have known I was in St. Louis and could have found me with my phone. Gabby and I use cell phones to track suspects all the time."

Gabby nodded. "So you think it wasn't because it was my laptop."

"It was the zip drive. With copies of the exact originals turned in from your *old* laptop ten years ago. It was still in the original envelope, sealed, with the original date. I made a copy of it at the evidence desk using one of the TSP issued drives. I signed for it, like we do everything, and told people where I was going. It was blocked off of the CF schedule three weeks ago. I even told Daniel McKellen that I was going to be up there. And when I expected to get there. I texted him when I got there, too."

"Why the hell for?" Chance asked.

"Because he's a friend and he was worried." She finally looked up at his brother. "*He* wants to be a whole lot more."

Chance's face got even darker, if possible. Elliot was surprised. Brynna had definitely baited the bear with that one. Did she realize that? "If he's not the son of a bitch who hurt you."

"He isn't. He's just a nice man who wants to get to know *me* better. He gave me flowers the day I left, you know. Those pink balloons right there are from him, too. He knows I like pink."

"Ok, back to what we're dealing with here…" Mel said in the awkward moment that followed. "So we know that anyone could have found Brynna easily. But not everyone could have altered that video."

"Not everyone who had access to it, anyway." Gabby shifted closer to Brynna.

"You're missing the obvious. Handley Barratt could have *paid* someone to alter that video and paid someone to switch it out." Chance grabbed the bottle of water on the table behind him and put it in Brynna's hand. "Drink. You can't afford dehydration."

She complied, but only after sending him a pointed look that Elliot had no difficulty interpreting. It stated clearly she was just humoring him. Brynna Beck was fully capable of handling his brother, wasn't she? For all her obvious vulnerabilities, she wasn't a pushover.

Elliot would never have thought it would be possible, but Brynna could hold her own with Chance somehow. A naïve, twenty-four-year-old woman with autism could wrangle his hard-as-nails brother with just a single look.

Probably all she had to do was look at his brother with love in those eyes of hers and Chance would be putty, just like Elliot was with his Gabby.

His Gabby. Just like Brynna was his brother's. Damn it; he was gone.

It was time he accepted it.

He wrapped his fingers in her hair as she spoke with Brynna in more detail about what would have had to be done to alter the video that sophisticatedly. Half of what they said didn't make a lick of sense to him, and he could tell the same was true for his brother. Mel was capable of keeping up, though, and she explained a few things in laymen's terms for them.

The sun was setting before Kevin Beck and his son-in-law returned to the hospital to take over guard duty from Mel.

Elliot called a nearby restaurant to make a quick reservation for the four of them—they were going to continue their discussion over dinner—and they headed to the parking lot.

Gabby was quiet, her exhaustion easy to see on her pretty face. Elliot pulled her closer to him in the elevator and brushed a kiss on her forehead. "We'll eat, then head home. I can tell you're exhausted."

She leaned her head on his shoulder for a moment. "I am."

"We'll figure this out, Gabs." Mel touched her shoulder briefly. Elliot looked at her—Mel's exhaustion was almost as visible as Gabby's. He got the impression she was holding *herself* together through the strength of will alone. This whole thing—it had to end soon, didn't it?

They'd parked the SUV in the closest parking lot, and Elliot scanned the area immediately after the exit quickly.

Mel made her way down the curb carefully, Chance staying close by. Mel snarked at Chance occasionally, but Elliot got the impression it was because of how protective she was of her younger sister. Family loyalty was strong in the Becks, for certain.

Elliot held Gabby's hand as they started across the parking lot. He wanted to keep her as close as he possibly could. Both to protect her, and because that was where he wanted her to begin with.

His body tightened in anticipation of just how he would be *showing* her how he felt about her in a few hours.

After she had rested a bit first, that was.

Life was too short for him to screw around with his future anymore.

This little blonde bundle of contradictions was all he wanted in his life. *Her*.

He got a quick kick out of imagining his sister watching out for him up above—he could just hear her wild giggles at the idea of her brother and her best friend.

He had no doubt she would have been thrilled with the idea.

Some of the torment he'd felt since her death lessened at that moment and he knew it.

He looked around at the parking lot again as the hair on the back of his arm stood up. As he felt eyes watching them.

There was a shadow on the hill three hundred feet away that should not have been there. And as he looked closer, a *glint* that he shouldn't have seen.

Shots came flying across the parking lot, just as Elliot crowded Gabby behind the concrete pillar of the portico.

Mel cried out behind them somewhere.

Fire burned through Elliot's shoulder. A fire he'd felt before.

Then he was falling; his weight taking her to the ground with him.

CHAPTER FIFTY-TWO.

* * *

CHANCE saw his brother go down and he didn't think. He acted. Brynna's sister was right there beside him. Right in the line of fire.

He dove toward Mel and took her to the ground, covering her with his own body. *They* were more exposed than Elliot and Gabby now. He had to get Mel back inside before the shooter tried again.

He risked a look over his shoulder at his brother. Elliot was moving, but there was no denying the blood.

Little Gabby, instead of curling up in a ball cowering like Chance would have expected, was tugging his brother closer to the hospital entrance, a look of determination on her face. She wasn't stopping until she got Elliot inside.

Elliot was on his feet, so some of Chance's worry lifted.

Ten steps more and Gabby would have Elliot safe inside.

Chance needed to get the woman beneath him there, too.

She hadn't been hit—there was no blood. But the woman was missing half a damned lung and could barely walk. Getting knocked to the ground could have done just as much damage as a bullet.

They were forty feet from the entrance, but twenty feet from the columns that provided some cover. "Can you run at all?" He knew the answer to that already.

He looked down at her, not missing the panic in the eyes so much like Brynna's. The sudden fear. Hell, even the gap between the front teeth was the same as her sister's. "Can't breathe…wind knocked…you're on top of me…"

"Sorry about that." Only choices he had were to either wait it out or scoop her up and run for cover. Neither was all that appealing. "I'm going to carry you inside. Keep your head down and hold on, ok?"

The panic was still there, and that's when he remembered. Brynna's sister had been shot outside a hospital just like this. Ambushed just like this. That she wasn't a screaming pile of hysterics right beneath him told him a lot about her.

He stood quickly and reached down to her, expecting a bullet to slam into him before he got her inside. He kept his body between her and the shooter. *She* was not getting hit like that again. Not if he could prevent it.

She didn't weigh much, and he ran with her inside, not stopping until he could put her down on a gurney. He looked at the doctor on duty—the same one he'd handed Brynna over to before. "I knocked her down pretty hard. She's having trouble breathing. She's been shot before, and I think she's missing a lung."

"We'll get her taken care of, Mr. Marshall." The doctor was already pulling his stethoscope up, as the orderlies rolled her down to an exam room. "Police have been called, and we're now in full lock-down."

Gabby waited outside it, and Chance knew his brother was in a room nearby. She looked at Chance and stepped toward him—covered in his brother's blood. "How is he?"

"They kicked me out while they do the exam. Mel…is Mel hurt? Did she get shot?"

"I don't know. I landed on her pretty hard. She was having trouble breathing. There wasn't any blood, Gabby. I don't think she was hit." She was alive. They all four were. "I'm going to get up to Brynna's room. Check on her and fill Beck in on what happened. Let him know his other daughter is down here."

"I'll stay with Elliot." She bit her lip after she said it and he understood. She was hurting *for* his brother, wasn't she?

Had she been the target? Or had it been his brother? Either one—if someone knew they were here at the hospital, chances were good they knew she'd been staying at Elliot's place.

Knew right where to find them if they went looking.

Easy damned targets.

"Gabby—you keep your head down. Stay right here until I get back. We're going to find another way out of this hospital; then I'm getting you and Elliot out of town for the night."

He didn't want to leave the hospital, but like it or not, Brynna was safer there guarded than Elliot and Gabby would be tonight.

But he had to check on her one more time. Just to make sure.

CHAPTER FIFTY-THREE.

* * *

GABBY prowled around the room, waiting. She wasn't very good at waiting, not when it was for something that mattered. Chance came back, looking all big, bad, and brooding. Gabby didn't know how to deal with him right them. She kept pacing.

"Sit down." Chance ordered after he'd dealt with the TSP who'd arrived. "They've agreed to move Bryn to an interior room."

"I'm sorry." Gabby sat. After about two minutes, she was back on her feet.

He had looked so pale, so broken.

Blood…

She bolted for the closest trash can, making it barely in time. When she finished, she fished a tissue out of her purse and a breath mint. It didn't help.

Chance was staring at her. "You ok?"

Ok? Heck no. "Not really."

"He's tough, you know. This isn't the first time he's been injured."

"Well, it's the first time I've seen it, thank you very much. I don't think it's a sight I want to repeat." And like what she'd seen ten years ago, this was something she would never forget.

Had he not pushed her out of the way, she would have been there bleeding right next to him. She shivered.

And once she started, she couldn't stop. She stayed there, tremors wracking her body, until strong hands wrapped around her and lifted her out of the chair.

Chance's eyes were just as green as Elliot's. Somehow that made this just a little bit worse. "He's going to be ok, Gabby. You can deal."

He hugged her tight, and she got the impression it was definitely something he wasn't comfortable with. But he was trying—that should matter, right?

She sucked it up and dealt. What other choice did she really have?

* * *

ELLIOT pushed himself up off the exam bed. "I'm finished."

"Sir…Chief Marshall, you shouldn't rush things. You need to give your body time to heal." The young blonde doctor tried to block his path to the door bodily. He admired her guts, but…he had things to do.

"I've been shot a time or two before." But never while the woman he cared for was watching. While she was threatened.

It didn't matter that he knew his brother was with Gabby, that Chance wasn't about to let anything happen to her, what mattered was that Elliot wasn't right there next to her, keeping her as safe as possible.

"I have things to do, Dr. McGareth. Sign me out. AMA, if necessary."

"I don't recommend that. Please reconsider."

"I won't be alone. And I've been hit worse than this before. A lot worse." It was his arm, damn it. Not like he'd taken another in the chest. "I have things I need to see to."

"I'm sure you do." The doctor stepped in his path again. He had no choice—if he kept going, he would be forced to knock her out of the way. "Look, the Becks are friends of mine, too. I want to go see how Mel is doing, myself. Work with me here. Let me *finish*. Then I'll bring Gabby back, and she can deal with you. How does that sound?"

Like the only option, he was going to get—unless he wanted to make one hell of a scene in the middle of the ER. How would that help anyone? "Deal."

He sat back on the exam table and the doctor returned to her task.

* * *

GABBY snuck into Mel's exam room. She'd heard Elliot talking with the doctor, and she'd peeked inside to see him without his shirt, getting stitched up easily. Lacy looked up and nodded, then waved her away.

He would be ok. And she wouldn't be a stupid wimp and bawl all over him like she wanted to.

Mel was being treated when Gabby slid in. The nurse stopped and glared at her. "Who are you?"

"Um…next of kin." She looked wide-eyed at Mel. Her friend was pale and shaken—and struggling to breathe.

"Can she stay?" The nurse asked Mel.

Mel nodded but didn't speak. She held a hand out toward Gabby. Gabby took it. "Your dad is on his way down from Brynna's room. He's taking care of insurance information first."

Finally, after a while, Mel was able to speak again. Faintly, but… "How's Elliot?"

"I think he's ok. Lacy's sewing him up now. Chance went back upstairs to sit with Brynna. I'm sure your dad will be here soon."

"They're keeping me here, Gab. They want to do tests after some swelling goes down."

"Swelling?"

"Around the lungs. Chance's shoulder hit me hard. He weighs a damned ton. Broken rib, they think…too close to the left lung. Can't risk puncturing it."

Gabby's eyes widened. Mel was missing half of her left lung anyway because of the damage from the bullet. "But you're going to be ok?"

"You know I will."

"Maybe they'll let you share a room with Brynna? I'll bring you yellow pajamas…"

Mel lifted a hand to her left side. "Don't make me laugh."

Gabby stayed with her friend while the nurses buzzed around and the doctor ordered tests for Mel. Kevin came hurrying in.

Gabby really felt for him; he was obviously worried about Mel now. First Brynna, now Mel. What was next?

Gabby waited until Kevin was finished hugging Mel, then excused herself to find Elliot again.

Chance found them in Elliot's exam room half an hour later. "It's all set. Let's get him out of here."

"What's set?" Elliot asked. The doctor—a friend of Jilly's Gabby knew and liked—had given him a shot of painkiller, and he was a bit clouded. But he clung to Gabby—and she clung to him. She needed to feel him, solid and warm beneath her hands. "What's the plan? I can't drive."

"You're going to do what you're told for once. I'm going to get you and your girl someplace safe for the night. Then we'll figure out tomorrow. I've borrowed us a car."

"Then let's get going," Gabby said. Elliot was leaning on her, and he was starting to get heavy.

"Let's go. We're going out the employee entrance."

Gabby recognized the car he led her to. "Ari's car?" Jilly's friend Ariella worked at the hospital as a victim's rights counselor part-time. "How is she getting home?"

"Bumming a ride from one of the doctors, I think." Chance didn't seem to care. "She volunteered the car. It suited our purposes. I'll repay the favor someday."

"Is it safe? Where are we going?" Gabby felt the fear again, as they got closer to the exit.

"Just get in the car. I'll get us where we need to go. It'll take us about an hour to get there, though. Why don't the two of you lay back and rest? Hell, keep your heads down, anyway. That will make us less noticeable if someone's waiting for us to leave."

"What did Erickson say?" Someone had called the shooting in while they'd been in the ER and Gabby had already given her witness statement to McKellen.

"Basically, we're going off the grid for the night. Until Elliot's head is clear. Then we'll figure out what to do next about that video."

"Elliot knocked me out of the way," Gabby said slowly. "I know that someone shot at me. Someone broke into my apartment, someone attacked my best friend and stole my laptop, and now someone shot at me. And it's all because of whatever *I* saw on that video ten years ago. But I don't have a clue what that is. What am I supposed to do, Chance?"

"You hunker down in the back of this damned SUV and keep my brother's head below the window line. I'll get you someplace warm and safe. We'll figure it out from there."

Gabby did just that.

CHAPTER FIFTY-FOUR.

* * *

ELLIOT opened his eyes when the car stopped. He took a look around and cursed. Cursed his brother up one side and down the other.

"I can't believe you brought her *here*. Damn it, Chance. Have you gone insane?"

"We need a safe place. One we're familiar with—and can defend."

"So you brought her here, to the very place the killers struck first? Did you even think about how that would hurt her?" The torture it would be to Gabby, to him? He hadn't stepped foot back in the house he'd grown up in since he'd went to get clothing to bury his family in.

"My first concern isn't how much pain your girlfriend has to deal with, but with the fact that she stays alive long enough to deal with it. It's not any easier for me to be here, either."

Gabby watched the two brothers.

And got angry once what they were saying sank in. As what she saw with her own two eyes started to make sense. She understood, she guessed. But… "This home has been in your family for two hundred years!"

Two pairs of green eyes looked at her. Elliot stepped toward her. "Gabby?"

"Your dad was *proud* of this place and the work your ancestors put into this ranch. And you guys just closed it off and walked away." Everything the Marshall family had been, everything Elliot, Sr. and his wife had stood for had been *family*. Home.

"What other option did we have? Every time we stepped in here we were reminded of them." Chance's words were harsh. Gabby refused to step back no matter how intimidating he looked at that moment.

"And every time *I* close my eyes I see Sara and Slade, and your mom and dad die. I *get* that you don't want those memories. But…this is wrong. It's too sad. And I remember your dad telling Sara that one day it would be *your* kids or hers or Slade's that played here next. And that's the way it should be!"

* * *

SHE looked at him with accusation on her face, and for the first time, Elliot felt guilt for the way they'd walked away from their home. "Gabby…it was just…"

"Easier. I get it, I do. I really *do*. But Elliot, this house meant *so much* to them. It seems wrong, somehow, to know that it's been abandoned. To know how much that would hurt them."

It had been, and it was evident. He'd paid someone to paint over the blood. To clean up the broken glass close up the house.

By that point, Chance had taken off for parts unknown, and Elliot hadn't seen any other option. And he hadn't been back, since.

Yet they'd been given offers on the property over the years. He just hadn't been able to accept. "We didn't abandon it."

"Don't lie. You're not very good at it." She walked over to the mantle where some pictures had once been displayed. They'd been destroyed ten years ago. He remembered each one of them perfectly. His senior photo, Chance's, and Slade's had set next to Sara's kindergarten one. His mother had always made a big production of changing the kindergarten photos to the final school ones when she'd receive them.

Said that it represented a new beginning for each of them.

Sara would never have a senior photo, and Slade's had only been two weeks old when they had died.

How did Gabby expect him to be able to look at this house and *not* remember the things that would never be?

She was right in a way, though. His ancestral home *was* made for a family and a large one at that. Five bedrooms, an office, a study, his mother's sewing room, those rooms were all on the basement level. The upper level had the living area, the formal front room that was part of the original structure, and the kitchen and dining areas big enough for large, elaborate parties.

That was just the house. The rest of the property covered fifteen hundred acres of prime farm and ranch land. His great-grandfather had once owned four times that area, back in the ranching heyday, but the fifteen hundred that remained in the family had been the original homestead.

Elliot had once felt that same pride.

The place was dusty, and nothing had been disturbed in the ten years it had sat empty. Everything would still be where his mother and father had left it. Who could fault them for not wanting to deal with it?

But it *had* been a decade. And the house deserved to be loved. Lived in by a family that would love it.

"Turn the lights on." Chance suddenly barked out. Elliot complied. They hadn't turned on the living room lights, just the foyer. The dark made it seem all the more overwhelming. "I've been paying the utilities. We've got lights and water. And we can check the generator. If it's working, we'll have heat. If not, there's wood out back, and I'll check the flue."

When the light flicked on, he wasn't so sure that was better.

Dust and cobwebs hung from the chandelier, and the rug that had once been light in color was dingy tan. Elliot didn't even want to consider the amount of work that was needed to be done just to make the place habitable for one night. What had his brother been thinking?

He asked just that.

Chance grunted at him, then stepped over to the window and looked out it. "I thought we needed a safe place to hole up. And figure out what to do next. That is, unless you trust the people you work with?"

Hell no, he didn't. The ones he trusted were right there in the room with him. And that was it.

"No. Everything needs to stay right here. With the three of us."

"You think someone at TSP shot at us?"

Wide-eyed fear flooded big blue eyes and Elliot went with his gut instinct. He pulled her against his chest using the arm that wasn't in the sling. He buried his fingers in blonde hair, and he kissed her forehead. "I'm just not being stupid, sweetheart. I'll do *anything* to keep you safe. Chance is right. This is where we belong tonight. A place we know, a place we can..." He'd started to say *defend* but stopped.

She didn't need to fear a second attack. Not tonight. He looked at his brother. Chance nodded. Elliot knew his brother understood. They'd do whatever they had to do to keep her safe. Protected. He rocked her for a minute, and she relaxed against him.

He felt warm curves and soft woman, vulnerable and sweet. She was just his *Gabby.* A part of his past, and the biggest part of his present. And he was damned determined to see she had a future. To see *they* had one.

He set her aside, then looked at his brother. "Check the windows and the doors. I've got the keys to Dad's study. I want to do a quick inventory."

"Understood."

Their father had been an avid gun collector, and as far as Elliot knew that collection was still secured in his father's study. He wasn't anticipating they'd need an arsenal, but he wasn't about to let them be ambushed without some way to defend themselves if needed.

His father's study was at the end of the back hall. But he wasn't willing to leave Gabby alone in the living room long enough to take a look for himself.

"Chance, take a look. See what's in there we can use."

"Bed, for one thing. Dad's couch folded out. We can drag a mattress in there to toss on top, if needed. There's just the one window. Big enough to get out of, if needed. And can be defended from the hallway."

Elliot glared at his brother when he felt the woman in his arms stiffen. Chance shrugged. "Better she knows the truth than you keep sugar coating everything."

"I'm not. But that doesn't mean you should continue rubbing it in her face."

She pulled back. "I'm ok. I'm not going to fall apart. I'm made of sterner stuff than that. I think. And this isn't any easier for you two, either. I'm not a wimp. You don't have to hide things from me. I kind of know what we're facing here, you know?"

But he wanted to. He wanted to put her someplace safe, where bad things could never touch her. He put his hands on her cheeks—her skin was so smooth and soft beneath his palms—and just held her for a moment. "We'll be ok."

Blue eyes were filled with hope. And even more frightening, *trust.* She was trusting him.

It made him feel ten feet tall and absolutely terrified. "We will. Stay with Chance, out here. I'm going to check the office, grab some sheets out of the closet. They may be a bit musty, but we have some time to run them through the washing machine and dryer before bed."

She nodded.

He needed a moment away from her, and he wasn't ashamed to say that. At least to himself.

Something about Gabby Kendall melted him to his very soul.

* * *

OLD washing machines that hadn't been used in ten years took a few moments to get started. Gabby had insisted on being the one to do it. She needed to get away from the intense gazes of the Marshall brothers before they had her falling into a babbling, crying mess.

She hadn't felt this crazy emotional since the years immediately following the murders. Was it just because of what was happening, the new threat, or the fact that the knights-in-tarnished armors were Sara's brothers? The last of what had once been her second family?

The sheets were light pink, with tiny red tea roses printed over them. Anne Marshall must have washed them over and over again. Used them to make her home comfortable and welcoming. The touches of Elliot and

Chance's mother were still there, underneath all the dust and sadness.

It made Gabby miss Anne and her own mother with an ache she could almost touch. She pushed those thoughts away by grabbing a broom from the back of the laundry room door and attacking some of the dust in the family room.

How many hours had she spent in this room as a girl? Sleepovers, after school hanging out time, massive study sessions? Just being there with people who cared about her and made her feel like she belonged, while her mom was busy working to support the two of them.

The things the Marshall family had given her would never be forgotten. And *they* shouldn't have been forgotten.

She wasn't stopping until the dust was gone, until this home they'd loved so much was just as warm and inviting as it had once been.

If their sons tried to stop her, she'd give them a real piece of her mind. Anne and Elliot, Sr. had deserved better.

And she'd see that their memories got that.

Elliot was the first to poke his handsome head into the room to check on her. "You ok?"

"No. Not at all. This place is filthy. Grab a broom." She pushed the one in her hands into his. "I'll start getting some of this dust up. I'm sure your mom had some better rugs somewhere. Guest room, maybe." She looked at the man who'd come up behind him. "You. Why did you turn the utilities on, but not bother to have this place cleaned?"

"Because…I was planning to come back here. Figure things out. Deal with the cleaning, then. That meet your approval, sweetie?"

"Not my place to approve or disapprove, but I'm not staying here with it all messy. And your brother needs to take it easy and let his arm heal. So…you…get the mop. I'll run your mom's vacuum over the place first, see what I can get out of the way. Then we'll make this place habitable."

"Yes, ma'am."

They worked in almost silence. She traded the duster she'd found for the broom in Elliot's hand. He didn't need to be using his injured arm cleaning, but he could dust one-handed. And she knew he wasn't the type to sit back and watch other people do the work.

No one had forgotten that the last time this place had been cleaned was ten years ago and that it was his mother's hands who had done it.

When they were finished, she looked at her two companions. Elliot was pale, but he was on his feet.

Chance's expression was hard as granite.

He scared Gabby sometimes. Had Sara's brother always been that intense?

She far preferred Elliot's calmer manner in things. Something about the way he reassured her just by looking at her, it settled her frazzled nerves and made her think—if just for a moment—that everything was going to be ok.

At least for the next little while. He was leaning against the old mantle, running a finger over the grooves that some long ago ancestor had carved.

For the longest time, she'd thought of what she had lost that day. But they had lost so much more.

And they didn't seem all that close now. Had they broken away from each other, too? How could she help fix that?

"Elliot?" She could start with the one who needed her the most. Gabby crossed the room and wrapped her hand around his uninjured arm. "Why don't you sit down for a while? You have to be hurting. The rest of this can wait."

"Can it?" He turned sad eyes toward her. "Maybe it has waited long enough."

She couldn't help it. He needed it, and she probably did, too. She hugged him. It took a moment, but his arms wrapped around her. And they held. Her head fit right on his shoulder, perfectly. He was the same height as Jarrod, the last man she'd been close to like this, but where her friend was leaner, Elliot Marshall was pure man muscle beneath his shirt. His heartbeat was right there against her ear, steady and sure.

Alive.

They both were.

CHAPTER FIFTY-FIVE.

* * *

GABBY watched the newscast on her first break the next day for anything about the shooting at the hospital. It was mentioned, but not with a lot of details. Elliot's doing, no doubt. Benny was in one of his moods—she suspected Brynna's absence really bothered him—so she kept herself busy on projects for the Major Crimes and Gangs units that required little supervisory oversight.

McKellen came in to ask how Brynna was and she told him what she knew. He smiled at her, and she was struck by how handsome he actually was. "She'll be ok, Commander McKellen."

"Of course. Thanks, Gabby. I…uh…suppose Chance Marshall is with her?"

"I think so."

"Great. He'll keep her safe, then, I'm sure. Can you tell her when you see her that I—we're all looking forward to her coming back to work soon. She's missed around here."

"I'll do that." Poor man, that was all she could think. He was a few years younger than Elliot, a few inches shorter but very handsome. He'd really cared about Brynna, hadn't he?

Before Chance.

Pretty sucky situation, wasn't it?

The newscast came back from commercial break and Gabby glanced at the television in the corner. Mel and Jillian's faces stared back at her. "Hey! It's Mel and Jilly."

McKellen turned up the volume. Jillian gave a quick update on Brynna's condition, and Mel thanked the public for their continued support and assistance as her sister recuperated. A local autism special interest group had even offered assistance with Brynna's hospital bill and to pay for in-home nursing, if needed.

It wasn't. There were plenty of people in Brynna's life willing to help her through this. Jillian was going to sleep in Brynna's room with her at night in case she needed anything then. Mel was going to be with her during the day. Jillian's friend, Dr. McGareth, was planning to come over at least once a day to check on her as well. They had Brynna covered, didn't they?

Because they loved her. They were family, even those who weren't tied by blood.

There was a reporter crammed up next to where Mel and Jillian stood next to the hospital administrator. "Is it true what happened to your sister and Chance Marshall has to do with the Marshall Murders? There's some speculation that she stumbled onto some crucial new evidence in her work with the TSP."

Mel sent the reporter a quelling look. "What we know at this time is that my sister and Chance Marshall were attacked by a trio of men in a stolen vehicle. As far as we know, the attackers were simply trying to cover their tracks and preserve their own hides. Any other questions about that should be directed to the Texas State Police."

"Does this case have anything to do with who shot you, Ms. Beck?"

“Of course not. The men responsible for shooting me are in prison, where they belong. Now, I’m sure you all understand, but standing here is rather painful for me, and we need to get back to our sister.”

“Rumor has it Handley Barratt of Barratt-Handley Enterprises is directly involved in the attack and the Texas State Police is looking for him. Is this true?”

Mel stilled. “If the TSP is looking for someone, shouldn’t you be asking the TSP? *I’m* hardly out there looking for anyone. I’d probably fall over if I tried.”

The crowd laughed lightly. Another reporter stepped closer. “Ms. Beck, if the Barratt family is involved, is there anything your family wants to say to them?”

“Only that we have complete confidence in Elliot Marshall and the rest of the TSP. Whoever was involved in the attack on our sister will get what they deserve. It’s just a matter of time. Thank you, ladies and gentlemen. But we really do need to get back inside.”

Gabby watched the rest of the newscast with McKellen at her side. He was frowning. “How the hell did Barratt’s involvement get leaked? That was something we were keeping under wraps until we knew more. Chief Marshall is not going to like this. Not at all.”

CHAPTER FIFTY-SIX.

* * *

ONE of the benefits of having almost unlimited amounts of cash was that Houghton could hire just about anything he needed to be done.

The Beck family weren't the kind to hide who they were from the world. Houghton took advantage of that.

He had spent the hours since the TSP had left his office internet searching every one of the key players in whatever it was that was going down. There was a lot of spec articles out there to search, too.

Elliot Marshall, head of the Finley Creek TSP, was the brother of the guy who had been missing with Brynna Beck. He understood Marshall's fury to some extent. When he'd found out about the guy's family, he'd really understood the anger. Had felt for the guy a great deal, honestly.

Houghton's own mother had been murdered when he was a toddler. He'd felt that loss in so many ways. Felt his own anger, still.

The FBI agent who had come to his office was connected to the Beck family somehow, from what he could find. And was damned good at what he did for the FBI. No clue why an FBI bigwig would be looking for his father, though. So many connections.

He wouldn't see his father railroaded by a bunch of cops and agents who were in each other's pockets.

But it wasn't the agents and Marshall he was concerned about.

He'd found nothing to indicate Brynna Beck was a liar. Or anything else than what she first appeared on the surface. She was a very pretty young woman in her mid-twenties. He'd studied her photo for a while, trying to figure out why she reminded him of someone.

She had a good reputation at her job, had developed software to help law enforcement agencies across the country, still lived at home with her father and three of her four sisters, and seemed to be as innocent and wholesome as a newborn puppy. She had a sister with the FBI—which explained his federal visitor. He'd also found mention of her social disorder that gave him pause. Made him wonder if someone was forcing this innocent young woman to lie about his father. Was she just a pawn?

Marshall and his brother, perhaps? Were they after a twisted sort of revenge for what had happened to their family a decade ago? Had they focused on his father for some strange reason?

Houghton knew what he was doing was risky. If someone caught him outside Brynna Beck's home, he'd probably be arrested. He could just imagine what the press would have to say about that. *Billionaire's Son Stalks Brynna Beck: New Angle in the Story!*

Bound to be a sensation.

They were already vilifying his father. It didn't surprise him that someone had leaked the information to the news station. Channel 7 KUFC was notorious for going after the big sensational cases quickly. Sometimes before the facts.

Houghton considered just buying the news station and putting some filters on the damned channel. He'd considered it before, when Channel 7 turned a bit trying.

Houghton's attorneys had told him to remain neutral and noncommittal if questioned about Brynna Beck. It was his best chance of weathering this storm.

He just wanted his father back and safe.

That wasn't so much to ask, was it?

A car parked in the driveway and three redheads climbed out. He recognized them from photos in the dossiers his people had provided him. The driver was around twenty-two or three, if he recalled correctly, and working toward a nursing degree. There was a girl still in high school; she was easy to pick out, complete with purple and black backpack.

And the elder Beck daughter was right there.

The one he was waiting for. Houghton smiled, seeing *her*.

He'd read the reports about her over and over, committing them to memory. Once he'd looked at the photos of her he'd been provided, his decision had been made. Once he'd confirmed she was the one he needed.

She was a truly beautiful woman. She'd lost weight since she'd been injured, though. He'd studied photos of her probably longer than he should have.

She paused and looked around like she was feeling his eyes on her. Houghton smiled; she'd feel more than just his eyes on her soon, if he had his way.

He watched her longer, ignoring her younger sisters completely.

Melody Beck used a metal crutch—he'd read the medical reports he wasn't supposed to have access to—and made her way carefully to the door. She wasn't fully recovered from the bullet that she'd taken a year earlier, and was still in therapy. He'd even researched the reputation of her physical therapist closely.

Everything. He wanted to know *everything* about her.

She was his ticket to fixing this entire situation. He *needed* this woman.

Houghton had been looking for *her* for a very, very long time. Eighteen months and two days, to be exact.

And now he had found her. Finally.

CHAPTER FIFTY-SEVEN.

* * *

HIS hands shook when he picked up the phone, but Benny forced himself to do it. Just like he'd forced himself to take a few shots at the Marshall brothers at the hospital. It hadn't been easy. But he'd did it. Just to scare Gabby off.

He'd never expected Brynna to survive what had been planned for her. Or Chance Marshall. He had looked at both of them with his own eyes for a few minutes the night before.

The trust Brynna and her family had in him had allowed *him* into the sanctum of Brynna's hospital room, had allowed him to sit with her and just talk.

She'd looked so young, so fragile, so damned vulnerable; he'd nearly been sick when he learned of how badly she had been hurt.

But she was supposed to be dead.

How was he supposed to be happy that she wasn't when she had the power to ruin everything he had built? Power in her tiny, scratched up hands?

He'd excused himself after half an hour—she was tiring, and refusing to rest. And already talking about when she returned to the TSP.

He didn't want her there; he wanted her to do what her father suggested and take a few months off to recuperate. Benny had told her that he would be happy to rearrange the department a bit, to give her that break.

But little Miss Hard-headed had turned his offer down, claiming that the only real way for her to heal mentally was to return to her routine.

Brynna clung to her routine like a baby monkey to its mother. Benny understood that.

The phone rang.

"*About time you called, Russell. We have a problem.*" The voice on the other end of the line was cultured, educated, and seethed with contained power. "*And you will be the one fixing it.*"

"Like what?"

He listened with growing horror as the plan was outlined, as just what the cost to him would be.

"I won't do it! There are too many other things that could happen. What if someone *else* walks in?"

"Those bitches hold the key to unraveling everything we have worked toward for years. I am almost at the point where I need to be, and I will not lose it because of some damned women. Get them out of the way, or I'll make it known to everyone you hold dear that you are the mastermind. You and that worthless brother of yours. But with him dead, who do you think will be the one to suffer most? You? Nora? Those pretty little daughters of yours? Now, what do you think would happen to them if Daddy is the one responsible for the Marshall Murders? It would destroy them, wouldn't it? Law school? Med school? What's little Addie's plans, Russell? Teaching little children? You'll ruin their lives."

"I'll do what I have to do."

But first, he had to *think.*

"This is exactly what you'll do. Everything you'll need is in the evidence room, right above your lab. Convenient, isn't it?"

CHAPTER FIFTY-EIGHT.

* * *

CHANCE watched from the front entrance as Dr. McGareth wheeled Brynna toward the exit. She was dressed in a loose knit dress that made her look young and pretty. She had big brown sunglasses perched on her nose, making her look like a little bug. He smiled when she tilted her head back and let the sun soak into her.

He had checked the perimeter of the hospital parking lot twice himself, and he had an old friend of his prowling around, as well.

He'd made the officers his brother had assigned within two minutes. *No one* would be hurting Brynna today.

Her father's SUV pulled up, and Kevin hopped out. He carefully lifted his daughter, even over her protests, and placed her in the backseat.

Chance walked up beside them. "I'll follow you back."

"Chance, I wasn't aware you were going to be here," Beck's eyes were suspicious. Chance understood —Beck didn't want him near his precious, innocent little daughter.

Innocent, like hell. She hadn't been well tutored, but she had been as into him as he had been into her. Every touch she'd given him had been full of need.

She'd needed *him* almost as much as he'd needed *her.*

"I'm trading off guard duty with Erickson for the next few days." A lie, but Chance didn't give a damn.

He was going to stay where he could watch over her, no matter how he had to do it.

Chance looked in the backseat. She was watching him, wasn't she? Those sunglasses didn't hide half of what she thought they did. "Brynna…fasten your seatbelt. I'll be around."

CHAPTER FIFTY-NINE.

* * *

GABBY spent most of the next three days with Brynna and Mel. Elliot had told Benny she needed a break, and her supervisor had agreed. He'd told her to go take care of her friend. To pamper Brynna and herself—that they both deserved it.

Said he'd see everything was taken care of at the TSP.

Elliot hadn't liked leaving her at the Becks, but he had. He'd kissed her goodbye at the front door each morning, then set his guards to watch over the both of them. Mostly it was Erickson, but Chance was there part of the time, though he spent most of his guard duty glaring at Brynna and making sure she barely moved at all.

Brynna treated him with polite courtesy—she was actually more welcoming of the big blond Erickson. Chance treated her with orders and frustration. Until she moved wrong or forgot her medication—*then* he was right there. Everyone knew Chance had it bad for Brynna. Except maybe Brynna—and Chance. Talk about clueless. Gabby felt torn loyalties—he was Elliot's brother, after all.

Chance caught Brynna off the couch around noon on the third day and went through the roof. Gabby and Mel escaped down the hall into Mel's room. Gabby collapsed on the bed, giggling. "Did you see his face?"

"She *threw* Cheerios at him. So classically Brynna." Mel's face was bright red, and she was pulling in a breath as she fought a laugh.

Gabby sobered as Brynna yelled that it had just been no-strings sex. "Glad your dad isn't here to hear *that*."

Mel's eyes widened. "Talk about an explosive situation. I think he's still convinced Brynna and Jilly are virgins."

This was so not their normal, was it? Brynna was still yelling, something she usually only did with her family. "Do you think she'll be ok?"

"What do you mean?"

"They agreed on no strings. That's not Brynna. Are we ever going to get back to normal?" She missed that, missed her home, missed what had been before. She loved being with Elliot; she wouldn't deny that, but as the days continued to go by without any real answers, she was starting to long for quiet nights watching movies or having pizza with Mel and Brynna, giggling and talking. Longed for Mel dragging the two of them to the mall to buy clothes they didn't need, longed for coding with Brynna just to see what they could do.

She wanted to be with Elliot out of free choice, not because it was the safest answer to a terrifying question. She wanted to be with him out in the open because they *both* wanted exactly that. Not hiding, waiting for the other shoe to drop.

"Oh, baby." Mel held out a hand. Gabby took it. "I wondered how long you'd be able to hide yourself away with Elliot."

"He hasn't mentioned any strings, either." And that was at the heart of her fear now, wasn't it? They spent their evenings together—and it was wonderful. But how could it last? When they weren't basically forced to be so close all the time? "I don't know what's going to happen. With him, with whatever *this* is that we've all gotten mixed up in. When—if—this all ends, what happens next? Will we ever get *our* normal back again?"

Mel stared at her for a long moment, as the shouting from the front of the house abruptly ended. "If you had a choice between *our* normal before and *Elliot* now, what would you choose, Gabby?"

She pulled Gabby into the hall. "Look at them, Gab. What do you think they'd choose?"

Gabby looked. Brynna sat on the kitchen island. Rice milk drenched Cheerios soaked into the back of her nightgown. Her Princess Toadstool nightgown. Brynna clung to him, her hands buried in his hair. Chance kissed her like his very breathing depended on it.

How she felt—how *he* felt—was pretty hard to miss, wasn't it?

That didn't mean there were *strings,* though. "I don't know."

"*This,*" Mel waved her hand around lightly "This *thing* we've been dragged into—it *will* end. Elliot will find the answers. When he does, go after your *new* normal. Don't let something incredible slip away because you're afraid. You'll regret it forever. Fear…fear robs us of the future, of the entire world out there. If you love Elliot and want those strings, go tie them yourself."

CHAPTER SIXTY.

* * *

SHE couldn't hide out at home forever. No matter how appealing that idea was to Brynna. She had a *life* that extended past what had happened to her. She would not lose track of that, of her goals, of what was important, because of fear.

What was it that Mel had said to her before, to Gabby? *Fear robs us of the world.* It had taken her a while to figure out what Mel meant, but Brynna finally understood it. Brynna didn't want to live in fear.

Not any longer.

The way she saw it, she had two choices. Stay at home under guard or go back to the TSP, where she was equally as guarded.

At least at the TSP she would be doing *something* besides eating Lucky Charms—she'd lost her taste for Cheerios, damn him—and watching mindless television.

Besides, she missed her life. Missed Gabby, missed Benny and Theresa and Haldyn and the rest of the people in her department.

She missed normal.

Gabby and Mel were cooking when she finished her shower and returned to the kitchen.

The cereal mess she and Chance had made was gone, thanks to Gabby. Brynna owed her one.

What had she been thinking? She should have known he'd not take to well to being challenged like that. Still, he'd made her so angry.

He had no right to tell her what to do. No right. Just because of what had happened in that cellar, he didn't have the right to tell her what she should do!

No one but her father had that right, and she was a full-grown adult. She'd stopped letting *him* control everything when she'd turned eighteen.

What was Chance playing at, anyway?

He had been just as adamant of the no strings thing as she had. So why was he trying to change things between them?

He'd told her after the kiss had ended that it meant nothing. And not to get *her* hopes up for something more. That he wasn't the white picket fences type.

It had taken her a few minutes to figure out what he meant by that. By that time the jerk was gone.

She was left standing there with Cheerios all over her butt. And her heart breaking in two all over again.

Mel looked at her. "You ok?"

"Men are stupid."

"Are they? Or just one in particular?" Mel hugged her. "If it's any consolation, I think you have him just as tangled and confused as you are."

"I'm not confused." Brynna refused to let herself be. "We made a deal that it was just sex. No ties. And just until we got out of the cellar. I don't understand why he thinks he has the right to tell me what to do. If I don't want to take a pain pill, I shouldn't have to."

Gabby wiped off the island and stared at Brynna. She couldn't put it into words, but something was bothering her friend, wasn't it? Sad, Gabby was sad, wasn't she? "Bryn, I think he just didn't like seeing you hurting."

"I'm going to hurt for a while. Someone sliced me up. But I'd rather feel *that* and still be able to think than be all foggy brained and useless."

"I know the feeling. Just don't push yourself too hard," Mel said. "You'll get better in time."

"I know." And the best way to distract herself was to get back to normal, wasn't it? "Gabs, when am I back on the schedule?"

Gabby gawked at her. "When you want to be, I guess. Benny has you blocked out for the rest of the month. Probably just need to call him."

"When do you go back?"

"I'm off the whole weekend. I got the ten shift on Monday."

"I'll see if I can go back when you do, then."

"Are you sure? I mean, why not take some time off?" Gabby asked. "Until Elliot finds *them*."

"I can help find them better at the TSP." Help find them and end this for all of the people *she* cared about. Gabby. *Chance.* All of them. "I'm going back. I'm going to work on that video until I have the answers."

"It's your choice," Mel said. But Brynna knew what her sister was thinking. Mel still wanted her to hide. To keep safe and let the rest of the world handle everything. Her eyes landed on the crutch that went with her sister everywhere; she saw how her sister had to lean against the counter just to throw the pasta in the boiling water. Remembered how fierce and strong her sister had once been.

Mel wanted to save the world, to protect her family no matter what. But when was she going to see that Brynna could stand on her own when it counted? When would she understand that the need to protect *her* family was just as strong in her as it was in Mel? "I'm doing this. I'm going back."

CHAPTER SIXTY-ONE.

* * *

GABBY didn't want to do this. The thought of watching that video again made her almost sick. She'd avoided it for ten years. Brynna curled up on her double bed, her laptop in front of her. Gabby took the left side of her friend. Mel took the right.

She wouldn't be watching it alone, would she? "We weren't supposed to be there that night, either."

"No," Mel said, shifting on the bed to get more comfortable. "But the three of *us* were going. For Sara."

"I was just waiting for my mom to get home from work to drive me."

"*We* were five minutes away. But Brynna threw a fit at the last minute. A ten or fifteen-minute fit. She saved our lives that night." Mel leaned her head on her sister's shoulder. "I've never forgotten that. How…random our very lives were at that moment."

"Why did you throw a fit?" Gabby asked.

Brynna was quiet for a long moment. "I don't know. I remember just sitting in the back seat and thinking that we couldn't go there. That we needed to be at home with Jilly and Syd and our mom. I wanted my mother so badly. By the time Dad had me calmed down, Mel was inside the gas station, and sirens came. After that, I just remember Jarrod carrying me inside our house."

"Dad followed the responders. We knew…when they turned off at the Marshalls' driveway that it was something bad. Dad handed us off to the first patrol officer he saw. It was Jarrod," Mel said. "He was twenty-two and grass green. It was his first week on the job. The first time he'd ever seen a murder scene."

"When…when dad realized they were all dead, he yelled at Jarrod to get us out of there fast," Brynna said.

"That night was when I decided to follow Dad into the TSP—as soon as I could."

"And she recommended *me* to Benny after I got my Associate's and decided not to go on for my Bachelor's. I already knew more than my professors at that point." Brynna wasn't bragging, Gabby knew. Her friend *had* surpassed the professors of computer sciences at Finley Creek University.

"That night changed *all* of our lives, didn't it?" Gabby looked down at Brynna's laptop. Glass and plastic and components she'd helped put together herself. Just a tool, but a laptop had changed her life so many years ago, hadn't it? "*We* were going to be there. Chance and Elliot were supposed to be there, too. The five of us could have died, as well."

"Sara and Anne would not have wanted us there. They would have wanted us safe," Brynna opened a search box and brought up the videos. "But they *would* want the answers, so none of us get hurt again. None of us."

Sometimes Brynna just nailed things dead-on, didn't she? "They'd want *all* of us safe. We're not safe now. Not like this. Not living with this constant fear, these shadows."

"Chance isn't safe. He's not going to ever stop. And I'm terrified they'll catch him and kill him," Brynna's whisper broke Gabby's heart. The fear…she understood it. "So how do *we* find the answers first?"

"By using our heads. Our skills. Even our hearts," Mel said almost grimly. "Combine what we know has happened now, with what happened then. We knew the vic—victims really well. We may have been children when we did, but we were never stupid. So load the damned video, Bryn, and let's do this. Together."

"I have two videos. The altered one and what I think is the original."

"Then we watch them both." Gabby pulled in a deep breath. The *Play* button was waiting on the screen. She reached over and brushed the mouse. Clicked.

The video started to play.

She hadn't recorded the first part of her conversation with Sara. The part where she'd been complaining about her two older brothers not coming home to her. That was a good thing—Sara's last words about her brothers didn't need to be remembered forever. That would just serve to hurt Chance and Elliot more than they deserved, wouldn't it? But she had hit the record button on her webcam just after she'd heard Slade scream.

She wasn't even sure *why* she'd hit that button. But she had. Slade had called out for his father to help him. His young voice was full of his fear. Gabby felt the tears start. She looked over at Mel and saw her friend wiping her own eyes.

She and Slade had been classmates and friends their entire childhoods, hadn't they? Gabby reached for Mel's hand. Anne screamed, yelled her children's names. Sara's terror had Gabby crying even harder. Brynna paused the video for a moment. There were tissues on the nightstand behind Gabby. She grabbed one and passed two more over to her friends. Gabby reached out and hit the button again. "Let's do this."

She forced herself to watch every second of the video. To try to detach somehow. The killers dragged Slade out of his bedroom. Pulled Sara away from the desktop they'd kept in the dining room. The webcam on Sara's computer had faced the rest of the great room. Faced everything.

The men argued. And then one shot Sara first. Then Anne and Slade together. Elliot's father stopped fighting then. They shot him next to his wife. He fell over his daughter's body.

He looked so much like *her* Elliot.

And then…a man leaned in front of the webcam and looked at the girl on the other side.

The *fifth* man.

His lips moved. But no real sound came out, just a static-filled whisper. What did he say?

He reached out and yanked the webcam from its perch. The video ended forever.

"Rewind that last part, Bryn," Mel said through her tears. "We need to know what he said."

It took them a few tries, but finally Gabby figured out what the fifth man said.

Fuck it all, Gabby!

The fifth man had called her by name.

Gabby had always thought they'd learned about her from witness reports or the media. But they'd known who she was all along, hadn't they?

Mel darted to the bathroom that connected her bedroom and Brynna's as fast as she was able—just in time to lose her lunch. Gabby curled her knees up to her chest there on the bed. Brynna just kept staring at the laptop.

Brynna still hadn't looked away from the screen. "I *knew* the fifth man said something. But I couldn't figure out what. I think I was more focused on *who* could erase a man from the file completely. I didn't realize..."

"It wasn't completely," Mel said from the bathroom. "You could sometimes see the shadows."

"That's because the tech ten years ago wasn't as good as it is today. If we hadn't already known, we wouldn't be predisposed to look." Gabby forced herself to straighten on the bed. To pull in some air. To remember that she was safe right then. "I never could remember how many men because they weren't always visible at once. I think I blocked out that man at the end."

"You were traumatized. Hell, so were we—and we didn't see anything. Except for Slade being loaded into the ambulance. Brynna practically went catatonic, Gab. For the whole next week." Mel settled into the desk chair next to the bed. "It was her first exposure to death at all. Except for a hamster or cat. Mom and Dad kept her sheltered from anything like that."

"Mine, too." Gabby pulled the quilt at the foot of the bed around her shoulders. "So. The fifth man knew *me* by sight ten years ago. What do we do now?"

CHAPTER SIXTY-TWO.

* * *

ELLIOT was a few minutes late to get Gabby at the Becks. When he walked in, along with his brother, the three women and Kevin were grim. Pale. Elliot tensed and looked at Gabby quickly.

Her eyes were bright red. She'd been crying, hadn't she? Brynna had her sunglasses on, but her normally pale cheeks were even whiter.

Mel just looked sick.

Kevin was tense and kept looking at the three women with a worried expression on his face.

"What the hell has happened now?" Chance asked, his attention on Brynna where she sat at the dining room table, with her laptop in front of her.

Gabby and Mel were cooking spaghetti in the adjacent kitchen. Gabby stopped what she was doing and threw herself against Elliot's chest. He looked over her head at Mel. "What's going on?"

"We watched the video from that day. Both the altered and unaltered." Mel dumped the dry pasta into the water. "And we found something."

"What?" Chance stepped up behind Brynna. He put a hand on her shoulder and leaned down. "Show us."

"No need. Not yet. After dinner." Gabby pulled in a deep breath. "It's simple. The fifth man."

"Explain," Chance said. "You." He pointed at Mel. "Not these two. You're the cop, boil it down for us."

"Not any longer, I'm not." Mel stepped away from the counter. "The fifth man looked into the camera and called Gabby by name, boys."

"I've probably known the killers all along. And I didn't remember."

Kevin patted her on the shoulder. "We probably all have known them, then, kiddo. Not just you."

"So there was a fifth man?" Chance asked.

"I wasn't wrong when I said so before." Brynna glared up at his brother. "There was a fifth man and a very sophisticated bit of editing. You can see him occasionally, even in the altered video. *If* you know where to look."

"I do not doubt you. I'm verifying."

"Unh huh. Anyway, how does this help us?"

"*You* not at all. I think your participation is over," Chance reached out and closed Brynna's laptop. "I think you, Gabby, and the rest of your family need to get out of town for a while. I have a cousin with a large spread eighty miles from here—complete with armed cowhands if needed. He's already agreed you could stay there. Let Elliot and I finish this."

Elliot had to admit that sounded like a good idea. If he had his way, he'd hide Gabby away until the threat was completely gone.

"Not happening. I'm going back to work Monday when Gabby does. I want my *life* back. I have goals. I'm not going to hide."

"Screw your goals. I want you *safe.* As far from these bastards as I can get you."

"I make my own choices, Chance. Not you."

"Don't start, you two. We're not having another food fight in here tonight." Mel put her hand on her hip and glared at them. "It took Gabby twenty minutes to get all the wet Cheerios up this afternoon."

Chance flushed.

Gabby giggled.

"Ok, apparently I've missed something." Elliot looked at his brother for clarification.

"Never mind." Brynna stood and went to the kitchen, completely missing the look of hunger on Chance face when his gaze followed her. "How much longer until the spaghetti?"

"A few more minutes. You going to make purple sauce?" Mel asked. She touched her sister's shoulder and squeezed. Comforted.

"I'll warm some up in the microwave for me." Brynna nodded, then grabbed plates from the cabinet. "I suppose *you're* staying, too?"

Chance nodded. "I want you to show me everything you found after we eat."

"Of course."

"Give me those." He took the plates from her. "Sit your ass down."

"I'm not helpless. And you don't have to curse all the time."

"You're stubborn, hard-headed, and contrary."

Kevin suddenly broke out into a coughing fit. Elliot looked at the older man and caught the humor in his eyes. Kevin was apparently enjoying the sparring, wasn't he?

"You forgot obstinate and determined." She smirked at him, and Elliot laughed

Gabby was still next to him. She stood and returned to the kitchen to drain the pasta for Mel.

Gabby was completely comfortable here, wasn't she? These people were her family. The love was something he definitely missed. His family had *loved* one another. For always. The ache to have that again slammed into him. The ache to have it...*with* her.

He slipped into a free chair as the younger two Beck daughters came in the back door. Mel tossed a head of lettuce at the elder of the two. "I think you know what to do. Syd, drinks."

"Crud, Mel, at least let us take off our jackets," Jillian said. Family. So normal. And so much like he and Chance belonged. Were welcomed.

Elliot hadn't felt quite so overwhelmed in a very long time.

CHAPTER SIXTY-THREE.

* * *

"**LOOK** out your window."

"What?" Benny stood and looked out into the alley that ran behind the annex. What he saw had his heart filling with horror.

"Get it set up, Russell. Get it done, and then I'll have Chuck let her go. Don't make me wait too long. You know how he likes young women."

He got just a glimpse in the backseat of the sedan waiting just outside the window.

His Alyssia. His baby girl.

In the hands of a sexual predator. One who had killed before.

Benny had shot Sara Marshall himself ten years ago—to keep that little girl out of the hands of the monster who now held his Alyssia.

The sick irony in that told its own story. What would Chuck do to Alyssia?

It didn't bear thinking about. He couldn't.

"I'll do it. As soon as Brynna returns to the TSP. She'll be here tomorrow. Don't…don't let him hurt my daughter. She's as innocent as you can get. What would come of it?"

"I have no intention of letting him harm her. We don't need any extra attention on you, or on him. You see to it that those two bitches are taken care of, and then we'll just let your little girl go with a very strong warning. She'll be just fine, and back in Mommy and Daddy's arms as soon as you uphold your part of the deal. Very simple, really."

* * *

BENNY spent the rest of the night after Nora retired thinking and planning. He'd covered Alyssia's absence by telling her mother that his daughter had stopped off at the TSP and told him she was going down to the Gulf with some friends from college for a few days. He'd told her that he'd given Alyssia some money and told his daughter to call if she needed her parents.

He hated lying to Nora and had rarely done so.

Worry for his daughter nearly consumed him. Love for his wife nearly destroyed him, and Benny couldn't stop himself from touching her, holding her, for one last night.

He saw his daughters off after breakfast with uncharacteristic hugs and proclamations of how much he had always loved them.

Benny knew he'd surprised them, but he brushed it off, stating he was just feeling his age.

Addilyn laughed at him, then hugged him a second time. Allana just grinned and told him that he was the most handsome old guy she had ever met.

Benny stood at the door and watched two of the four most important pieces of his life drive away.

He hit his knees when the fear for Alyssia overwhelmed him again.

Nora had left an hour earlier for her shift at the hospital.

It was just him.

He had less than an hour to do what he had to do at the house before he had to head to the TSP.

Brynna and Gabby would be coming in for the ten a.m. shift.

Everything needed to be in place long before then.

The supplies he needed were already in his car. He wasn't stupid enough to wonder how they had arrived there while he slept. Benny knew what he had to do.

But first…he needed to write to Nora, to tell her the *why* behind everything.

To tell her…that no matter what happened he loved her and the girls.

And to tell her about Alyssia and how he was trading Brynna and Gabby's lives for that of their daughters.

Because there wasn't anything he wouldn't do for his girls.

CHAPTER SIXTY-FOUR.

* * *

KEVIN drove Brynna in the next morning. He came into the lab and said hello to Gabby and to Benny. Their supervisor was flushed and harried, so Kevin didn't linger. Gabby and Brynna didn't, either.

Both were aware of *why* Brynna had truly returned. They'd discussed it among themselves and Mel the day before. Brynna hoped to use her breaks to clean up the unaltered video, using the TSP's more sophisticated programs. They'd considered sending it to her older sister in St. Louis but decided that would take too long.

Gabby was to help make sure Brynna had *time* to do the cleaning. Gabby was also going to get copies of everything the TSP had on file about the Marshall murders.

They were going to compare the TSP files to the original FBI files Gabby's stepfather had agreed to fax Kevin privately that afternoon.

Chance had taken off to wherever he holed up when he wasn't tormenting Brynna to gather everything he had amassed over the past decade. Elliot had sent him to empty their father's personal safe of any remaining paperwork, as well. Chance had vowed to be back in time to pick Brynna up after her shift ended. He was taking his guard dog status seriously. No one had argued with him—even Brynna.

Everyone was finally going to pool their resources and knowledge.

Brynna was assigned to her regular workstation. Gabby got the small laptop station about eight feet away. Most of the work done on that computer was audio. She'd spend most of her shift with sound-cancelling headphones. It wouldn't give them much time to talk; that was for sure. She *would* be able to run the audio from the unaltered video, see if she could clean up the fifth man's last words.

Maybe she'd recognize his voice or something.

If they figured out who *he* was, they might be able to tie him to Handley Barratt or something. Benny closed his door for the first hour of their shift. It was going to be just the three of them for the first three hours of the shift. Theresa was scheduled to come in at noon.

Gabby reviewed the first audio file on her list—for the gang unit—and paused between it and the next. Something had been tickling her brain since the day before when they'd watched the videos.

She pulled off her headphones and spun her desk chair around. "Bryn?"

Brynna jerked around with a guilty look on her face. She pulled a memory card from her computer and shoved it into her pocket. "What? Sorry. Guess I'm nervous. Aren't I?"

"I think we both are." Gabby thought for a moment. "What if it wasn't Handley Barratt who had the video altered? Isn't he super tall? None of the men in the video were that tall, were they?"

"No. He was at least six-five, Gab. Taller than Chance." Slade and his father had been the same height, close to Elliot's height. She and Brynna had used what they knew of Slade's height and weight to compare to the killers on the video. None of the men had been taller than six-one or six-two.

Elliot's brother was an inch shorter than Elliot, who Gabby thought was six-four, or so. "So if *he* wasn't one of the men in the video, why would *he* erase the fifth man?"

"Someone else did it."

"Someone who could access the file *from* the TSP. Someone who could do that ten years ago—and someone who could know that *you* signed the zip drive out now. Who knows Elliot is back and with *me*. Someone with the skills to alter a video like that." There were only five in their department that had been with the Finley Creek TSP long enough. One was a woman. Gabby didn't think any of the killers in the video were female. So that left them four choices, didn't it?

"We need to get to Elliot *now*." Brynna stood up just as Gabby did. "Let him know."

Gabby turned toward Benny's office. "Bryn—there's only *one* who would have known *me* ten years ago like that. Just one, who has known *everything* you and I have done since Elliot came back. We need to get upstairs now."

Benny's door opened. He looked at them, and Gabby *knew* he'd listened to what they'd said.

"Benny?" Brynna said. "What are you doing?"

"I'm sorry, girls." He held something in his hand. A cord? A remote? "I am so sorry."

He pushed a button.

CHAPTER SIXTY-FIVE.

* * *

ELLIOT was finishing his discussion with the superintendent and the brand new mayor—Handley Barratt's nephew, Turner. It had made for a tense few minutes. Turner had been the assistant mayor until two days earlier when Mayor Jacobi died from a sudden aneurysm. Elliot had just stood up when the building shook around them, and the glass of Elliot's office windows shattered.

"Everybody get out!" Erickson yelled from his position by the window. "Annex just blew!"

Gabby. Elliot was already moving. "Gunnar, get people outside! Now."

He was going straight down. He wasn't stopping until he got to Gabby's side, until he found her and Brynna.

Officer Journey and Jarrod were running behind him. "Foster, Journey! Take the second floor of the annex, search for survivors!"

Gabby's lab was on the *first*. The back of the first. That's where he was going, and damn what anyone else thought.

People were evacuating from the main building per standard procedure. The TSP building consisted of five floors in the main structure, basement, and the two-story annex. He knew how many rooms were in the structure, how many departments, and how many people were on the clock every single day.

Today was no exception.

Journey tried to protest his order—it was her job to keep him safe, and he knew it. He waved her on. "Go!"

He took the service stairs, aware of the people running behind him. The instant he got close enough to see the lab, Elliot knew Gabby and Brynna and anyone else who'd been in the computer forensic lab were most likely dead. It looked like a war zone. Like a bomb—that was exactly what had happened, wasn't it? Where was she?

The glass doors were gone, the walls between each tiny department were buckled and cracked, and none stood more than two feet high now. The sprinklers still rained down, but they wouldn't be enough to stop the destruction. Debris piles were everywhere and as high as his shoulder. Were Gabby and Brynna underneath some? Being crushed?

The computer lab where Brynna and his Gabby spent most of their time looked like a tornado had ripped through it. Gaping holes were all that existed of the ceiling now; the rooms themselves were half-walls and destruction.

But where were they?

Had someone already pulled them out?

"Gabby! Gabby! Answer me, damn it!"

He grabbed a piece of debris, sheetrock, and heaved it out of the way. He'd dig her out with his bare hands if he had to.

Her office would be toward the back southwest corner of the building's footprint, but she preferred the conference room in the center. Where should he look first? A mountain of debris and rubble stood between him and that corner. The only full wall that remained was one that blocked his path.

Elliot grabbed another piece of the rubble. He'd clear a path around the wall if that's what it took.

Hands wrapped around his arms and jerked. He looked into Erickson's face. "She's in here!"

"Who?"

"Gabby. My...Gabby. And Brynna. They're in here somewhere. I have to find them." He wasn't leaving them. He wouldn't think about what it would mean if he'd lost her. If he'd failed her and Brynna. "I have to. They're going to be terrified!"

Erickson bent down and grabbed a huge piece of metal that had probably once been a computer. "Then let's start digging. I'm here as long as you need me."

Elliot yelled again, then listened. Hoping.

He heard nothing. They kept digging.

The fire alarms continued to shriek, but the flames were dying down thanks to the sprinklers.

The explosion had been contained in the annex. To the forensics labs and the two rooms flanking them, to evidence storage above.

Had anyone else been down here?

The forensics department was usually empty this time of day, wasn't it? With only a thin skeleton staff to run tests when absolutely necessary? They didn't have a large-scale forensics department. But there should have been at least one more person, besides Gabby and Brynna and Benny, right?

Most of the time the first floor labs were relatively empty. Just the way Gabby and Brynna liked it.

He prayed it was empty today. That somehow they weren't in there.

CHAPTER SIXTY-SIX.

* * *

GABBY looked straight up. Through the hole in the ceiling. Plaster ceiling tiles were still falling. She raised an arm to cover her face protectively. She rolled on her side, pulling her knees beneath her.

She kicked something soft. Brynna's bag. And that was when she remembered.

Brynna. Dear heaven, where was Brynna?

The alarms rang, drowning out everything else. The sprinklers were mangled but still managed to rain out overhead.

Smoke still blocked her view.

She crawled to where she thought the door was. Toward where Brynna had last been. Where they both had last been.

Was her friend dead? What had caused the explosion? They didn't keep chemicals in the computer lab. There wasn't need. And the floor above them housed the evidence storage. Unless there was something up there?

She heard shouting from somewhere. Then the rapid report of what she recognized as gunshots.

Dear heaven, was the TSP under siege? What were they supposed to do?

Brynna. She had to find Brynna. And the door.

She wouldn't let herself think of Elliot or Jarrod or Benny or anyone else who worked on the floors above her. Right then, she'd focus on Brynna. Gabby must have been knocked half across the room from her desk.

The sprinklers were doing their job; smoke was clearing. There was a dark shadow toward the front of the room. The shadow moved, crouched low. Over Brynna. Who wasn't moving.

Gabby coughed and hurried closer. She froze when Benny looked over at her. When she saw what he was doing to Brynna.

Their boss's hand covered Brynna's mouth and nose, squeezing. Was he suffocating her? "What are you doing? Let her go!"

"I thought you were unconscious." He tightened his grip. "It'll be easier on her this way. She won't be hurting anymore."

"Let her go." *No.* It couldn't be Benny. He'd given her the position, had mentored her over the last four years. He treated her and Brynna like they were his own daughters. Why would he be hurting Brynna? Gabby shook her head. The pain—it was almost overwhelming.

Gabby jerked closer to her friend, nearly tripping on what remained of a chair.

Brynna was completely still beneath his hand.

"Let her go, Benny! You're hurting her! You're going to kill her!"

"I meant to. Damn it, Gabby, do you think I *wanted* the two of you involved? She's been through enough recently."

"Then why? Please, Benny. Let her go." Gabby grabbed the chair. "Just turn around and get out of here. I won't stop you. I just want to help her."

"The two of you should have left enough alone. The past is in the past. Why did you drag it all up again? Why did you look at Marshall and suddenly grow a damned spine? And Brynna, as curious as a little kitten! I *never* wanted to have to hurt either of you! But they made me do it." His free hand slipped into his holster, and he pulled his service weapon free. "I am sorry about this. I know you never truly knew...They have Alyssia now. I have no choice."

"You were one of the men on the video, weren't you? One who went after Elliot's family. Why? Why Sara?"

"We didn't know she'd be there. Or her brother. We thought they were planning to be out of town with their mother. That house they had in the gulf. When we realized...well, things had to be done, didn't they? Just like now. I'm sorry, Gabby. I promise I'll make it quick. For both of you."

"What you did will never be right. Get your hands off of her!"

"Gabby, we both know you're not going to stop me from doing anything. All anyone has ever had to do was say *boo!* to you and you freaked."

"*Because* of what happened ten years ago. *Because* of what *you* did." He'd taken one friend from her. She'd be damned if he was going to take Brynna. Gabby shook, now from rage instead of fear. At that moment, she wanted Benny to *pay* for everything he'd done.

To pay for what he was doing to Brynna.

Brynna still hadn't moved. She wasn't going to just stand there and do nothing while Brynna died beneath his hands.

She swung the chair at Benny's shoulder, knowing not to go for his head. Too easy to miss the smaller target.

She honestly waited to feel a .38 tear through her flesh at any second, but it didn't.

Benny stumbled away from Brynna.

Faced the most immediate threat against him.

Her.

"I don't want to do this. The bombs…they were supposed to kill all of three of us. Quickly. So the two of you didn't suffer. I've always liked you. Loved both of you girls."

"Sure you have." She held the chair up between them. It wouldn't stop bullets, but maybe she'd get lucky. Not die right away.

But if he killed her, who would help Brynna? Elliot would be coming. Jarrod, McKellen, Erickson—they were coming. She just had to keep herself and Brynna alive until they got there.

No. Gabby wasn't about to give up.

She stepped back and threw the chair at him as hard as she could. Straight at his face.

She'd only have a single opportunity to grab his gun.

Hopefully, it would be enough.

CHAPTER SIXTY-SEVEN.

* * *

HER tears burned her eyes as she clawed at Benny's arms. He had his hands around her throat and was choking her. She didn't know where the gun had ended up. Her second blow with the chair had gotten her lucky, and Gabby knew it. The gun had flown out of his hand and landed somewhere in the destruction.

Gabby raked her hand down one of his cheeks, leaving furrows. It did little good; Benny wasn't going to let go. Not until she was dead. She tried to bring up her knee, but he stopped her.

He was that desperate, that determined. Benny blocked her, knocked her to the ground with a backhanded blow.

People were shouting on the floors above them, as they tried to find their way into what remained of the annex's two floors.

Even if she screamed, would anyone be able to help her?

She kicked and scratched, but it did little good.

Her last thought before she lost consciousness was of Elliot. Of how much she would have liked the opportunity to love him.

CHAPTER SIXTY-EIGHT.

* * *

EVERY part of her that she could think of hurt, but Brynna rolled onto her side anyway. What had happened?

She had been talking to Gabby, the both of them trying to pretend that it was just like any other day at the TSP. Brynna had never been all that great at pretending. She used to think it was just her, but after meeting her sister Carrie, she suspected a lack of artifice was just a part of the Beck genes.

Someone cursed, and she forced her eyes open the rest of the way

Gabby screamed.

Brynna's gaze found her. *Beneath* Benny.

Benny held Gabby by the throat, madness in his eyes. Just like she'd seen in those men in the woods. Madness, or was it evil? How was someone supposed to tell the difference?

Suddenly everything made a sick sort of sense.

Benny had *known* every move she and Gabby had made. Because he'd kept them close, watching, all these years.

There was a gun nearby. Why was there a gun? Was it loaded? Brynna screamed, loud and long and as hard as she could. Benny jerked toward her.

They needed that gun. Brynna could use a gun. Her dad had made them all learn years ago. Brynna had hated it then, but she understood his logic behind the lessons now.

His hands came off of Gabby's neck. Brynna looked at the hell that surrounded them.

"Get the gun, Gabby! Get it!" Brynna yelled.

People were yelling from somewhere. She knew they were coming for them. Benny reached for Gabby, and she tried to pull away. People were coming to help.

If Benny didn't kill them first. "You'd better run, Benny. They're coming for you. Do you want to go to jail, Benny? Do you?"

If they kept his attention divided between them, they *might* have time to stay alive. Might.

Brynna pulled herself to her feet, but Benny was on her, yanking on her shirt until it ripped. He forced her to the floor. She cried out.

Fire ran through her back and into her side, robbing Brynna of all breath.

Something dug into the flesh of her side. Brynna kicked at him.

Brynna shot out her foot and it connected with the target. The small, deadly metal. The gun skittered across the floor.

Right toward Gabby. "Gabby!"

CHAPTER SIXTY-NINE.

* * *

THANK God Brynna was ok. That was the only thought Gabby was capable of making right then.

She screamed along with Brynna, hoping that the man wouldn't be able to deal with the both of them at once. That might be able to buy them time. Elliot and the others would be coming for them, right?

Time, they had to buy themselves some time. Keep his attention divided between them.

She knew the procedure, and knew Elliot would say screw procedure. He was out there, trying to get to her. She had no doubt about that. They just had to keep Benny from killing them before help could arrive.

"You're a bastard, Benny!" She yelled it at him, then grabbed a hunk of wood and heaved at him.

But it didn't matter. Benny had Brynna cornered, and was doing his damnedest to shut her up.

He struck Brynna, and she fell. She keened from pain. The sound was so horrific Gabby knew she would never forget it.

Brynna didn't get up again.

Gabby screamed. She grabbed a remnant of a two-by-four or a two-by-six—she never could remember the difference between the two—and swung it at his head.

He held up a hand to protect himself. The board cracked against his exposed palm instead of his head like she wanted. She tried to swing again.

Benny yanked the board from her grasp.

It wasn't any use. He was bigger, stronger, and had spent the last twenty-plus years as a police officer. He'd been fighting since before she and Brynna had taken their first breaths.

The only way they had to get out of this was if they could attack him together.

But Brynna was down—and not getting up. Gabby yelled again, hoping someone would hear, hoping it would distract Benny, hoping it would goad Brynna into getting back on her feet.

She yelled again as he turned toward her.

Why wasn't he running? Or did he know they were trapped and his only hope to survive was to kill them and make it look like the explosion had done it?

Brynna rolled on her back, proving she was still alive for the moment. She screamed.

Gabby yelled.

This time, *someone* yelled in return. Yelled her name, yelled Brynna's.

Gabby knew who it most likely was. Help was on its way.

She just had to keep herself and Brynna alive until their rescuers got there.

CHAPTER SEVENTY.

* * *

GABBY grabbed the gun, somehow. She wasn't sure how it had happened, but it had. Brynna yelled and then it was there.

Her stepfather had made sure she knew what to do with a weapon if she ever touched one.

Benny stopped. "Give it to me, Gabby. Right now. Give it!"

"Don't be stupid, Benny." Gabby's hand trembled, but she kept the gun aimed right at his chest. *Center mass, center mass, center mass.* "I will shoot you. I will."

"Sure you will. Tell me, Gabrielle—have you ever even stepped on a butterfly? I know you. Every little thing about you. I've watched you for *ten* years, after all." Benny walked closer. Brynna was directly behind her, the wall trapping them. She was crying, hurting. "You'll hesitate, and I'll walk right up to you."

"You really think that's who I am? That I'll let you kill me. Kill my *best friend,* without stopping you? There is *nothing I won't do* to protect the people I love. You took Sara from us; I'm not letting you take Brynna! Maybe you think I'm a wimp because I value life more than you, but...too bad. You'll get over it—in hell. Where you belong."

He lunged toward her arm.

Gabby pulled the trigger, and pulled and pulled some more until the gun was empty.

CHAPTER SEVENTY-ONE.

* * *

WHEN the gun was empty, and Benny was lying in a growing pool of blood, Gabby dropped the weapon and fell to the ground next to Brynna. "Brynna..."

"I'm bleeding. I'm hurting. But I'm alive, Gab. We're alive. And he's...he's dead, isn't he?" Brynna's voice was getting higher in pitch, and *now* Gabby saw the signs of panic hitting her friend.

"Where's the blood?" Gabby turned Brynna away from Benny's body. "Where are you hurt?"

"Here. I...think...it's deep. And it's really bleeding. Bleeding. Metal went through my side. I'm bleeding really badly, Gabby. And I'm scared. Scared. Scared. I want to get out of here."

"*Stop*, Bryn. You *can't* panic right now. You can't. I can hear help. I can hear Elliot. He's coming for us. He's coming." Gabby pressed her hands over Brynna's side. "You can't twig out, Bryn. I...need you to stay right here with me until Elliot gets here. With me, ok."

"I love you, Gabby. Have I ever said that? When I thought he was killing you...it was just as scary as when Mel almost died."

"I know. I felt the same. You're my best friend, Bryn. And I love you. We need to get out of here so we can tell Mel that, too. Mel is probably on her way here to get us out of this, but I think—" Gabby's breath stuttered out. "I think we should save ourselves this time. Just to prove we can, you know?"

"Why did he do it? He was our friend for years, wasn't he?"

"I don't think he was ever anyone here's friend. I think he was just out for what he could get. And you and I—we had skills he wanted. And he used us. Watched us."

"But not anymore."

"No. Not anymore. *We* stopped him. Together."

CHAPTER SEVENTY-TWO.

* * *

ELLIOT pulled the sheetrock from the pile and tossed it to the side. He had a fist-sized hole in the rubble when he heard the sounds of a gun, just on the other side of the debris. For a moment his heart stopped.

Just stopped in his chest. A gun made it damned clear it wasn't an accident, didn't it?

Was that what his father had felt at the moment his mother had been murdered?

Was that why the elder Elliot had just stopped fighting for that moment, long enough to follow Elliot's mother to the grave?

For the first time in ten years, Elliot actually understood his father a little better.

"Gabby! Answer me, damn it!"

Elliot kept digging, aware of Foster and Erickson, and he didn't know who all else, right beside him. Digging. Evers, McKellen, Callum. Even the new mayor of Finley Creek was pulling rubble out of the way.

His people, going toward the gunshots rather than away. Because some of their own needed them.

Elliot yanked on another piece of drywall as first responders surrounded them. Someone pulled on his arm, trying to force him to stop digging.

Elliot jerked away. “Gabby's in there! Gabby and Brynna!”

The guy in the fire helmet tried to reason with him. “I understand, sir. But we're trained in this type of rescue. You have to let us do our jobs.”

“We heard gunshots. Last I heard, fire and rescue weren't into gunmen,” Foster said. “That's our deal.”

“Keep digging,” Elliot ordered his people, though he knew the words weren't necessary. The people with him were the ones he could trust.

The only ones at this point.

He and Erickson grabbed a large piece of pipe. It was hot to the touch, but Elliot didn't care. “On three!”

They moved it aside as much as they could.

And then there was a hole big enough for a smaller person to get through.

“Keep digging,” Erickson said, putting action to his words.

“Thank you.” Elliot had his own hands around more drywall.

“Not everyone in the TSP is bad, Marshall. Not everyone. Keep that in mind.”

Elliot dropped to the floor and shined the flashlight someone had handed him toward what used to be the main conference room. Debris had shifted, making a small tunnel next to what had once been the outer wall. If someone could get to the door, they'd have an escape route. He measured with his hands. *He* would never fit. He was too damned big to be able to even try.

* * *

GABBY finally let the tears flow when she saw the beam of light suddenly appear near the bottom of the rubble separating them from the people digging them out. She saw the path and knew what she had to do.

"Brynna's bleeding!" she yelled as loud as she could.

Gabby was terrified of moving her hand in case her friend bled to death right in front of her.

Gabby pulled her own shirt off, revealing a white tank top. She ripped the already torn sleeve free. "I'm going to tie this around you as tightly as I can. Can you crawl, Bryn?"

"I don't know."

"We'll need to get you out of here; most likely on a stretcher. I don't think we can wait for them to make a larger opening." How much blood had Brynna lost already? Her friend was already fading in and out of consciousness. How much longer could she last?

Gabby looked around. There had to be a way to get Brynna out of there. There had to be.

There was the storage cart—or the bottom of it. The thing had been sheared off near the bottom. Leaving the wheels intact. Would it be strong enough to hold Brynna's weight?

Gabby looked back at the tunnel. How long was it? How wide? Did they really have a choice? She tried to guess from what she remembered of the room before Benny had blown it to hell and back. She had counted steps during thousands of her danged panic attacks. She *knew* how many feet were between them and freedom. She *knew* she could do this. "I'm going to get us out of here, Bryn. I promise. See this board there? I'm going to get you on it. Do you think you can help me?" Gabby grabbed what remained of one of their computers and pulled the mostly intact Ethernet cable free. She pulled the board over the bottom of the cart and tied the board in place as fast as she could, using the cord. She looked for another cord and found one beneath a piece of ceiling tile. "We'll slide you right out. Think how proud Mel's going to be when we get ourselves out. No waiting around to get rescued. I'm tired of being a weenie; fear robs us of the world, Brynna. That's what Mel says. No more being big chickens, Bryn. We're going to get out of here."

"Then let's get out of here," Brynna said, then cried out as she rolled to her side. She crawled toward the makeshift stretcher, slipping once in her own blood. Benny's, where the two puddles had started to pool together.

Gabby would never forget that sight as long as she lived.

"Bryn, I'm going to see how big the tunnel is. See what we have to do to get out, ok?"

Gabby laid down on her stomach near the source of the light. It was wide enough, she thought, for her and Brynna. No one bigger. Definitely not Elliot.

It *was* up to *her* to get them out, wasn't it? But how?

Thankfully, Brynna wasn't very big. Brynna laid on her back, and Gabby wrapped the Ethernet cord around her own hand. She'd crawl, then pull. No matter what she had to do to get them to the outside. She yelled to whoever waited on the other edge. "We're coming out right now!"

The front entrance of the annex was at least thirty feet from where she thought she and Brynna were. Thirty feet, under a pile of debris—wood, plaster, ceiling tiles, wires, glass. Could they do this?

She looked at Brynna. Brynna was barely moving. Was she even still breathing?

Gabby had no choice.

The sprinklers still rained overhead, but the remaining smoke burned Gabby's eyes. Gabby pulled on the cord, ignoring how the rubber coating burned the skin of her palms.

Brynna dragged in a broken breath and cried out as they got nearer the entrance of the tunnel. But her left foot came off the board. She used it to help push herself closer. Some of the strain in Gabby's arms lessened. "We'll do this, Gab. Make Mel proud."

Even if Gabby had to pull her the entire way, she was getting Brynna through this.

Crawling through rubble was something Gabby never thought she would ever have to do in her life. Brynna was able to help some. It was slower than Gabby wanted, and real hell on her knees and on her hands. She'd crawl a yard then pause long enough to pull Brynna the same distance. She'd wrapped the cord around her left wrist so she didn't lose her hold on it and the rubber burned and abraded her skin as she pulled.

The opening was only a little over two feet wide, and maybe eighteen inches tall at its absolute widest point. At its worst point, Gabby had to crawl at a weird angle. She scraped her arms on broken drywall and insulation a thousand times. She just prayed there were no exposed electrical wires to catch them up. Then they'd both be dead, no question, right?

Brynna's body was almost scraping the debris, and she had to turn her face to the left, but they kept going. What other choice did they have?

Gabby kept talking, telling Brynna they were ok, over and over and over. She'd pause and push debris out of the way, praying it wouldn't bring everything down on them. But it didn't.

Near the halfway point, the opening got tighter. Gabby had to almost lay down. There wasn't a lot of moving room. The only solution she had was to scoot herself around and inch her way backward, her head millimeters from Brynna's. She couldn't see Brynna anymore. It was far too dark. The light was at her feet, behind her. "Well do this, Bryn."

Brynna didn't answer.

She coughed. Was there enough *air* in there for them both? She didn't know. She dragged in one last breath, then held it. Brynna needed what oxygen was left a bit more than she did right then.

CHAPTER SEVENTY-THREE.

* * *

ELLIOT saw the feet first. “Everyone stop moving!”

The responders around them froze. A small foot came out of the tunnel. He recognized the blue pants as the same ones Gabby had worn that morning. “Gabby!”

He wrapped his hand around that ankle, and then the other one. He pulled gently. The threat of her being crushed by the debris at any moment was very real. They needed her out of there and as fast as possible. Her, Brynna, Benny. Anyone else who was left inside.

But thank God she was moving under her own steam.

She weighed far more than she should have. Gabby was on her stomach and covered in blood. Elliot’s heart froze in his chest. She looked worse with every inch of her he pulled free.

There was a two-inch gash near her temple. Her hair was filthy and blood-soaked. So much damned blood.

She was covered in it.

“Brynna! Elliot, get Brynna!” She was crying, sobbing, yelling. “Get Brynna out.”

She was clutching a cord. And pulling. The cord was wrapped around her left arm so tightly the skin was turning purple. Elliot cursed and tried to get it off.

And then he saw what the cord was attached to. Saw carrot hair and a thin body. Saw why she was so frantic. He dropped to his knees beside Gabby and wrapped his hands around the other woman's shoulders, and pulled. Took his first real good look at Brynna. "She's not *breathing!* Get the damned paramedics in here *now!*"

CHAPTER SEVENTY-FOUR.

* * *

PARAMEDICS were everywhere, but she and Brynna were the only ones with major injuries from the blast. After her friend was loaded into the first ambulance, Elliot ushered her to the second, after asking if anyone else was in there with him. All she'd been able to say was that Benny was dead.

They cut the computer cord from around her wrist and pulled it gently away. Gabby yelped at the burn. Elliot was there next to her, holding her other hand. It was ragged, and the nails were torn. But she wasn't letting go of him. The second paramedic wiped the blood from her forehead and applied pressure to the gash.

She was injured, but Gabby knew she would live. But Brynna?

Her last sight of her friend had been paramedics performing CPR until they got a pulse back, then whisking her away.

Gabby looked at Elliot, seeing the fear in his green eyes. She loved his eyes. Loved *him*. "I love you. I was afraid I wouldn't get the chance to say it. I love you."

She broke into a coughing fit before she could say anything else, but it was enough. She'd told him. Nothing could ever take those words away from them.

Gabby finally gave in to the pain in her head. She collapsed on the gurney and let the darkness carry her off.

* * *

ELLIOT couldn't take his eyes off of her. The paramedics worked quickly, stopping the blood from the gash on her forehead, and cleaning the wounds on her hands.

Around her neck, the skin was red and inflamed. Welts were visible already.

They arrived at the hospital within minutes, and the first ambulance was still unloading Brynna. Elliot had almost forgotten about her.

He would have to call his brother and let him know what had happened. Before Chance learned some other way. And someone would have to contact the Becks. Let them know that Brynna was hurt. Again.

He'd failed to keep her safe, failed to keep Gabby safe. The shame of that would never go away.

They rushed both women into the ER. Straight to Dr. McGareth…and Brynna's little sister.

Jillian took one look at Brynna and screamed her sister's name. McGareth grabbed her arm and shoved her gently toward the intake desk, where the hospital administrator was standing. "Fin! Take care of Jilly now."

McGareth flew to Brynna's side, and the nurses and doctors jumped into action.

They pulled Brynna down the hall and away.

Gabby was taken into the second exam room, and a crowd of people separated her from Elliot.

It went against every instinct he had to let her go.

CHAPTER SEVENTY-FIVE.

* * *

GABBY came out of it in the exam room, with the doctor over her.

Gabby didn't get a chance to speak with anyone until after she'd been treated, admitted, and cleaned up of all signs of the explosion.

No one would tell her how Brynna was. Or if Brynna's family was there.

They'd even separated her from Elliot.

Gabby waited until she was finally alone in her hospital room, then slipped from the bed. It was her hands and head that were injured, not her feet.

She was going to find Elliot and going to find out how Brynna was doing.

She made her way right back down to the emergency room, dressed only in her underwear and a hospital gown. She held the back together with her least injured hand—her left hand and arm were wrapped in bandages because of the abrasions from the cord.

Something had changed in her in that rubble, and she knew it. No longer would she *ever* let fear or anxiety keep her from doing what had to be done. From living her life. Those bastards who'd taken Sara from her wouldn't take another moment from her *ever* again.

Jilly's friend Lacy—Dr. McGareth, the same doctor who had sewn up Elliot when they'd been shot at—was at the admin desk. She looked up at Gabby. "So, here you are. We had word that a patient escaped. When I heard the name and description, I figured where you'd end up."

"Brynna? I need to know how Brynna is. Where are Jilly and Mel?" And Elliot? She had no doubt *he* was looking for her.

"They are upstairs in the waiting room next to the surgical wing. I'll walk up with you. I want to check on her myself. I had to let Dr. Jacobson take over once we had her stabilized."

"How is she doing?"

"I can't give you too many specifics, Gabby. But she's going to be ok." She grabbed a wheelchair and pointed at it. Gabby didn't argue. Lacy pushed her toward the elevator. "Brynna's tougher than people think."

"Yes, she is." Gabby thought of how hard Brynna had fought Benny. How if it had been for the two of them working *together* they would never have stopped him. "Today just proved it."

They'd kept each other safe.

"I have a feeling you are, too, Gab." Lacy wheeled her into the waiting room where the Becks were spread out. Chance was there, as well, and the look on his face was one of such torment Gabby almost *felt* his pain. He looked up at her, and she knew he was blaming himself for not being there.

Elliot called her name from just outside in the hall. Lacy stepped back and went to the surgical intake desk down the hall. He leaned over her.

Gabby wrapped her arms around Elliot's neck and hugged him for a moment; then she pulled away. She looked at Mel, who sat near the door. "Brynna?"

"She's in surgery. But she's breathing on her own. Now."

Kevin came to Gabby and crouched down in front of her. His face was pale and his eyes ravaged by tears. She reached a hand out and touched his cheek. "I'm sorry, Kevin."

"Don't be, honey. You saved her life in there."

"She saved mine, too." Gabby's voice cracked as the tears threatened. "Benny…"

"What happened in there, Gab?" Mel asked. "What did he *do?*"

Elliot's hand was warm on her shoulder. "They've pulled Benny's body out. The questions are starting. Do you feel up to telling us?"

Gabby thought for a moment, then nodded. Best to get it over with, wasn't it? "Yes."

"*Benny* was one of the men who killed Sara and the others. He was a part of it. The fifth man…it was Benny. He didn't tell us why. And he didn't care at all that he was going to kill Brynna or me. I…I…shot him. He was going to kill us today because he said someone had his daughter Alyssia, and I killed him instead."

How could he be like that? She'd worked with him almost every workday for the past four years, Brynna just as long. They'd laughed together. She'd taken him dinner when his wife had been in the hospital six months earlier. Brynna had collected his mail for him when he'd taken his wife on a three-week cruise two months after that. They'd thought he cared about them.

But he hadn't.

His wife. Who was going to tell his wife what had happened? Tell her that *Gabby* had been the one to kill him. "I did it, Elliot. I did it. He was coming for Brynna, and I stopped him. He said he cared about us and wanted it to be *quick* for us. To not make us feel the hurt. I pulled the trigger until the gun was empty. Just like Artie taught me to. And then Benny was there, dead. And Brynna was hurt, and we were trapped, and I didn't know how to get her out."

"But you did. You kept her alive, sweetheart. Don't forget that. Start at the beginning. When I dropped you off this morning."

"We talked to Benny, but he was in one of his moods. Or so we thought. Theresa wasn't supposed to come in until noon, so it was just the three of us in the conference room. We got set up, worked for a little while. Talked about the video between ourselves. We decided it had to be someone *still* in the department. There were nine possible. We narrowed them down in under a minute. We were scared and going to come tell you what we figured out. Then Benny came out of his office, and we knew he'd been listening. Knew *he* was the only one who could have known what we were doing now *and* knew me back then. That's when the…He pushed a button and—just like that—the room exploded around us."

Jilly gasped and shivered. Mel cursed. No one else made a sound.

"I was knocked out, I think. And so was Brynna. When I opened my eyes, I was near the back wall where I think I'd been thrown. Benny…Benny was leaning over Brynna. She was close to where we'd started out, but I wasn't. I thought Benny was *helping* her at first. But he wasn't. He was hurting her. Choking her."

She paused, then. "I yelled at him, and he stopped. Came at *me*. I was trying to fight him, to keep him away from her. She woke up. He didn't know which of us to come at first. So we used that to keep him distracted. We could hear you calling, digging. So we kept him split between us. Brynna started throwing things at him when he came at me. When he went after her, I stopped him. We kept doing that, hoping to buy us some time. And then he pulled the gun."

Gabby drew in a breath, tried to keep herself calm while she told them all. "He wanted us to just *let* him kill us. Because it served his purpose. Somehow the gun ended up on the ground. Brynna kicked it toward me. He had her cornered. She couldn't get away from him. He hit her, then shoved her down hard. She cried out, and I got the gun. He looked at me, and he came at me. I aimed the gun. And I pulled the trigger. Until he was dead."

Brynna's sisters were all crying. Gabby was too, but she was barely aware of it.

She'd killed a man who was trying to kill her and her best friend. He was dead. They weren't. That was what mattered. *That* was what mattered; not that she had killed a father of five.

There were so many questions they still had to answer, weren't there?

"He was dead, and Brynna was bleeding. We knew…we knew we couldn't wait until Elliot got us out. There was too much blood. We knew Elliot was out there, though. Knew he and Jarrod and the others were trying to get to us, too. But Brynna couldn't crawl out. She was hurt so bad. So we made our own stretcher. And…and we crawled out. We crawled out. I was afraid the tunnel wouldn't be big enough, and it almost wasn't. I had to crawl backward and pull her. She'd stopped breathing. I knew she had."

She drew in another breath and forced herself to go on. "Benny's dead and we aren't. But…I still don't know *why* he did it. Not really. He said…he said he hadn't *known* Sara and Slade were going to be there that night.

But he hurt them anyway. And he was going to kill us. He said his daughter was missing; someone will need to find her. Alyssia. The entire reason we were in his department was so he could watch us all this time, wasn't it? Elliot, I just...don't understand what we're supposed to do now."

"Now, Gabby?" Mel's tone was harsh as she knelt the best she could in front of the wheelchair. "Now you *live.* You keep going, you love. You be *you.* No matter what!"

Gabby wrapped her arms around her and just held her, while they both cried.

CHAPTER SEVENTY-SIX.

* * *

SHE was holding herself together, but Elliot knew it was just a matter of time before she cracked. She was his Gabby, after all, and he knew her well. Stronger than she thought she was, but there was a core of goodness in her that would make something as horrific as a cold-blooded killer in her world more than she could ultimately process.

He wasn't too proud to admit that he was terrified of letting her out of his sight. He should never have assumed that just because she was inside the TSP building that she was safe.

Bennett Russell was someone they'd thought they could trust.

Hell, the man had even gone to Elliot's high school and college graduations. He had been almost a part of the family.

The betrayal stung, and Elliot knew it. But nothing would ever compare to how terrified he had been at the moment a fucking explosion ripped through his building.

He didn't think he had breathed until he had seen her crawling through the rubble. He had been certain she was dead.

Instead, it was Brynna Beck fighting for her life, again. Because of whatever had happened ten years ago. Would it ever make any sense?

Elliot stepped out into the hall and told Callum and Evers to get started hunting for Benny's family, his daughter Alyssia in particular. If she was missing…she needed to be found. The two men left to get started. Elliot returned to Gabby's side.

Gabby's attending physician arrived, looking for his lost patient. She didn't want to leave the waiting room, and she told him that. Elliot held up a hand to stave off the argument. "We'll watch her closely, but she needs to be here with her family right now."

Dr. McGareth came up behind the other doctor. "I'm off the clock, Dr. Devall. I'm staying with the family. I'll keep an eye on Gabby."

The older doctor didn't approve, but he allowed it. Gabby needed to be there with Mel and the rest of the Becks. So Elliot would make it possible.

She loved her friends and wanted to be there with Brynna's sisters. With the people she loved. So he was going to make that possible.

Elliot looked at his brother. Was Chance going to be able to make it, if Brynna didn't?

CHAPTER SEVENTY-SEVEN.

* * *

BENNY had tried to strangle her. She had bruising and damage to her throat. She'd hit her head hard enough to have a concussion. Her left arm was sprained, the right palm was raw and bruised. Her lungs were filled with dust from the explosion and debris. She had multiple contusions and lacerations, though none were too deep. Only four required sutures. She had scorch marks on her arms and about an inch of her hair had been burned. She'd have to get it cut eventually. There were some second-degree burns where sparks had landed against her skin while she'd been unconscious. She had a nasty scrape on her right arm where she'd run afoul of some broken drywall in the tunnel of Hell.

It was all Gabby could do to stay sitting up in the wheelchair while they waited for word on Brynna. Word had gone out about what had happened. Cops were gathering at word that an officer was down. Brynna Beck may have only worked forensics, but she was still considered one of the TSP's own. They had calls from all the TSP posts from Galveston up through Wichita Falls. And when one went down, they all came running. There would be questions. Elliot could only hold them off of Gabby for so long.

Erickson was already waiting to take Gabby's full statement about what had happened. Thankfully Elliot's former partner was high up enough on the hierarchy that it would do them some good. He'd been in the waiting room, sticking close to Chance. Elliot appreciated Erickson's unwavering support. He owed the man, didn't he? Erickson had had the presence of mind to record Gabby's explanation with his smartphone. To video her. It was a start. He wanted someone he could trust on Bennett Russell's history. Officer Journey showed up with what seemed to be half of the Finley Creek TSP. "Everyone likes and respects the Beck family. With what they've been through recently...well, we're here to help. However, we can."

"Bennett Russell. Find out everything you can about him. Quietly. Don't let anyone know I've put you on it. And watch your back. He might not have been the only one in the Finley Creek TSP that was involved."

"Understood." Journey hesitated for a moment.

"What is it?"

"Benny...it was bad in there, sir. I went in after Gabby came out. Russell was serious about taking them all out himself included. It was divine intervention that *one* of his explosive devices was a dud. He used three. One in his office, one in what we've identified as Brynna's workstation and one in the conference room. The one near Brynna didn't go off; if that one inside that computer had worked—*both* Brynna and Gabby would be gone. If there are others involved still inside the TSP, they're serious about this. And I don't think they'll stop until everyone who can identify them is dead."

"Understood. Watch your back, Magda." Elliot looked at the green uniforms surrounding them and at the plainclothes detectives trickling in. For all they knew, the rest of the men they were looking for were already right there in front of him. "It may only get worse from here."

Who the hell could they trust?

CHAPTER SEVENTY-EIGHT.

* * *

GABBY leaned her shoulder against Mel's, wanting to give her friend as much support as she could. Mel laid her temple against Gabby's for a moment. She wasn't alone.

Neither of them was.

This wasn't over. Benny and the man Chance thought Brynna had killed and Handley Barratt—they were only *some* of the men who had killed Elliot's family. They still had to figure out who the rest of them were.

If they ever did.

How were they supposed to keep digging into the past when they really didn't know when to start? They were going to have to go over *everything* Benny had touched in more than thirty-five years with the Texas State Police.

It was going to take time and effort and finding people that they could trust.

Elliot would have to figure out a way to fix Finley Creek.

Finally, after what seemed like about fifty lifetimes, the doctor came in the waiting room. Gabby did her best to hold Mel's hand, even with the bandages wrapped around her fingers.

"Doctor? My sister?" Mel asked, standing.

It would always be Mel, wouldn't it, who faced things head on? Did anyone else hear the fear in her friend's voice? Gabby stood and slipped her arm around Mel's waist. Mel's father stood on her other side, Jilly and Syd beside him.

How did Mel do it? Gabby knew the other woman felt just as deeply as anyone else. But whenever there was a storm, Melody was the calm. Somehow she *always* held herself together until *after* the trouble ended. Gabby knew the truth, though. Sometimes her friend used her control to deal with the fear.

The doctor was the same who'd treated Brynna the week before. Gabby thought that was good—he'd know exactly what she'd been through recently.

"Brynna is a remarkably strong young woman. I won't lie—we did have to give her a hefty transfusion. And we almost lost her on the table once or twice. She'd lost a lot of blood, had been deprived of oxygen for a few minutes, her lungs were full of debris from the explosion, and with the infection last week, today was very tricky. If she'd been any later getting here, it would be a different story. There wasn't a great chance she'd be strong enough to survive the damage, as it was. But she has. Thankfully the metal missed anything too vital. We did remove her appendix because it took the brunt of the injury. She's still under sedation and will be at least until the morning. But barring any unforeseen complications, she should be just fine. However…she's going to have to be watched closely for signs of infection and for pneumonia from the debris in her lungs and chemical burns. She did inhale a bit of insulation, as did *anyone* who was in there today." He leveled a look at Gabby. She nodded. "In the meantime, we're going to keep her quiet and let her body *heal* from all she's been through in the last few weeks."

Mel practically wilted, until her head was resting near Gabby's shoulder. Gabby tilted her head to rest on her friend's. "She's going to be fine."

The doctor nodded, then frowned at Gabby. "She'll be fine. And I suggest you get back to your own room now, Ms. Kendall. We frown on patient escapees around here."

"Thanks, doctor," Elliot said. "We'll take care of her."

Gabby barely heard him. Mel and her father were hugging each other, and hugging her. And she was clinging just as hard to them.

CHAPTER SEVENTY-NINE.

* * *

ELLIOT waited until Gabby was back in her own hospital room and Brynna Beck was moved out of recovery before he looked at the one other man in the world he trusted besides his brother. He stood in the hall outside Gabby's room, speaking as quietly as possible. "Russell was only *one*. Brynna Beck killed one last week and identified Handley Barratt as another. We have at least two more out there."

"Where's that dumb brother of yours? He finally upstairs with his woman?"

His brother. Who Elliot suspected had deep feelings for the woman who'd almost died today. "I'm not sure. I'm going to try to find him. He...cares for Brynna. This is probably eating him alive."

"Anyone know where Handley Barratt is? The son?"

"Swears that he doesn't. And nothing we've been able to find proves differently."

"So you have a few snakes in your midst."

"Who the hell knows? Apparently, that's all Finley Creek has."

"You going to take the time to clean house now?"

"Damned right I will." And on that he was certain. People—*good* people—were getting caught up in shit that they didn't deserve to.

Brynna Beck would have been all of fourteen when his family was killed. Fourteen. There was no damned reason she had been pulled into the past. No reason she had been threatened today.

Yet she had been.

Just like his Gabby.

Elliot was going to end that as soon as he could. He looked at his former partner. "I want *you* to start going through every damned case that ever went through Finley Creek TSP, starting at least thirty-five years ago. *Find me something.* Anything."

"Thirty-five years is asking a lot, El."

"Focus on anything connected to Bennett Russell. There's something there. And someone needs to find it."

"You know I've got your back. But keep your ass safe, too. And that pretty girl of yours. Bravest woman I've met in a long time. Well, one of the two, anyway. Too bad you saw her first. And Chance her best friend. Still, there's always one of the sisters. Congrats, man. You're a lucky bastard."

"Thanks. I just want to get this cloud over our heads gone, so that we can focus on what *we* need to do next. I'm never letting her go again."

"Can't say I blame you." Erickson paused for a moment. "So shouldn't you get your ass in there with her? We both know time is fleeting. Screw this shit, let her know how you feel *now*."

Elliot thought that was damned fine idea.

* * *

GABBY knew when she opened her eyes just exactly who it was that she would see. He had his fingers in her hair—like he'd done so many times before. Elliot definitely liked blonde hair. Or maybe it was just *her* hair he liked so much? She smiled at that thought. "Hi."

"Hi. How are you feeling?"

"Better. How's Brynna?" From the angle of the sun coming in the room, Gabby guessed it was early morning. She hadn't meant to sleep for so long. The doctor had given them word about Brynna near ten the night before.

"She woke a few hours ago. She's in pain and groggy. But she was able to give Erickson and one of the regional commanders a statement about what happened. It corroborates with yours. And the security cameras were left intact. We saw what happened."

"And Benny?"

"He died instantly, Gab. He didn't suffer."

"Is it bad that I almost wish he had? What kind of a person does that make me?

"No. I think it makes you human. Real." He slipped his arms under her back and knees and lifted her over the bedrail. "You did well. You and Brynna both. You stayed alive."

"Do we have any idea *why* he did what he did?"

"No. Not yet. But we have him. We *know* he was involved with what happened ten years ago. And we know Handley Barratt was involved somehow. We are connecting the dots now."

"I guess I just don't understand why."

"Maybe we never will. But we'll find the answers. I can promise you that. This is more information than we had ten years ago. Places to start, anyway."

She heard the determination. He wasn't going to stop with just Benny or the Raymund guy, was he? He was going to find his answers, and she couldn't blame him. "So what do we do next?"

"We? *You* are stepping away and staying nice and protected. The regional commander is getting pressured from the commissioner to get this cleaned up. Or they're talking about closing the Finley Creek district."

"We can't do that!" The TSP was the smallest branch of law enforcement in the state, but that didn't mean that they weren't an important part of the law enforcement community, providing support to the other organizations and handling their own heavy caseloads. To close the Finley Creek post—that would have a huge impact. "What would happen to everyone at Finley Creek?"

"Those that pass the Internal Affairs review will have the option of transferring to the Dallas/Ft. Worth or Abilene or Lubbock or Amarillo posts."

"Hell of a commute. I don't want to move, Elliot. I like where I'm at."

But then again...where she was at didn't exist anymore, did it? "He destroyed the lab, didn't he? Everything."

"Yes. But he didn't destroy you or Brynna. And that is what matters."

"How much damage did the rest of the building get?"

"Not much. Russell accomplished his goal—he took out every piece of computer equipment in the lab. And a third of the evidence storage above."

"But what about what wasn't in the lab?"

"What do you mean?"

"Brynna was there—but she *always* has more than one computer. She cloned her laptop hard drive and mine and gave them to her sister Carrie for safe-keeping. Yesterday evening, before we came back to work today, we wanted to just be sure we didn't lose anything we'd worked on. Whatever we had in the lab, she gave to her sister. Everything. We just didn't feel safe having it at the TSP. So if there was something Benny wanted to be hidden, we'll find it. Eventually."

"It'll take time. But that's professional, Gab. We've brought in people to help us. And we'll do it. But right now, I want to talk about something else."

His words were so serious that for a moment Gabby started to panic. "Are Brynna and Mel ok? Did something else happen? You're scaring me, Elliot."

He smiled. "Nothing else has happened. This is just not professional. It's personal."

Gabby sat up. His hands were there to help her, just like she'd expected. His touch lingered. "What kind of personal? You're not going to pull what your brother did with Brynna, are you? No strings, no matter what?"

Green eyes widened. "Hell, no. Chance has his own demons to deal with. Just like I've had mine."

"Had?"

"The demons of the past will never be able to compete with what I want for the future. For us."

Dear heaven, what was he saying? Gabby was certain she was about to start babbling again, wasn't she? "And...and what do you think that's going to be?"

"Simple. You, me. This huge old ranch house that needs a family again. *My* family, if you're willing. I believe you know the one I'm talking about. We've both been there before. That is...if you can see yourself living there after what happened there."

"Are you saying what I think you're saying? Because I have some ideas, but I don't want to say something totally stupid, if it's not close to what you mean."

"I think we both know what I am trying to say here, sweetheart. You and me...I...you make me alive again,

Gabby." He put both hands on her cheeks and kissed her lightly.

Gabby lost all ability to talk. To even think of words. "That... How...Elliot...I..."

He laughed. "Can't think of anything to say, sweetheart? What *I* am saying is that I want you to move in with me. To marry me. Be with me forever. To show me that there is more to life than the damned TSP. To fill that house with love again. The way it should be."

"You're serious." Her heart threatened to jump right out of her chest and land at his feet. She couldn't think of anything she had ever wanted more than to share that kind of love with a man just like Elliot. *With* Elliot, forever.

"Why wouldn't I be? You mean the world to me, Gabby. I didn't realize that was what I needed until I almost lost you. I know we haven't been together very long. But we both know what can be lost by waiting. I'm not going to wait another minute to tell you how I feel."

"Then don't. Use lots of words." Gabby wrapped her arms around his neck and tucked her head on his shoulder. "I want to hear lots of them."

He laughed. "I love you, Gabby Kendall. I want you to move in with me, marry me, and help me make my family home into *my* family's home. Do you think you can do that?"

"I can't think of anything I'd rather do more." And she couldn't. She loved the man holding her, and always would. And he was right; they should seize every moment together they could. They both knew how precious time with someone you loved actually was.

Gabby wasn't ever going to let *him* go. Ever. And she told him that, over and over.

EPILOGUE.

* * *

BRYNNA managed to avoid pneumonia from what they'd inhaled, but Gabby hadn't been quite as lucky. Probably because Brynna hadn't been breathing as deeply while in the Tunnel of Hell, as Gabby would probably always call it when she thought about it. The hospital kept her for three days.

Jilly had begged and pleaded with someone—probably Fin—to get Gabby into the same room as Brynna. They were both going to be under guard for quite a while if Gabby had read Elliot's expression correctly. He was going to do whatever he could to keep her safe. And she was going to let him. Hopefully with the TSP after Handley Barratt and Benny dead, the rest of the killers would take off instead of coming after her and Brynna again.

She and Brynna were both bruised and battered and had concussions—Gabby's was actually more serious than Brynna's. But they were going to live. Both of them.

Brynna woke fully on the afternoon of the second day.

Calling for Chance.

Gabby had pretended to be asleep while Elliot's brother had reassured Brynna that she was safe. Gabby watched the two through her lashes. The depth of emotion in Chance's eyes when he'd looked at Brynna had floored Gabby.

It was the same expression that had been in Elliot's whenever he'd looked at Gabby since he'd pulled her the rest of the way out of the rubble. One of devotion and hope and fear and intensity. Love.

Elliot loved her.

She didn't doubt that at all, even though they'd been with each other less than two weeks.

And Gabby loved him.

Everything else was going to figure itself out, somehow.

Elliot had stalled on connecting Benny to Handley Barratt. But he hadn't given up, and she knew he wouldn't.

It was going to take time—to make the connections, to rebuild the computer forensics department, for her and Brynna to heal.

But they would.

And Gabby wasn't going to let *fear* guide her through life again.

Love was a much better choice; she thought as Mel came in. Her friend hugged her and then her sister. "Well, so now what do we do? Where do we go from here?"

"We just keeping going forward, Gabs. One day at a time."

That sounded like good advice to Gabby. They'd all just have to keep going. Together.

The Finley Creek series originated as a spin-off of the PAVAD: FBI Romantic Suspense Series. For more of the Beck family, check out their first appearance in WANTING (Carrie and Sebastian's book), how they help out in RUNNING (Al and Seth's book) and see Mel get shot in REVEALING (Paige and Mick's book).

And don't forget to check out when Elliot met Paige and Sebastian in PAVAD: FBI Case Files #0001 "Knocked Out"

Keep Reading for a sneak peek at the next two books in the

FINLEY CREEK TSP

Series!

SHELTER FROM THE STORM

&

THE PRICE OF SILENCE

SHELTER
FROM
THE
STORM

FINLEY CREEK TSP

BOOK 2

COMING
OCTOBER 2016

***Brynna Beck** had plans for her future, and those plans did not include working for the Finley Creek branch of the Texas State Police forever.*
Nothing was going to deter her from her goals. Until a ten-year-old cold case resurfaces. One with massive *implications for the entire Finley Creek TSP.*

Brynna had loved the family killed almost as much as she loved her own. That mattered enough to have her changing her plans—just for a little while. When Brynna discovers new information, she gains the notice of men who will stop at nothing *to protect themselves. Even if it meant silencing Brynna forever.*

*Former Texas Ranger **Chance Marshall** had spent ten years searching for the men who'd slaughtered his family. He had found nothing. Until Brynna demands his help.*
She'll share what she knows—if he agrees to drive her home, three states away. She has the information he needs, but she'll only share it with her boss, Chance's brother.

A band of killers stops them, determined to keep Brynna from sharing just what exactly she knows.
If Chance wants to stop the killers, he'll have to keep the beautiful, maddening redhead safe…while the storm rages around them.

CHAPTER ONE.

* * *

THERE was a strange woman sitting in his car, demanding he take her home with him. Any other night and he might just have considered it.

But not tonight. Not when his brother was counting on him to keep the woman his brother loved safe.

"Get out of my car." Chance Marshall leaned over the redhead who had instilled herself in the passenger seat of his rented SUV. She didn't back away.

There was no way in hell he was taking this woman back to Texas with him tonight. He didn't even know who she was. Not really.

Just a vague family connection that she had claimed. If he *did* know her, it had been well over ten years since he'd seen her, hadn't it? Why had she climbed into his car and refused to get out? What was he supposed to do with her?

"No. And don't curse at me. I don't like it." She leaned her carrot-red head back against the seat. "Get in the car, Chance. Or don't you care that I found something that may help you? May help your brother?"

Chance had never laid his hand on a woman before in his life—with a few notable exceptions while on the job with the Texas State Police and the Texas Rangers back in the early days of his career—but this woman left him no choice.

He grabbed her arm with one hand, then slipped his other hand under her long skinny legs and gripped. He pulled.

She got caught in the seatbelt. She hooked her arm around the headrest. He cursed again. Then again when she laughed. "I do not need this right now. Get *out*."

She smiled, then pushed the sunglasses up to rest on the top of her head, revealing pretty light brown eyes. "Tough. Gabby's my best friend. One of my only friends, to be honest. If she's in trouble, I'm going to be there."

Gabby was the woman his brother had feelings for, the woman his brother was going all ape-shit overprotective over. The woman some asshole had terrified. Threatened. The fact that this girl mentioned Gabby and the trouble the other woman was in told him that she probably was a genuine family connection. And a very loyal one, apparently. He admired the sentiment, but the stupidity...it was beyond foolish. "Don't be a damned idiot. What are you going to do to protect her?"

Light brown eyes bore right through him. "Whatever I have to. Gabby's my best friend, Chance. And I love her."

For the life of him, he thought the girl meant it. And she was a girl in a lot of ways. At first glance, he'd thought she was younger than she actually was, but she was still a good decade younger than him. And innocent. Very naïve.

What the hell was she thinking getting in a strange man's car this way? Didn't she have any more self-preservation than this? "What's your name? Why did you track me down?"

"You don't remember me. That's ok. I'm Brynna. I was just a little girl when we knew each other. My father and mother were good friends with your parents. But you were a teenager when I was there the most. And then...after you had moved out, I was there quite a bit. We didn't see you very much. Which was ok, because I know you never liked me. I never really liked you, either."

He vaguely recalled a bunch of redheaded girls in his parents' home. Had she been one of them? "Why are you really here?"

She stared at him for a moment out of those disconcerting eyes. This girl-woman had eyes that could twist a man's gut into real knots, didn't she? "I've found something, I think. And Gabby said you were nearby."

"So why are you in St. Louis?" How the hell had this creature found him? He'd always paid cash for everything, and there wasn't anyone other than his brother that he'd told where he'd be. And even that was just an occasional occurrence. He wasn't exactly the type that was easily tethered.

"My sister is here, with PAVAD. Have you heard of it? I tracked your cell phone to find you after Gabby told me you were up here when we were chatting online earlier today."

Of course, he had heard of the FBI's PAVAD division. He had contacts in every federal agency in the country—contacts he'd deliberately cultivated in his work—and he'd heard quite a bit about the relatively new FBI unit that was supposedly unstoppable.

He'd used this trip to speak to a St. Louis field agent who'd worked the murder of Chance's family ten years earlier. Chance had been called up to speak to a grand jury about a previous kidnapping case he'd worked as a private investigator.

Ten years ago he'd been assigned to the same team as Art Kendall. Chance had wanted to get the guy's impressions about that day.

He wasn't so sure he trusted the reports the Texas State Police had given him.

And Chance would be following every lead, no matter how long it took. "Aren't I just the lucky one?"

He'd met with the field agent after the man's shift had ended, which was why Chance was in the FBI parking garage at nearly eight at night. The parking garage shared with PAVAD. Had the girl been waiting for him all this time? In a dark garage, alone? With little defenses?

Damn it; the girl-woman needed a keeper.

She blinked up at him, the dim light of the interior lamp her skin glowed and her eyes were remarkable. What was it with those eyes of hers? They were gorgeous but made him feel like a damned slug. "I don't really understand sarcasm. At least, that's what I've been told. Why are you lucky?"

Was she for real?

"Never mind. Other than Gabby's friend, who are you exactly? What do you know about my brother?"

"I have something that is extremely pertinent to the murder investigation that I know you are still working. But I need to speak with my bosses before I can share it. But I didn't want to wait to talk to Benny. I wanted to talk to the chief of my TSP post. Your brother. Elliot. What I found is going to be hard on Gabby. I was chatting with her to check on her, and she said you were up here, too. I don't drive. You are going back there. It was logical that we ride together. So I found you myself." She grinned at him, revealing a beautiful smile complete with a tiny gap between her front teeth and dimples.

"So you came up this way to show me?"

"No. Not exactly. I was here anyway; I was visiting my sister and brother-in-law, who both work with PAVAD. I need to get back to Texas tonight. And I need to check on her. On Gabby. She tends to freak out over scary stuff like this. Since it's about your family, it made the most sense that I find you and you drive me home. See. Logical. Logical."

"Let me get this straight...Gabby's with my brother. I know that part. But you aren't capable of finding your own way home? How exactly is that working out for you?"

"I *have* found my way home. You. I don't drive. I never learned. We have a common purpose. You want to catch the bastards who killed your family. So do I."

Why did the word *bastard* coming from her lips sound so wrong? Because of the sweet doll-like appearance? The obvious innocence on her face? Chance pushed those thoughts away. This girl was bound to give a decent man fits. An honorable one. He wasn't the least bit decent, and he was for damned sure not honorable. He didn't have the time to screw around with this girl. Woman. Girl-woman—it suited her better.

But he doubted he was getting her out of his car anytime soon.

"Of course I want to find the killers."

"So do I. So does Gabby. And your brother, too. Shouldn't we work together on that? I'm very good at what I do, you know? Some of my work is now being used by the FBI. By the FBI. It's cutting edge, or so they say. You drive me home; I'll work in the car. I share what I have; you do the same. An *I-show-you mine, you-show-me-yours* kind of thing. Except with clothes on."

Seriously? This girl-woman was just asking for trouble someday, wasn't she?

"Who controls you? You have a family out there? One of your sisters? Parents? Handlers?" Someone had to. There was no way this creature had been released on the unsuspecting world completely on her own, right?

She stared at him for a moment. "I don't think I understand you. I live with my father if that's what you're asking. My mother died five years ago. Five. He's home now. He and your dad were partners twenty years ago, you know?"

"*Beck*. You are one of Kevin Beck's daughters." That made things perfectly clear. He'd met Kevin Beck on many occasions, and had liked and respected the man. Beck had been a little younger than his dad and had four or five kids, all a little younger than Sara and Slade. And all girls, he thought. All pretty red-haired girls who gave everyone who knew them fits. *This* was one of them, then. He tried to recall if any had had hair quite that carroty. There had been one. And he hadn't liked her when he'd been a teenager, had he? Something about her had annoyed the hell out of him back then. "Your dad should have whipped your ass *years* ago. You *don't* get into strange men's cars. I'm surprised you didn't know that."

She looked at him like he was the idiot. "You're not strange. Well, not unknown strange, I mean. You may do weird things that I don't know about, though. I guess you could be strange that way. I've known your family my entire life. Known you. Known you. You poured pancake batter on my head when I was six. Which was really mean. And your brother is with my best friend right now. See? I do know you."

"Still. You don't know me now. I could kill you, beat you, rob you, rape you, assault you right now and then dump you along a dark road somewhere. Or bury you. Where you'll never be found. Have you thought about that?" He leaned down in the open passenger door. Because the girl was for damned sure not getting out. And now that he knew *who* she was, he couldn't just kick her to the curb and let whatever happened to her happen, could he?

Kevin Beck had been his sister's godfather. His parents had reciprocated with the Beck brat closest in age to his sister...the one with...the carroty red hair. *This* girl. Damn it.

That meant something to Chance. It had to.

Like it or not, he was stuck with her for a while, wasn't he? At least until he delivered her to her father, along with a clear lecture to her and a reprimand for the older man for letting her out of his sight long enough for her to get her into trouble.

He got close enough that he could see the faint flecks of gold in those peculiar brown eyes of hers. She didn't so much as flinch away, though he knew having him in her personal space like that had to bother her. Hell, it would bother him. But this one was an extremely cool little customer. "What do you say about that?"

"I'd say I've already texted my sister Mel and told her where I was and who I was with." She smiled at him like she'd won something. "And Jarrod. I texted him, too. He gets a little freaked out if he doesn't know where I'm at or what I am doing. Especially this late at night."

"Who's Jarrod?" Boyfriend, possibly? She was a damned beautiful—if irritating—girl-woman. There had to be a guy involved somewhere.

"Jarrod's with the TSP. Detective Foster." Chance remembered him; he'd met Foster hanging around Gabby. For some reason, he couldn't see this girl-woman with Foster, though. The other guy was too hard, cynical to be with a girl-woman like this. "In your brother's post. He's a detective. And a friend. But...shouldn't you get in and start driving? We have a long night ahead of us. And I think it's going to storm some more."

"It's not going to storm."

"Oh, I think it will."

***

IT stormed. Chance should have known it would. It didn't seem to bother his companion, who'd slipped earbuds in delicate little ears.

Something about Brynna Beck bothered the hell out of him. Made him a bit snarly. And if she was the Beck he was remembering, always had. Whenever she'd been around, she'd grate on his nerves to the point he'd want to scream.

It was the way she looked at him, the way she talked. She used to repeat everything anyone ever said in a monotone, like a voice recorder. It had driven him nuts. As had the way everything normal had seemed to bother her as a kid. He tried to recall the last time he'd seen her—had she been at the funerals? He didn't remember. No surprise—he'd buried four members of his immediate family that day.

He looked at her—she had to be around twenty-three or twenty-four. A little younger than his sister Sara would have been. Kevin Beck had brought his family to Chance's college graduation, hadn't he? That was the last time he remembered seeing the Beck family, when he'd been twenty-two.

So this girl would have been about twelve then. He vaguely recalled a thin little girl hiding behind sunglasses and headphones. She'd told him congratulations, then followed her older sister to the duck pond nearby. He hadn't given her another thought since then.

This was that girl.

He looked at the sunglasses on her head. The headphones in her ears. Some things hadn't changed, had they?

She shifted, and he was just able to make out the full-grown female curves in the dim glow of her laptop.

Well, some things *had* changed over the last ten years, hadn't they?

She thrummed. Practically vibrated in the passenger seat of the rental. Her bag was at her feet, and her fingers typed at the speed of a freight train. She'd occasionally hum, little sounds of concentration that seriously pissed him off. Made him wonder when else she would hum. *What* else would please her enough to have her making that sound.

Did that damned Foster make her do that?

She'd promised to show him hers. He was manfully keeping his thoughts on the professional, rather than the other areas of his body that idea, that image, flooded. Trying to, anyway.

This was his parents' goddaughter. That they'd been dead ten years mattered little to his body.

Kevin Beck's annoying little daughter. Hell. He'd never had a thing for younger women before. He wasn't about to start now.

He shifted a bit in the driver's seat.

Beautiful, intelligent, loyal...and apparently as mad as the hatter ever was.

So why was he having so much trouble keeping his eyes on the road and off of her?

She finally pulled the earbuds from her ears and sighed, about four a.m. He'd decided it would just work best if they drove straight through the night. He'd expected his companion to fall asleep, but she hadn't. "Yes, Gabby has to have what else I need. Damn it. I didn't want to have to show her what I found. It will upset her too much. Gabby gets upset a lot."

"And what is that?"

"You know about the emails Gabby's been getting, right? I've been looking for three years to find some connection between the IP address and the Finley Creek Texas State Police branch. I've found nothing, and I haven't told Gabby. I don't want her getting scared again. It's almost like someone knows exactly what I am doing as I'm doing it. Even though I'm not *supposed* to be working on the Marshall case, and I've told no one. Not even my sister, Mel. But I've checked every computer I use. Mine, Gabby's, my personal ones. If they're using spyware, I can't find it. And that means they are very, very good."

"That confident in your skills?"

She blinked at him again. Did he have moron written on his forehead or something? "Well. *Yes*. I've designed some seriously kick-ass software for law enforcement—as has my older sister, Carrie. We know what we are doing. I gave her a cloned hard drive from both mine and Gabby's laptops. She hasn't been able to find anything, either. But I know something has to be there. But I can't find what. Can't find what."

"And that's why you have that sticker over the webcam?"

"Yes. And after what Gabby told me happened to your sister...how the killers saw Gabby, too. Well...I'm not stupid. Not stupid at all. I don't want someone spying on me. But this is Gabby's laptop. Benny has mine today; he's upgrading it. I borrowed Gabby's. We built them together. Together."

Chance looked away from her for a moment. His sister Sara had been killed while on a live webcam feed to her best friend, Gabby, ten years ago. Gabby had hit record as she'd called 911. But it had been too late for Chance's family.

All he had left was his brother Elliot.

"You've been friends for a while?"

"Four years. We met once or twice with Sara when we were kids. At your mom's house. But Mel was more Sara's friend than I was. I was too young. But Gabby and Sara...They were older than me."

"Yes." Gabby had been his sister's constant companion from about the age of ten or eleven, he thought.

"I'm younger than Gabby. Mel's older—she and Slade were the same age. Whenever we'd visit your house, I'd stay in the kitchen with your mom while they played. Mel and Sara and Slade. They'd play with Jilly and Sydney. My other sisters."

"But not you?"

"Too loud for me." She said it so matter-of-factly. "I'd rather make cookies with your mom. She didn't talk to me like I was weird. And she wouldn't let them be loud in her kitchen. She was my friend, too. I loved her, a lot. I still miss her."

"Me, too." There was something in her tone that told him far too many people probably had looked at *her* differently. "Why weird?"

"I wasn't quite as good at communicating back then as I am now. You know that. You used to laugh at me for it. I remember."

He winced. He couldn't remember it, but he probably had when she'd annoy him too much. Most of the time he'd just tried to stay away from all of the little kids running around his parents' house. Now he wished he hadn't. He wished he'd spent as much time with his younger brother and sister as he possibly could have back then.

It was easy to miss what you'd lost, wasn't it? Rather than appreciate who you had. Chance had learned that the hard way.

The last words he'd ever shared with someone in his family had been harsh. An argument with his youngest brother Slade over something so stupid he barely remembered it.

What he remembered most about that kid was signing the hospital paperwork to cut off life-support and letting Slade die three days after their parents and younger sister.

"It's ok. I've forgiven you for it. You weren't the first. Nor the last. I'm weirder than most women. And I know it."

She was very direct. No artifice. He had to admit that was a bit of an oddity. "I see."

"I don't think you do. Ever heard of Asperger's. You know, kind of like autism? Although they are lumping it in with autism now."

Who hadn't? "Yes."

"I'm on it, you know. The spectrum. For years I thought I was the only one in the family. Then two years ago we found my missing sister. I'm not. Carrie's just like me. Only she has Pervasive Developmental Disorder-Not Otherwise Specified. PDD-NOS. I am high-functioning. So is she. We don't know who is higher-functioning, though. Probably her. She's lived on her own before. Before she got married. I haven't. I've always lived with my father. But Carrie was lost for so many years. She didn't have our family like I did."

Chance was having some trouble keeping up. But Asperger's explained a lot, didn't it? "Ok, missing sister? How was she lost?"

"Carrie was kidnapped by a murderer when she was nine. He took her to Oklahoma, and she went into foster care there. Then she ran away when she was fifteen and lived on the streets. I saw her in a computer forensic trade journal and recognized her. I mean...she looks just like me and everything. So I did some digging—" Which Chance took to mean hacking. "In her files. She's a year and a half older than Mel."

"I'm sorry for what your family went through." He'd never heard anything about Beck having a missing child out there. Had his father and mother known?

"We didn't know about Carrie. I mean, my dad and mom did. They did. But not the rest of us. But we've found her now. We saved her life when that murderer tried to kill her again a few years ago. We got there just in time to help save her and some other people. She jumped off a roof and landed at Mel's feet. I was down on the street, by all the sirens. I could just see the fire. It was terrifying. My dad was up there, too. He almost got shot. Now she's married with a baby. My niece Madeline."

"I'm glad it worked out for you." Family sagas and drama just pissed him off. He wanted no part of them. Not that he resented people who had those kinds of connections—but he didn't want to hear about them. To be reminded…he was a bastard, and he knew it. "So what did you find on that laptop?"

"Oh. I have to show you mine first, huh?"

He wished the interior light was on, that he could see her face. Did she realize what kind of sexual innuendo she kept using? Chance knew himself as exactly what he was—he was a damned caveman at times. Especially when it came to females and sex. She'd gotten him thinking of one thing with her *I-show-you mine* earlier.

Damn it. This woman—she still grated on his nerves but in an entirely different way than she had as a child. Did she realize that?

Somehow he doubted she did.

A keeper. The girl-woman needed a keeper.

"Do you realize how that sounds?" He pulled the car to a stop at the intersection. From what he could tell they were just south of Tulsa. He hadn't taken the direct route. Chance never took the direct route—it was safer to go an alternative than what people would have expected. He knew that. But they also needed to stop.

They needed food and a break. A restroom. Caffeine. Then they'd keep going.

She turned toward him, just as headlights flooded her window. Headlights that weren't stopping. "What—"

Chance grabbed for her, knowing as he did that it wouldn't matter in the least.

He was too damned late to get her out of the way.

Something crashed into the passenger side.

Into Brynna.

Her scream was a sound he would never forget.

* * *

THE
PRICE
OF
SILENCE

FINLEY CREEK TSP

BOOK 3

COMING
DECEMBER 2016

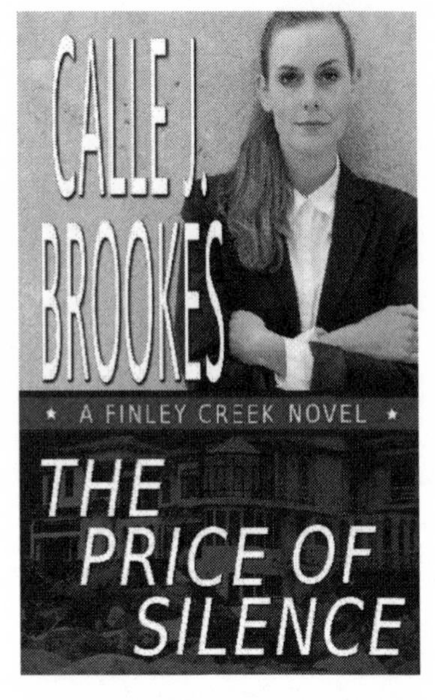

She was the one who had always done the protecting…

***Melody Beck** had spent her life taking care of others—especially her younger sisters. When one of her sisters is attacked and nearly killed, Mel is determined to find out why and who.*

All signs point to the richest man in Texas, billionaire Handley Barratt, as being the mastermind behind the attack. And on Barratt being involved with the infamous Marshall Murders, a ten-year-old cold case that Mel would never forget. She had been friends with the victims and their deaths had been what led her to join the Texas State Police.

Going after Handley Barratt was going to be extremely difficult, though. In more ways than one. Going after Handley Barratt meant dealing with his son…The one man she was trying hard to forget…

The world was claiming his father was a killer…

His father was an honorable man and he'd raised Houghton to be the same. What had happened to his father had to be a set-up and only link Houghton had was the name of the woman who'd been attacked, who'd accused his father.

It wasn't Brynna Beck who drew his attention, it was her older sister—the woman he'd shared one heat-filled night with eighteen months earlier. The woman he had never forgotten, or stopped wanting.

But as Houghton schemes and manipulates to get Mel back in his arms where she belongs, the real mastermind responsible for the Marshall Murders is getting closer. Only this time he's focused on Mel and the sisters she'd do anything to protect…

CHAPTER ONE.

GET *up, little* *one, get up.* His whispered words echoed around the dim interior of the car as he sat watching the redhead fifty feet away.

Houghton Barrett watched the woman struggle to navigate the simple sidewalk and his heart broke for her. When she fell he almost bolted from the dark sedan and lifted her back to her feet.

He knew her story. He had her medical files in the briefcase on the passenger seat next to him. He knew everything about her, about her father, about her sisters, and her brother-in-law. Over the last several days there wasn't a single scrap of information about her family that he hadn't poured over, memorized. Every photo of all of them, every mention in the media.

Everything.

His world centered on information that family held. He'd been watching them every second that he could. The younger two, he'd discounted. The one was barely twenty-three and working on her nursing degree; the other was still in high school. That left one in St. Louis, who had discounted for simply being too far away.

Brynna was the next one; the one who had just been found after nearly being killed. She was still in the hospital from what his sources had told him.

And her sister was right in front of him.

Melody Beck pulled herself back to her feet, but the groceries she'd been in the process of carrying inside were more of a struggle. She couldn't balance both the food goods and the crutch that he'd watched her lean so heavily on.

She should have someone to help her. It was obvious she was too weak to do anything significant, though this was the first time he'd witnessed her actually falling.

Too weak to defend herself if trouble came. That made it easier for him, didn't it?

Houghton definitely meant her trouble.

He zoomed in on her face, seeing her lips moving. She was cursing; but it wasn't just anger he saw. It was pain. Fear. Fatigue.

And stubbornness. He'd watched her for a few days; it wasn't the first time determination had been all that kept her going. What had she been through these past eighteen months?

She managed to get most of the groceries back into the bag, but a lone cantaloupe had escaped her. She stood on the sidewalk for a moment, obviously debating whether to attempt to bend down and get it or say to hell with it.

Finally she gave up and started the slow process of inching her way toward the door. Every laborious step she took tore at him for what he was going to have to do to her.

It must be a living hell for her, struggling to barely walk after a life, a career, of such a physical sort. And she *had* been a very *physical* sort. She looked nothing like the former cop he knew her to be. Instead she looked weak, vulnerable, an easy damned target.

She fell again, this time catching her weight on the front of her palms. He sucked in a breath. When she turned her palms over to inspect them it was clear they were torn and scraped. He raised the lens to focus on her face—tears.

It was the tears that did it.

She didn't deserve to cry over the groceries. He didn't want her to cry over anything.

If he went over there to her, she was likely to shoot him on sight.

It's what he would have done, facing the son of the man who'd—allegedly—kidnapped her sister and almost killed her.

Rumor had it Houghton was as dirty as his father. Damn them all.

Her sister's words had dealt Houghton's company a serious blow. But it had found him *her*.

What in the hell was he supposed to do now?

* * *

MELODY Beck assumed life would get better. It just sucked in that particular moment. She even knew *she* would one day get better. It was just going to take time.

She wasn't even supposed to be able to walk. The fact that she could was a miracle in itself. One she was extremely grateful for.

But some days she was just more tired than others. And clumsier. Today had been a particularly rough one. She'd gone back to therapy after missing two appointments the week before when every moment of her waking time had been devoted to finding her sister.

Not to mention her own twenty-four hour stay in the hospital after someone had nearly shot her, and her rescuer had thrown her to the ground and covered her with his own body. The bruised ribs had been a concern for the doctors and they'd kept her as a precaution.

Her sister was safe. The man who'd saved her—and carried Mel back into the hospital—was safe. Their best friend Gabby was currently safe.

It was going to have to be enough for now. Mel had used up her share of miracles for a while.

She just hoped it was Brynna's turn for a few miracles. Brynna and Chance.

The look in Brynna's eyes as Chance had left her hospital room had nearly broken Mel. Such devastation. She'd always known her sister could be hurt so easily, but what she had witnessed today was never going to be erased from her memory, from her heart.

And it had been so much worse for Brynna.

After their father had arrived to stay with Brynna, Melody had escaped to run to the store—and to take a breath. To decide what they would be doing next.

Two of the men who had kidnapped and threatened her baby sister was still out there somewhere. The other was probably dead.

She was so proud of what Brynna had done.

Melody was going to use every resource she had from her days with the Texas State Police to find the bastards and make them regret ever looking at her sister as collateral damage in whatever war they had with the TSP, and the Marshall family.

She may be worthless in a physical fight these days, thanks to a bullet, but she still had what lay between her ears.

She unlocked the door and stepped inside the foyer of the house where she'd lived most of her life—she'd had an apartment near the campus where she'd gotten her degree but had returned home to help when her mother was ill—and tossed her keys to the table next to the door.

She was on cooking duty for the foreseeable future. And that meant she'd make the best damned dinner for the people that lived there with her that she could. Jillian and Sydney, her two youngest sisters, would be home within the two hours. Their father would probably stay with Brynna as long as he could.

The sister closest in age to Melody hated hospitals—they were a sensory nightmare for a woman on the autistic spectrum like Brynna was.

Possible complications of being sliced open with a penknife demanded Brynna stay where she could be monitored. They all understood that. No matter how Brynna didn't like it.

But her sister hadn't been fighting the hospital when Melody had left; she'd been lying there. Bereft over a wild renegade of a man who would never be the kind to settle in one place, no matter what a woman like Brynna could promise him.

Melody didn't doubt the depth of her sister's feelings for Chance. Brynna felt deeply—she just had trouble showing that, at times.

Worst part of it was, she was certain the man in question loved her sister just as much as Brynna loved him.

But he had still walked away.

What would that do to a woman like Brynna?

Melody was afraid she already knew the answer to that. Devastation. Chance Marshall had broken her sister into a million little pieces. And Melody didn't know how to fix her.

She didn't know how long she stood by the stove, thinking. Worrying.

Hard hands went around her waist and covered her mouth. The intruder yanked her back against a hard, strong chest. Mel tried to pull in a breath, but couldn't. "If you scream, I may hurt you. Do you understand what I am saying?"

She nodded and ruthlessly shoved back the panic. She had to keep a clear head.

The hand around her mouth slipped down to grip her waist. Mel looked down. Saw the gun. What did he want? Who was he?

The only weapon she had was her forearm crutch, if she could bring it up between them…And there were knives in the block five feet away. If she could get to one of them...

Who was she kidding? She could barely walk, let alone defend.

In the current physical state she was in, she was no match for an armed attacker. No matter what it was he wanted. "What do you want?" She kept her voice from trembling somehow.

"Turn around. We're going to make this as easy as possible." He slipped back a half a foot or so and then the gun was away from her side. Somehow.

"M-make what?" Where was the strength and calm that had been drilled into her at the Academy and in her days with the TSP?

"We need to talk, you and I." His hands scorched her even through her clothing when he turned her around more quickly than she could handle. She lost her balance and fell against him. He straightened her quickly.

"Hold out your arms." Mel looked up—a long way—up into the intruder's face.

"What are *you* doing here?" It was a beautiful face, one designed to stay in a woman's mind long after she'd seen it. She should know—she still dreamt of it at night.

Houghton McKinley Barratt, heir to the Barratt-Handley fortune. Son of the man responsible for the kidnapping and near murder of her sister. Brynna, who had hurt no one in her entirely life.

Houghton Barratt, the last man Melody had slept with before a bullet had changed her life forever. It had only been one night, but…

She struggled in his arms, trying to push his hands away from her, as some of the fear left her. Some. He still had a gun, after all. And he was still a Barratt. "Let me go, Houghton, and I won't call the police."

"Of course you will, little one. Do you think I don't know about your family now? Your ties to law enforcement?" His dark eyes were cynical and hard. Cold. Nothing at all resembled the hungry lover who'd made her forget one of the worst murder investigations of her career. He slipped the gun into the holster he had in his pocket. "Hold out your hands."

"Rot in hell, Barratt." She lunged for him. She knew he was quick—and probably had two bodyguards waiting outside. Surprise was all she had on her side.

It didn't do a damned bit of good. Her attack didn't even budge him an inch. Houghton was six and a half foot tall and in excellent physical shape.

Houghton caught her up and carried her into the dining room, completely ignoring how she twisted and bucked. He dumped her back on the dining room table where half her sister's science project was still laid out. "Had to make it difficult, didn't you?"

She wanted to scream at him, to curse him, but she couldn't. The air had left her lung-and-a-half when he'd dropped her against the tabletop.

Not that it took much to do that to her these days. A bullet through a lung left its mark for a long time, didn't it?

"I don't *want* to hurt you, Mel. But you're going to do what I say." He grabbed the hand she tried to punch him with and held it flush against the table. Then the other one. "I need your help, and you owe me for just walking away that morning."

He pulled her wrists together in front, then wrapped them quickly with duct tape.

It had little yellow ducks on it. That stuck out with her. Yellow ducks, of all things.

His eyes were dark and cold, missing the warmth that had been there before. Her fear rushed back, doubled. "What are you going to do with me?"

* * *

Made in the USA
Middletown, DE
18 December 2017